THE
VOICE
MAIL

JACK E. DAVIS

The Voicemail

Jack E. Davis

ISBN (Print Edition): 978-1-66789-211-5

ISBN (eBook Edition): 978-1-66789-212-2

CONTENTS

CHAPTER ONE

My name is Samantha Harris and one cold November morning, I was awakened by my dog Daphne licking my face, which she typically did every morning around 5:45 like clockwork. Daphne was a miniature dachshund, all brown with a long pointy nose, short stumpy legs, and a grey patch of hair on her head. She was a girl's best friend, especially here lately. Tragically, it was just the two of us after my dear husband Jack died one year earlier in a car accident. Jack and I were high school sweethearts and we married right after graduation. We were just two weeks shy of our twentieth wedding anniversary when Jack succumbed to his injuries. He was my rock and when he died, I felt like a shell of my former self—like a piece of me was missing—and I didn't think I could go on without him.

The day Jack died, I had been writing my manuscript for another novel all day; I had already written a few books and was somewhat of a celebrity here in St. Lux, Michigan. However, that day I distinctively remember Jack yelling into the office where I sat working while Daphne slept under my desk near my feet, "I'm done with yardwork Sam, and I'm on my way to the supermarket.

You need anything?" "Well, of course," I jokingly replied, "the register would be nice."

Sadly, I rarely, if ever, broke concentration when I was working on a new novel and usually when I wrote, everyone around me fell into oblivion. I hate to admit it but when I was in the zone with my writing, I don't think I would've even noticed Daphne doing a handstand right in front of me. But that day something was different. I got up as Jack was putting on his coat and told him I loved him, hugged him, and gave him the biggest kiss on the cheek before he left the house.

Jack was on his way to get a bottle of our favorite wine to go with the steak dinner he was preparing. If I'd known "be back in fifteen minutes" would be the last thing he said to me, I would've held him just a little while longer. I've often beat myself up for letting him go out that door. *How could I have been so consumed with my book?* I thought to myself. It was hard not to question everything I believed in during that time, and I've often wondered if God had a bigger plan for me. A bigger plan for why I was here and my loving husband Jack was gone.

Although life hasn't been the same since Jack's death, I was starting to resemble my old self again. I was back to work at Holcomb Elementary where I taught second-grade English. I loved being able to shape and mold a young child's mind, especially at that age when structure plays such a pivotal role in determining who they become. Also, I went skydiving with one of my best gal pals, Maureen Smith. Maureen was Jack's half-sister on his birth mother's side. Since Jack was adopted out of foster care when he was around age three, he didn't know of any siblings. We found out about Maureen a few months before his death when she phoned us out of the blue. Unfortunately, Jack didn't know too much about that part of his life; he'd only mentioned his birth mother, Harriet Smith, a handful of times and he never knew the name of his biological father. It took Jack a few weeks to warm up to Maureen, but when I finally convinced him to give the relationship a try, he and Maureen got along swell. Jack would often tell me I was too trusting of people, especially when Maureen initially reached out to us. However, those fears diminished over time once they formed a sibling bond that even I couldn't break.

Lastly, I even began writing again, although this proved to be much more difficult than piecing together lost childhood memories or jumping out of a plane. Writing has always been incredibly special to me. Something that I greatly enjoyed but, subconsciously or otherwise, I now associated it with my husband's death.

I remember I was still at home in my office writing when I received a phone call from one of our longtime friends, Sheriff Rodney Lucas. He was calling to tell me Jack had been in a terrible car accident. A phone call that I remember all too vividly; a phone call that changed my life forever. I didn't know the severity of Jack's condition at that time; I just knew he needed me by his side. Then a few seconds later, Sheriff Lucas informed me that Jack was being transported to Oak Grace Hospital just outside of St. Lux.

However, all I could do in that moment was stare down at the scribbled-on paper that covered my desk. The paper with the make-believe families I created. *This type of life-changing accident was supposed to happen in stories; this terrible thing is what I usually made up in my imagination,* I thought to myself.

With tears welling up and holding Daphne in my arms, I asked the Sheriff, "W-Will my husband be okay?" But, of course, at that time Sheriff Lucas didn't have much information other than reassuring me repeatedly that Jack was a fighter. We talked for maybe another minute but for what seemed like an eternity before the Sheriff offered me a ride to the hospital.

"I-I can drive myself there, Sheriff," I whimpered like a small child.

"Nonsense," he replied. "You're in no condition to drive anywhere. I'll be right over, Sam." Sheriff Lucas said firmly, then we disconnected. The next thing I remember is Rodney pulling into the driveway about the same time I was putting down the phone. St. Lux was a small town but he must've been driving a hundred miles an hour to get here so soon. I knew he was Jack's best friend and cared for him deeply, but all I could think about in that moment was my dear friend Kathleen.

Kathleen was Sheriff Lucas's wife and the four of us all met while in high school. While there, we were known as the "final four" for years, and truthfully, I didn't want Kathleen receiving that same phone call that I'd just gotten. I put Daphne down as she whined a little, presumably picking up on my own state of shock. But I remembered to thank Rodney as I got in the car, then explained the irony of speeding while going to meet Jack at the hospital who was just in a car accident. Rodney understood, smiled, and agreed as we backed out of my driveway and headed towards Oak Grace.

At the hospital, the receptionist lady at the front desk let us know that Jack was in the operating room. We both sat quietly in the cold, empty waiting area until Rodney was called away on another police matter. When he ended his call, I was still sitting in my chair with my hands covering my face. I'm not sure what I was even thinking in that moment. I just felt the chaos of a million tangled thoughts, and I was unable to make sense out of any of them. Rodney walked over to let me know he was leaving but would try and make it back before Jack got out of surgery. Then he knelt in front of me taking both of my hands and we said a prayer together. Afterwards, his phone started to ring and I jumped nervously, as if it could be Jack calling, saying he was alright. However, Rodney interrupted my fantasy when he said it was work calling again. After his phone call, Rodney asked if I was going to be okay and I shook my head yes, then he proceeded on his way.

It seemed like a few seconds later Jack's surgeon was tapping me on the shoulder. I tried asking if everything was okay, but the words wouldn't come out. However, before she said a word her facial expression exposed the truth and something in my heart told me nothing would be okay from that day forward. Then Dr. Jones informed me that Jack's internal injuries were too severe and there was nothing more they could have done. She told me Jack died on the operating table, and immediately I felt something in me died too.

I did sense his presence around me for a few seconds as if his spirit was saying goodbye. But after that, I was sure he had left for good.

Maybe it was survivor's guilt, but I stopped doing anything that brought me joy. No friends, no vacations, and I was like a zombie at work. Kathleen and Rodney would often invite me out, but I was almost afraid to see them as it would heighten my loss and theirs too. I didn't even write again for the next year, mostly because I didn't want to go back to that dark place I was in when I first learned of Jack's accident. It was like I couldn't concentrate and would have to relive the same morning of Jack's death if I put myself back in that writing chair.

But eventually, I realized Jack was gone, and I was doing him a disservice by using his memory to rationalize my fear of moving on. So, I redecorated the office and emptied myself of that painful reality so that the imaginary world could flow through me again. And just two days before everything went haywire, I went down into the basement and grabbed my old desktop computer. I had packed it away right after Jack's funeral and hadn't thought of it since. Tired and out of breath after carrying it up the basement stairs, I placed it back in my office on the wooden table Maureen and I had picked up from the local thrift store just a few days earlier.

Right then, all the ideas and characters I had in my mind for the past year started to come to life on paper. I hadn't realized how being so deeply invested in this one thing could completely take my mind off all other problems. I started to notice how therapeutic writing really had become for me, and honestly, it made me feel whole again, even if it was just for short spurts. However, while I was still lying in bed thinking about becoming a better person, I glanced at the clock on my nightstand and realized that it was almost 6:00 a.m. Poor Daphne was not impressed and started to let me know that she'd been waiting forever for her breakfast kibble, even if I knew it was only fifteen minutes since she jumped into bed with me and proceeded to give me the dog's version of a wet willy.

We both got out of bed and I slipped on my pink bunny slippers, then I walked into the bathroom to grab a tube of ChapStick. The weather today was cold, but very dry. Daphne—like every morning before—ran to the patio doors to bark at the squirrels that had gotten too close to the mound of tree branches she hid near the back deck. So, I started pouring her a bowl of her favorite granola, and as soon as she heard the first piece fall from the box she ran over. I barely had time to stand back up and she was completely done. Daphne was only fifteen pounds, but could eat more than anyone I'd ever met.

Afterwards, I walked into the kitchen turned on the coffee pot, grabbed an apple from the refrigerator, and clicked on the morning news. I absolutely loved watching the segment they recently added about local heroes making a difference in their community. Today's story was about a teenager named Sean who would go around after school and paint murals over the graffiti that covered some walls in the neighborhood.

As the camera panned to Sean during his introduction, I thought. "What an unusual coincidence." Just yesterday I saw this same young man as I sat on my front porch while playing fetch with Daphne. I knew he was a teen, but he looked fairly small for his age. He was barely a hundred pounds, had a huge earring in his ear, and wore a white t-shirt that read in big bold letters, "*Not just a little bit, but a lot.*" It must've been a generational thing because I didn't get it. But what struck me as odd, as I sat there playing with Daphne on my front porch, was how I noticed the kid really hustling across my lawn once she started to bark. I remembered his face because I thought it was a bit funny that a boy his age would be so frightened by such a small dog. Nevertheless, I sat there completely floored and glued to the television screen for the entire segment because of this young man's artistic talent. "What a gift," I said to myself.

Since St. Lux was such a small town, I thought I knew everyone but I'd never met this young man before. The locals here were such busybodies, especially this one group of older women in their eighties, who I called "The Grey Cougars," because they all had grey hair and would constantly flirt with Jack, even if I was with him. Well, I hadn't heard these ladies mention a new family moving into town, so I found it was a bit strange for someone who wasn't a local to be on this news segment about local heroes. However, at the same time, I thought this young man was truly a diamond in the rough. It was heartwarming to see a kid so gifted uplifting his community. Believe it or not, that was the whole reason I decided to become a teacher after all. I knew the world needed more people like this young man and I wanted to play a part in that.

Sadly, Jack and I knew we couldn't have children biologically and we had discussed becoming foster parents before his death. We were trying to start the process of adoption shortly before he died and we had considered fostering teens because, for one reason or another, it seemed like St. Lux was attracting more and more young runaways, and because Jack had grown up in foster care, I knew he wanted to help in any way he could. Now, I just hoped that this Sean wasn't another runaway teen.

After pouring a cup of coffee, I went into my office and began writing. Daphne soon joined me, resting near my feet under the desk. The news was still on in the kitchen, so I heard my good friend and chief meteorologist Tom Miller say that it was going to be a chilly thirty-five degrees today but may warm up to forty-five by noon. I instantly thought to myself. *I couldn't be happier that I scheduled all my errands for tomorrow when it would be an unusually warm 65 degrees and sunny.*

Daphne, on the other hand, although not a fan of chilly weather, couldn't go a day without her walk around Heather Creek's Trail. The trail led to the local bark park where every dog in town got their exercise. Daphne soon ran to the closet and brought back the bedazzled sweater I'd made for her a few winters ago, and I laughed and gave her a pat on the head because an appearance from her sweater normally meant she was ready for a walk. I told Daphne to give me a few minutes, and I was twenty minutes into writing chapter three when my cellphone began to ring.

I thought to myself that the interruption was a few minutes late. Normally, I didn't get these many ideas down on paper before someone sensed I was busy and called. I looked at the caller I.D. and noticed that it was Jack's half-sister, and my dear friend, Maureen Smith.

"Hi, Maureen," I said with the biggest smile.

"Good morning, Sam," Maureen replied. "I know it's early but you promised that you'd go with me the next time I went power walking."

"D-Did I say that?" I asked hesitantly.

"You most certainly did, Sam, and it's not up for discussion. I want you looking as good as you're starting to feel!" Maureen shouted. "I was just calling as a formality," she laughed.

"But it's so cold out this morning, Maureen," I said, lethargically. "Matter of fact, I just heard Tom say it's only thirty-five degrees today."

"Oh, please," Maureen said in a flippant dismissive kind of tone. "Tom Miller, I think, he got that weatherman job for his looks more so than his abilities. I wouldn't be surprised if it was eighty degrees and sunny out. Besides, the colder, the better, for power walking," Maureen said firmly. "It'll give your immune system a well desired boost, so I'll just slip on my shoes, Sam, then I'll be over in a jiffy," a now cheerful Maureen said.

"Okay, I'll see you soon," I replied, then we disconnected.

I loved Maureen to pieces although she would constantly put me in the middle of her bickering with Tom because she felt that he'd made a pass at me at Jack's funeral. However, I was too stricken with grief to notice or even care at that time. Honestly, Maureen showed signs that she could be a handful in the brief time Jack and I were getting to know her, but she also showed that she was a loyal and true friend. After Jack's funeral, she stayed with me day and night for three months, waited on me hand and foot, and helped me find myself again. I credit Maureen with giving me a new lease on life and helping me see that it was okay to smile again even though Jack was gone.

Jack and I went out on a few dinner dates with Maureen when we first met her in order to get to know one another a little better. We found out she never married, didn't have children, and only learned about Jack after her mother confessed, while she was on her death bed, that she'd had another child years before. *What a weird way to find out you have an older brother*, I thought. I couldn't imagine having siblings I didn't know about. So, I didn't pretend to know what the two of them were going through. I just wanted to be there for them.

I eventually forced myself up from my desk and walked into my bedroom with Daphne following behind me as she was so desperately ready for her walk. I knew Maureen would be pulling up any moment. St. Lux was approximately twenty square miles, so you could practically go anywhere in ten minutes. Moreover, Maureen's apartment was just a mile or so away, so it never took her long to arrive.

Maureen was really into physical activity and was a very fit woman. She stood six feet tall with long curly black hair, big broad shoulders, and a six pack to boot. She was in her mid-thirties, about five years younger than Jack and I, and if you didn't know her just to look at her was physically intimidating. She obviously took exercising seriously, especially since she moonlighted as a personal trainer on the weekends. However, in reality, Maureen was a sweetheart, and she left her hometown of Norfolk, Michigan, which was about two hours north of St. Lux after she sold her mother's house. She came to St. Lux to meet Jack but liked it so much she decided to stay. I was glad she chose this area to call home as I knew everyone in town but didn't have many girlfriends. Unfortunately, our friendship hit a rough patch after Jack died. As I was grieving over losing my husband, I failed to realize Maureen had lost her brother. Subsequently, when I finally came to terms with being a widow, I looked up and Maureen was still there. In some weird way, I guess maybe because they were siblings, it felt like I still had a piece of Jack right here with me.

I like to tease her now by saying she got me over the grieving phase by treating me like one of her fitness bootcamp clients. Whatever her method was, I was grateful to have her as a friend. I no longer had Jack but I now had a sister, the sister I'd longed for as a child. Sadly, as the youngest of five children, all older brothers, I didn't get much girl time. To fit in, I either had to be as tough as my brothers or be overlooked, and it felt nice to be close to someone again and not to have to be so tough all the time.

I stood in front of my dresser in my bedroom and grabbed a pair of black leggings. Then I threw on a black sweater that was hanging in my closet. I looked in the mirror as I was getting dressed and thought, *you should be so proud*. You've done a complete 180 since Jack's death. My skin was glowing again, my nails were now healthy after all the biting, and my eyes were no longer red and swollen when I got up in the morning from crying myself to sleep. I had a new attitude and nothing was going to ruin my day. Not the weather, not Maureen and Tom's bickering, heck, I didn't even care that I put my writing, once again, on the back burner.

I grabbed a red scrunchie off the bathroom sink and pulled my brown shoulder length hair into a ponytail. I did a small shimmy for my audience (that'd be Daphne), then I put on my smoky black eyeglasses. Next, I sat on my bed to lace up my athletic running shoes, the ones that I normally only dare put on when I'm feeling carefree. I struck a pose in my bathroom mirror with all five foot three inches of me, loving what I saw staring back. I put my left hand on my hip, my right hand on my back, while my glasses were hanging just off the bridge of my nose. Then I strutted back into my bedroom as if I were the most fashionable model this side of the Mississippi. I felt in charge, that is, until I got hit with a dose of reality. And accidentally tripped over one of Daphne's toys and fell to the floor. I laughed so loud I scared poor Daphne. *I haven't laughed so hard since before Jack died,* I thought. But boy, did it feel good.

As I was picking myself up off the floor, Maureen was ringing the door-bell, and of course Daphne ran over and gave her usual *enter-at-your-own-risk* bark. As I opened the door to let Maureen in, I noticed she was dressed as if it was really eighty degrees out. She wore tight, black, running shorts, a small t-shirt, and a black baseball cap. I asked if she was cold and if she needed a sweater from the bedroom, but she declined. She said she always overheated when power walking and wanted to play it safe today. She then knelt on the kitchen floor to play with Daphne for a while and I remembered she told me she had a similar dog, but he passed away right before her mother did.

As I stood there watching the two of them play, I thought, *How could such a good person get so many bad breaks?*

However, before I got too emotional, I offered Maureen a cup of coffee and she asked for it black with no sugar like every time before, then we sat at my wobbly kitchen table and chatted for a while before heading out. By now it was 6:30 a.m. and I was starting to wonder why I'd ever gotten up so early on a Saturday morning when I didn't have school.

After Maureen finished her coffee, she asked if I had anything edible in the refrigerator she could snack on. She liked to tease me because a month prior I got rid of all the unhealthy goodies throughout the entire house and brought in health-conscious food for the new diet I had recently started. "Grocery shopping is actually one of my errands for tomorrow," I said. "I don't think you'll like anything I have in there now, but I can pick you up a few extra snacks tomorrow, so the next time you come over you won't have to eat what you like to call scraps of unpalatable mush."

"No-no, I don't want to be a hassle. I was only teasing," Maureen laughed.

"Tell you what," I said. "How about we stop by Susie Sweets on our way back from power walking. It's right along the way. I won't get anything but I'm certainly not breaking any rules if I watch you pig out." Maureen agreed and we both had a chuckle.

I finished my coffee, then put Daphne on her leash, and we all walked over towards the front door. Through my big picture window, I saw a man in the empty field across the street watching my house with a pair of binoculars.

He looked so comfortable as if this wasn't his first rodeo. I asked Maureen if she knew who he was, but neither of us could get a good look at his face because we were so far away. Instinctively, as we walked out the front door I looked over at the area where I'd seen the man, but now he was walking away. Unfortunately for him, he turned and looked directly at me and I couldn't believe it. I could see a little bit clearer now and it looked like Sean, the same young teen from the news this morning.

Why would anyone be casing my house? I thought to myself. I knew St. Lux had recently seen a spike in crime since Sheriff Lucas retired, but this was extremely odd. I was more than a little perturbed at the thought of someone spying on me, but two potential sightings in less than a day of the same young man had me thinking this was more than sheer coincidence. I normally would distance myself when I see trouble is brewing, but something in my gut told me this young man needed help. I knew this Sean wasn't a local, so why was he here in St. Lux? How long had he been watching me and what did I possess that was so coveted?

CHAPTER TWO

I decided to tell Maureen about that kid Sean from the news earlier today and that I was sure it was him watching us from a distance. She suggested we take the longer route to the dog park and stop in the empty field where we had originally seen him.

I was hesitant initially, living out here all by myself, but Maureen assured me that if I ran into any trouble in the future, she was just a phone call away. I knew that to be true from previous experience. Besides, by this time curiosity had gotten the better of me as I wanted to know who this person was, and more importantly what he wanted from me.

We headed over in the direction of the empty field. With Daphne nudging out in front, sniffing the entire canvass as if she was a police hound searching for drugs, we came across the area where Sean appeared to have been, and we saw two empty soda cans and some loose candy wrappers, which may have suggested he was there for quite some time. Maureen convinced me that Sean was just another runaway who we scared off and that he probably wouldn't be back since nothing else seemed disturbed in the area. I reluctantly agreed, and we continued towards the park.

By now it was almost 7:30 a.m. and we had just arrived at the dog park. There wasn't anyone else around besides the two of us, so I let Daphne off her leash and began to throw the ball I'd placed in my pocket before leaving home. As I watched Daphne chase the ball in the gated area of the park, I couldn't quite shake the feeling that something bad was looming.

I hadn't felt this way since the day of Jack's accident. Something was still gnawing at me about being so closely surveilled. However, I promised myself a good day and with those so few and far between, I figured Maureen's speculation about a runaway teen would have to be satisfactory for now.

As I continued to play fetch with Daphne, I noticed Maureen doing some stretches to keep loose until we took off again. Unfortunately, I recognized a pattern with Maureen of late that bothered me. Whenever the conversation went too deep, she would often make herself scarce to avoid the subject of family coming up. I didn't know if it was too painful for her to talk about and I didn't want to pry, but Maureen wasn't just an old friend whose past I had no ties to. She was my dead husband's long-lost sister which meant her past was also Jack's past.

However, Maureen never talked much about her childhood, nor did she mention her mother very often. I assumed in the beginning it was because of how raw the emotions were at that time, and considering Maureen found us shortly after their mother's death, Jack never felt the need to pry or ask too many questions about that part of her life either.

But at this point, it was well over a year since her mother's demise and although Jack was gone too, I knew he wanted closure for that missing part of his life even if he was too stubborn to ask. So, I took the risk and asked Maureen if she knew the motive behind her mother never telling her about Jack.

"I guess it was just too painful for her," she replied. "Although she gave him up and chose to keep me, I would imagine the thought of him brought up too many memories that she just wasn't ready to deal with," Maureen answered intensely.

"Well, I guess I can understand that" I concurred, patting her on the shoulder.

"But hey, while we're on the subject, I do have a confession, Sam," Maureen professed.

"What is it? I asked.

"Well, I don't know how to tell you this, but I need you to promise me that you won't get upset," Maureen pleaded.

"Well, of course, I won't," I said in a worried tone. What's got you so upset?" I asked, hoping that whatever she said next didn't ruin our friendship because I have to admit I had never seen Maureen so visibly shaken.

"W-Well, I do have this locket of Mom's," Maureen whispered softly. She went on to say she had a photo of Jack and their mother inside that says, "forever my boy." "Honestly, on her death bed she asked me to find Jack and let him know that he was always in her heart, but I just couldn't bring myself to part with her locket so soon after her death. It was only a few months later that Jack died, and I never got the chance to give him the one thing that possibly could have stirred up some old memories."

"Oh, I just feel so awful about that," Maureen cried out as her eyes welled up with tears.

Oh my, I thought. Part of me was furious at Maureen for withholding such information that could have been beneficial in helping Jack heal while the other part just wanted to console my friend.

I held my arms out and Maureen just fell into them as if she was a five-year-old child. I could tell she had been holding this secret in since Jack's death, and she looked as though she had just released a huge burden off her shoulders. We both stood there holding each other while crying for the next five minutes before I asked Maureen if I could see the photo of a young Jack she had in their mother's locket. She handed it over and I unclasped the lock and looked inside.

There was little Jack sitting on his mother's lap. He had to be around two years old when the photo was taken. Harriet, Maureen and Jack's mother, looked much older than I'd presumed. She looked to be around forty years of age in the photo.

I clutched the locket close to my heart for a few minutes, then handed it back to Maureen. I told her not to worry about the secret she'd kept, that we'd always be friends, and that we'd get through this.

"Besides, you've got a more pressing engagement with a jelly donut right now," I said gleefully.

She smiled as she continued to wipe tears from her face and she let me know that I wasn't just her friend but I was her family.

"I totally agree!" I said with a smile.

A few minutes later, we were walking as slow as turtles to accommodate Daphne's short legs. We got about half a mile down the trail when I saw one of the most beautiful young women I'd ever seen in my life coming towards us.

She looked like a movie star and dressed the part. I was baffled as to why she was here in St. Lux when she looked like she should be on a runway in Paris, but we continued walking. Daphne on her leash ran over towards the young lady as she walked by and then sat on her shoe. Daphne was smart as a whip but couldn't contain herself around high heel shoes for some reason.

The woman couldn't have been more gracious. She was dressed in black tights, a black vest, an extravagant fur coat, and four-inch heels while advertising impeccable makeup. She even wore my favorite perfume (Bare Witness), which somehow smelled better on her. She started to laugh as Daphne wiggled onto her shoe. I apologized profusely before shooing Daphne away, but then the woman stopped me, knelt to pet Daphne, and said, "Oh, don't worry about it, these shoes are rags anyway. Besides, this dog has got to be about the cutest thing I've ever seen," the woman added. "What's his name anyway?" she asked.

"Oh, it's a girl." I replied. "Her name is Daphne."

The woman who looked half my age, giggled, then said, "Daphne, that's my mother's name." I had a chuckle as well before I told the young woman that I named Daphne after a childhood friend (although I called this friend Dee on most occasions). But, sadly on my ninth birthday her parents decided to move away and I never saw her again. I told the young girl my name was Samantha Harris and I also introduced Maureen, who looked less than impressed with the woman's fashion statement. She politely reached out her hand and said, "Nice to meet you, Samantha Harris, I'm Ronda Evans."

I guess I was too mesmerized by her beauty to notice before, because for the first time since we'd been talking, I thought I heard a slight southern accent, *Ahh I'll bet she's from Tennessee too,* I thought to myself. I usually had a pretty keen ear for that particular regional dialect, partially because our new Sheriff Philip Hawkins and his late wife Julia were originally from Tennessee, and when they spoke they had that same charming accent. I asked Ronda what brought her to the small town of St. Lux, and why she was going through the dog park in such expensive clothing. She gave a half-smile and said, "I thought this was a dog park but I'm a bit lost. Can you help me, Samantha?"

"Well, you ran into the right girl," I said. I know this area like the back of my hand. St. Lux wasn't a large city by any stretch, but if you weren't a local you could certainly get turned around.

"Whereabouts you headed?" I asked.

"Well, you see, I'm here in town from Nashville for a few more days, and I'm on my way to meet a friend for lunch," Ronda said. "I'm coming from the Pelican Hotel over on Morton Avenue and I'm supposed to meet someone at the Steamy Brew coffee shop on Wren Drive."

"I know exactly where you're headed!" I said, buoyantly. "It's not that far. You simply need to continue down this trail, make a left in half a mile, walk down about two minutes, and you can't miss it. I go there nearly every day and they have the best coffee in town," I said with enthusiasm.

"Oh, thank you, Samantha," Ronda shouted. "You're a godsend."

"Not a problem," I replied.

"Ooh, by the way, Samantha, I love that scrunchie," Ronda said, flattering me. "I had a multitude of those that were similar in style I brought with me from home. You know the ones strong enough to keep every strand of hair in its place while simultaneously making a fashion statement. However, the strangest thing happened on the plane ride here," Ronda said, while appearing to still be pondering what had occurred. She went on to say that her carry-on bag was stolen from the overhead compartment while she slept in her plush first-class seat. She didn't seem overly concerned with the lost property, and quite honestly, she appeared flattered that someone would even go through all the trouble just to have a personal possession of hers.

"You wouldn't happen to remember where you got those scrunchies, would you?" Ronda asked. "I'm going shopping later to try and recoup a few of the items that were stolen and I'd love to add a bunch more hair accessories to my collection."

"Oh, really," I said cheerfully. "Well, Ronda I just may be your lucky charm today because I actually make and sell these all over town," I said, with exaggerated pride in my voice.

"No way!" Ronda yelled out in excitement. "Cost is no issue," Ronda proclaimed. "I'll take ten of every color. I have a few girls that I'm currently sponsoring and I'm sure they'll love them as well," she stated.

I told Ronda I wasn't sure if I had that many off hand, but for five dollars a scrunchie I would certainly work through the night to produce them. Ronda was adamant about receiving those scrunchies before she left town and asked if she could give me her number, so I could call when they were ready. I instantly started checking my pockets for my phone and realized that I'd left it in my office, which unfortunately meant I had no way to save her information.

Before I could mention that I misplaced my phone, Ronda saw me in a panic while searching for it and shouted out, "No worries, I've got mine." As she pulled her phone from her coat pocket, she asked me to store my number, then said she'd give me a call in the morning for my address to see if her order was complete.

As she continued to talk after she handed me her phone, I soon realized that I couldn't work such a fancy piece of equipment. I didn't want to interrupt the story she was in the middle of, nor did I want to admit how perplexed I was trying to work such a pricey device. So, embarrassingly, all I could do was call my number in hopes that she would see it later and save it from her call log. At the very least, I figured she'd have quite the chuckle at my expense once she realized what I had done. I handed Ronda back her phone and she said she'd touch bases with me tomorrow, then ran off to meet her friend at the coffee shop.

Once Ronda was gone from view, I walked over towards Maureen to tell her the good news. She had gone over towards the trash can just off the trail to dispose of a slice of pizza someone dropped on the ground. Just a few feet from Maureen, I raised both arms, jumped in the air and shouted, "I'm going to be rich! If I could get some publicity from someone like Ronda wearing my scrunchies, this could be a crucial breakthrough," I told Maureen.

Maureen, always the skeptic, responded with disapproval. "Well, if she could influence the masses, she wouldn't be here in St. Lux traipsing around a dog park now, would she?"

"Be that as it may," I retorted. "When I was putting my number in her phone she told me about her huge following on *instagraph*, and how she had gained nationwide admiration because of it."

"That's Instagram and they're called 'followers.' And that makes her an Influencer," Maureen said as she laughed.

"Well, whatever her cult calls itself," I said, "it's far more people than I could ever reach by myself. So, it couldn't hurt to try."

Although Maureen was one of the people who initially helped me out of my depression after Jack died, I knew ultimately it was up to me to keep moving forward and to have no qualms about doing so.

As we continued on our journey, I noticed Daphne's tail flailing about and her ears sticking straight up and I knew that tail wag could mean only one thing. We were getting closer to Susie Sweets. The further we walked, the more I could smell the pastries in the air. *Oh, how I've missed them,* I thought to myself.

I had been so good all last month with denying myself any food with flavor that I knew just the smell of fresh pastries would make me gain five pounds. We stopped in front of Susie Sweets and I chose to wait outside with Daphne while Maureen went in to place her order.

As I was waiting, I saw Susie Lynn pull up in her one-of-a-kind all-pink electric car. Susie had taken over the pastry shop when her father died and she changed the name from *Phenomenal Pastries* to *Susie Sweets*. Before running into Ronda, a little while ago, Susie was the most extravagant person St. Lux had to offer.

She stepped out of her pink car wearing pink Crocs, pink jeans, a pink crop top, and flaunting pink streaks in her otherwise blonde hair. Susie was nothing if not eye-catching. She saw me and demanded I come over.

Oh no, I thought to myself. Susie Lynn was as stubborn as a mule when she didn't get her way, and she could hurl insults that would make the raunchiest comedian blush.

As I walked over, Daphne began to bark at Susie whom she'd met several times before. I knew dogs were color blind but I would've bet my bottom dollar that Daphne's dismay had something to do with all the pink.

As I reached Susie, I picked Daphne up just to calm her from barking.

"Aw shucks, I thought you were someone important," Susie said cruelly.

"Oh, well hello to you too," I replied. "How's your better half, Peter, and those gorgeous stepchildren of yours doing? I saw you guys posted the most amazing pictures of your family vacation. It sure did look like a fun time," I said.

"Well, of course it did. Yours truly was in the photos," Susie boasted. "However, I sure am glad to be back home. I spent the entire time worrying about the shop. Well, hey, I know you never have much going on in your life, Samantha," Susie—tactless as usual—said. "How about next time I get you to look after the store while we're gone!"

I had recently started to meditate when I changed my eating habits. So, I was well equipped to let more than a few of Susie's unwarranted insults roll off my back.

"I'd love to care after your shop, but you know I have a full-time job as a schoolteacher," I reminded her.

"Oh, I just assumed that didn't take up much of your time since kids that age usually just color on walls and imitate purple dinosaurs," Susie boldly stated.

I smiled through gritted teeth while trying to say as eloquently as the moment would allow that it did indeed take time and lots and lots of patience. *Almost as much patience as dealing with you*, I thought to myself. Susie, usually out of touch with reality, somehow sensed resentment in my last statement and abruptly yelled, "Well, you didn't have to come over here to try and start a fight with me, Samantha."

Typical Susie, I thought to myself. After you would call her out for insulting you, then she would seemingly make everything your fault.

A few minutes later and somewhere mixed in the hurtful comments, Susie insisted that I double the scrunchie order she'd placed last week. "Are you expecting I double the order in the same amount of time?" I asked.

"Well, if it's not too much trouble, Samantha," Susie said. "My daughter's school is now taking the whole fifth grade class on the girl scout expedition and it's now more girls than we originally thought," Susie complained.

The girl scouts, how admirable, I thought. Even if it did just come out of Susie Lynn's mouth.

"Well, I can't always complete scrunchie orders because I have a day job," I reiterated to Susie. "However, since this is a special occasion, I'll make an exception, and I'll have your order ready by next week," I said, hoping that would be the end of it.

By now Maureen was walking out of Susie Sweets with a donut in each hand. I told Susie that I needed to meet back up with Maureen, but I'd certainly phone her when her order was ready. I gently put Daphne back down and we headed over towards the store entrance.

"What'd the Wicked Witch of St. Lux want?" Maureen asked.

"She actually wanted to double her order!" I said in a panic. "Between Susie the other day and now Ronda this morning, I'm not sure if I can keep pace with customer demand."

"Do you want me to go tell the Witch to get her hair accessories elsewhere?" Maureen said audaciously.

After a brief delay and a slight giggle, I told Maureen that wouldn't be necessary. "Besides, it'll be good business to get my merchandise out there. I guess it's just a little overwhelming to think about," I whispered.

I turned and saw Susie walking towards the store entrance with baking supplies in each hand, so I held the door open for her without so much as a thank you in return. However, while looking inside, I noticed the big donut-shaped clock on the far wall. The day sure was getting away from me. I thought

I'd better get moving if I wanted to give myself any chance of completing Ronda's order by tomorrow.

It was already after 11:00 a.m. and I didn't want to miss the opportunity to earn some extra money while also getting my merchandise in the hands of two very fashion-forward women. So, I told Maureen I was going to scurry back home to get ahead of some of the orders that were placed last week. Then I gave her a hug and Daphne and I walked the short distance home.

We made it back in less than ten minutes and I entered after Daphne, then set the alarm. I went downstairs into the basement and began to sort through all my fabric scraps. I knew there wasn't enough material for everyone in my order log, but I figured these pieces would at least get me through the night. Ten minutes later, I had one bedazzling scrunchie down, and according to my records, two hundred and nineteen to go.

The next time I looked at my watch it was well after 6:00 p.m. I had worked almost an entire eight-hour shift producing scrunchies. That was until I heard my phone ringing upstairs. However, the basement was in such disarray with boxes of material everywhere that I didn't dare think about running through this trip hazard to see who was calling. Mainly because I figured it was my mother. We had talked last night before she and my dad left for their fiftieth wedding anniversary to Jamaica.

During our conversation last night, she mentioned that she'd give me a call this evening before they went out to dinner. I loved my mother, but for some reason, even though I was nearly forty years old, she possessed the unique ability to scold me at every turn for not joining the family practice and becoming a doctor like all my brothers had. So, I decided to steer clear of any hassle and call her back when I had both the time and energy for a lecture.

I finally made it upstairs and went into the kitchen to make myself a sandwich. By now it was going on 6:30 p.m. and staying up after midnight the night before was starting to take its toll. I finished off my turkey sandwich at my wobbly kitchen table and decided to take a nap for a few hours. I had planned on pulling an overnighter making scrunchies. So, I figured a quick cat nap would be beneficial for someone like me, seeing as how I hadn't stayed up all night since my twenties. I walked into the living room to lay down on the sofa, then Daphne joined me a few minutes later curling up next to my feet.

I slept longer than I'd planned because it was almost 10:00 p.m. when I woke up. I stumbled into the kitchen still in a haze and poured myself a glass of iced tea, then I gulped it down because I had a feeling it was going to be a long night. Next, I turned on my computer and programmed it to play smooth jazz throughout the entire house. I turned on the television so the news could play in the background. I wanted to be certain that the weather forecast for tomorrow hadn't changed. Before heading back downstairs I walked into my office to see if I had any extra sewing materials in the closet. I quickly realized I didn't have any material, but I heard my phone chime with a voicemail notification while I was in my office. *Could this be another order someone placed while I was asleep?* I thought to myself.

I loved making scrunchies but lately it was starting to feel like more work than I could handle. I picked up my phone and called my voicemail, then entered my code and I was flabbergasted by what I heard. Evidently, I was listening to a murder that had taken place right over the phone! I could hear a woman pleading for her life and someone else in the background, who I assumed was her tormentor but I couldn't make out what they were saying. I couldn't even differentiate whether it was a man or a woman when they spoke.

Whoever it was, they began to yell abruptly but all their words were completely muffled. I assumed the woman in trouble covered the phone somehow so it wouldn't be seen, but in doing so I could hear her perfectly clear while everything else was completely distorted. The woman began begging for her life and I hadn't the slightest idea how to help her. I didn't know who she was or if she was even here in St. Lux or why she called *my* number.

The voicemail went on and the woman began to cry and say she just wanted to go home. I was in total shock and I couldn't believe what I was hearing. She then said she wouldn't tell anyone about the other murders and cried that if she could just leave, then she'd go home and never come back. About two seconds later, I heard her let out a deafening scream that made my eyes fill with tears.

What was going on there? Could she have been fighting for her life in that moment? Did she need medical attention? Oh, how I didn't want to imagine what was happening to her.

The woman, sensing she couldn't get out of the situation she was in, began to bargain with her captor.

"If you name your price, I'll make sure you never have to worry about money again," she said. However, sadly I got the feeling that her captor wasn't interested in her riches.

The next thing I heard was the woman ask, "How would you make this one look like an accident, obviously no one will ever believe I harmed myself and you know the cops will tie my death to all the others."

"Tie her death to all the others." I repeated. *Were random people being targeted for some reason, and was I in some sort of danger?* I thought to myself. After all, it seemed as though whoever this woman was, she was giving me clues. Could it be that big of a stretch to think maybe she was trying to warn me somehow?

Then finally, something I could understand, and I'm sure it didn't come from the distressed woman. I clearly heard someone whistling in the background as if they were thoroughly enjoying what was taking place. However, it wasn't just a random whistle. They were whistling the melody to the song "Anything You Can Do I Can Do Better," which I recognized from the TV show *Glee,* because Jack and I use to watch it faithfully every week. Oh, the stark terror this woman must've been experiencing in that moment! It was almost too much to imagine. And right before the voicemail cut off, I heard a loud boom that sounded like fireworks going off. Then I heard what I perceived to be someone gasping for air, followed by complete silence.

Sadly, with my knees feeling weak I sat down on the couch, completely frozen and unable to comprehend what I'd just heard. My thoughts were running randomly in my head. Who was this woman, and why did she sound so familiar? I thought. Should I call the police, and what would I say if I did? Would they even believe me? Would they think it was all just a prank?

I paced back and forth in my living room until my feet were raw, then I noticed the television from the corner of my eye. The news was still on, and I instantly realized why the voice was so familiar. David Holtz, our local anchorman from Channel 18 News, was reporting a story that developed a few hours earlier. My heart sank as I turned the volume up. To my dismay on the television screen was a picture of a young lady who David referred to as Jane Doe. She was shot once in the chest and died instantly, he reported. David went on to say that the deceased had no I.D. on her person, and that Channel 18 News received an anonymous phone call earlier in the night informing them of the location where they could find the girl's body. He said they also found a photo of the girl that the killer left behind for some reason. It was clear Channel 18 used the photo they'd received from the killer in hopes of someone coming forward and identifying the slain girl. *Oh, my that loud boom that sounded like fireworks going off must've been a gunshot.* I thought to myself.

As tears filled my eyes, I knew it had to be her who I'd just heard on my voicemail. I was aware right away that this wasn't some well thought out prank, and unfortunately, I knew she wasn't a Jane Doe either. I recognized exactly who this woman was! It was Ronda Evans. The beautiful young woman from this morning in the dog park who was extremely nice to Daphne and I. A feeling of unease overtook me the longer I stared at her photo. Then I remembered Ronda mentioned that she was meeting a friend at the Steamy Brew Coffee Shop.

Could this person be involved? I thought to myself. Who was she meeting and had she made it there, was the question. I couldn't believe that someone would want to harm her in this way. *Who was her murderer?* I thought. *And who were the other victims Ronda mentioned? Is this the reason for her murder—that she knew too much? Why had she called me instead of the police?*

There were so many questions, but absolutely no answers. Well, no answers for now, but I certainly planned on getting to the bottom of this awful tragedy.

CHAPTER THREE

After I'd paced the room, I sat down in my chair in a state of disbelief and thought I'd better contact Sheriff Lucas with this information right away. As I dialed the police station, a sense of calm came over me. I knew if anyone could get to the bottom of this, it'd be the Sheriff. After the phone rang several times, Charlie West finally answered. Charlie attended my church and had just recently graduated from high school. He thought he'd make a fine police officer one day. Unfortunately for him, no one else echoed that sentiment. However, Charlie stuck around the police station answering phones and running errands, hoping one day he'd get his big break and solve a major case.

"Hello St. Lux police department Officer West, umm Charlie West speaking. How may I help you?" Charlie asked.

"Oh, Hi, Charlie, this is Samantha Harris. I was hoping to catch Sheriff Lucas. He wouldn't happen to still be in, would he?" I asked.

"Well, hello there, Sam," Charlie replied. "I'll take it you had quite the day calling in asking for a retired Sheriff. I would imagine He and Mrs. Lucas are still somewhere in the Florida Keys enjoying their vacation, but I can get Sheriff Hawkins if you'd like to speak with him," Charlie said.

Oh geez, I thought to myself. I had completely forgotten that Sheriff Lucas retired nearly two months ago, and Philip Hawkins was the town's new Sheriff. From our few interactions I knew Philip was certainly a no-nonsense, take-no-prisoners, do-it-by-the-book kind of guy, and his reputation preceded him. So, I figured he'd be just as determined as Sheriff Lucas would've been to get justice. "Yes, Charlie," I replied swiftly. "I'd like to speak with Sheriff Hawkins. I need to report a murder," I murmured hesitantly.

"OH, GEE WHIZ, A MURDER!" Charlie shouted out. "Is there anything I can help with, Sam?" he asked.

"Maybe later, Charlie." I replied promptly. "Right now, I may have vital information involving a young woman who was fatally shot earlier tonight, and I'd like to hand it straight over to the Sheriff," I said firmly.

"Oh wow." Charlie said in a hushed tone. "You're referring to the Jane Doe victim from earlier tonight. I'll go find the Sheriff right away, Sam."

As I sat waiting for Sheriff Hawkins to come to the phone, I tried not to replay in my mind all the terrible things I'd just heard on that voicemail. However, all I could think about was how sweet Ronda was in that brief encounter we'd had this morning, and how her family back home must've been worried sick from not being able to reach her.

After a few minutes, Charlie came back to the phone and said Sheriff Hawkins was gone for the night and that his Deputy Randall Hicks was unfortunately out on a call. He informed me of the Sheriff's wishes not to be disturbed at home unless it was absolutely dire. Then I remembered not long ago while at church, Charlie boasted about nabbing a shoplifter who stole a fifty-cent candy bar, and he subsequently called the Sheriff, at home, in the middle of the night to brag that he'd single-handedly apprehended St. Lux's candy bar bandit. I now understood why Sheriff Hawkins had this 'do not disturb rule' in place.

I told Charlie not to worry about calling the Sheriff this late at home, partially because I didn't want to add to Charlie's already extensive list of infractions. Moreover, I wasn't exactly sure what I'd say at this point. I didn't really know Ronda personally, so I had no inkling of anyone who could've been responsible for her death, and I certainly had no clue why I received that voicemail, but I felt like there must be more to the story. So, I let Charlie know that I'd be in first thing in the morning to speak with Sheriff Hawkins and told him not to mention a word of our conversation to anyone. He agreed, and we disconnected. I realized I had a terrible case of the shakes as I put my phone down.

Now it was almost 11:00 p.m. and I wasn't sure if it was the iced tea, the nap, or the unfortunate circumstances I now found myself in but I was wide awake, and it looked like Daphne was also. She ran over to me and turned belly side up, so I knelt down to start our nightly ritual of 'rub the belly.'

As I stood up, I noticed light coming in the front window from outside. All I could think about was how bad Maureen scared me just a few weeks ago on Halloween, when she stood outside this very window wearing the most hideous mask I'd ever seen while tapping on the glass with a strobe flashlight in her hand.

As I walked over to the big picture window to close the curtains, I noticed the glare was coming from the streetlight directly across from my house. The light must've been broken because it started to flicker on and off every few seconds. *Thank God,* I thought to myself. I wasn't sure if I could handle another scare from anyone tonight. As I pulled the curtain closed the flickering light came back on, and I saw the silhouette of someone in the same empty field where Maureen and I had seen Sean this morning. *Was I going crazy?* I thought. Who would want to spend their days and nights watching me? I taught second-grade English for goodness' sake. My life was as dull as they come. Well, I was no longer certain that it was just a young runaway who'd been outside my house earlier today. If the traumatic voicemail of Ronda's brutal murder wasn't enough, now I had someone getting dangerously close to stalking me.

I called Maureen up in a frenzy and told her someone was watching my house again, and that I was on my way over to her apartment. She said I was much too distraught to get behind the wheel of a car and to just sit tight, and she'd be over in five minutes. Well, I didn't exactly have time to mention that awful voicemail nor the anxiety I now felt having heard Ronda's last moments before her death, but I'm sure Maureen sensed something more sinister than a midnight creeper from my tone.

Soon after we disconnected, I saw Maureen walking up my driveway as I looked out the window. I don't think I've ever been so happy to see someone coming over to my house so late at night. I disengaged the alarm and opened the front door before Maureen had a chance to ring the doorbell. Then I pulled her inside, turned the alarm back on, and told her to look out the window over at the empty field with me to seek out any movement. We watched for at least ten minutes and didn't see anything, so we walked into the kitchen and I offered Maureen a glass of iced tea. As I poured her drink, I asked her how she got here so fast on foot. Maureen mentioned she was already out on one of her nightly runs and was just up the road when I called her.

"As a matter of fact, Sam..." Maureen said, "During my run, I saw that rent-a-cop Charlie West. We chatted for a while and although he offered me a bottle of water not even five minutes before you called, my mouth is still extremely dry. So could you be a lamb and put a rush on that iced tea?"

Shortly after I joined Maureen at the kitchen table and handed her a tall glass of iced tea, I then tried to make sense of this irrational day. However, before I could get a word out, Maureen sensed that I wasn't in the same mindset since we'd last seen one another just a few hours earlier. She then asked if the shadowy figure had really gotten me this upset, or if it was something more I hadn't told her.

"There's something more," I responded. "There's a lot more."

"Well, what is it, Sam?" Maureen asked. "What's got you so on edge?"

"Do you remember the girl from the dog park earlier today?" I asked. "Remember I told you she wanted to buy a bunch of my scrunchies!"

"Umm yeah." Maureen responded. "Little Miss Hot Pants! What about her?" Maureen asked.

"W-Well...she's dead," I whispered, realizing my voice was going to crack.

"WAIT, WHAT?" Maureen shouted. "Dead! How could she be dead?" Maureen asked frantically.

"Trust me she's dead because I heard her on my voicemail being tortured and eventually killed, and I've been a complete wreck ever since," I said emotionally. "Then that creeper outside didn't help matters."

"Whoa, calm down," Maureen said, as she cut me off by throwing up her hands. "Take a deep breath, Sam. Now, one problem at a time. How do you know the girl from the dog park is dead?" Maureen asked in a caring voice.

I explained everything in depth to Maureen, then I let her listen to the voicemail for herself. *God help us all,* I thought as I watched Maureen's posture completely crumble while she sat there listening to Ronda's untimely death. I heard Maureen let out several audible gasps as the voicemail played on. When it ended, she asked how I knew the distressed woman on the call was Ronda when she never said her name. I pointed at the television as I rewound the news back to the Jane Doe story.

All the color drained from Maureen's face, and she just about fell from her chair before I extended a hand to her shoulder to catch her fall. I asked if she was okay, and if she'd eaten anything all day.

"How embarrassing, I'm supposed to be the tough one," Maureen said as she sat back up in her chair. "I am a little light-headed, so I guess I could go for one of your famous turkey sandwiches if it's not too much trouble."

"No trouble at all, it's my pleasure" I replied. "One finger-licking Samantha Harris Turkey Sandwich coming right up," I fervently announced.

And after I finished making Maureen's sandwich at the kitchen counter, I placed it in front of her. Poor thing must've been starving because she gobbled it down in about three bites. She then finished off her glass of iced tea and was now starting to get her color back.

Maureen then asked if I'd called the police with this information I knew about Ronda. I told her I called but couldn't get through to anyone of importance, so I was going to the police station first thing in the morning.

"NOT WITHOUT ME!" Maureen shouted. "It's just awful what's happened to that poor girl, but I wouldn't dream of making you go through this alone," Maureen said.

"That would be great, Maureen," I responded. "I really could use the extra support. I'm not certain but I think whoever killed Ronda could now be after me," I suggested.

"Why on earth would you say that?" Maureen asked.

"Well, you heard the voicemail, Maureen," I said, suddenly feeling frantic again. "Ronda mentioned other victims, so it's not past the realm of reality that whosever is responsible for her death could be on some sort of murder spree. Maybe a serial killer! And we still don't know anything about this creeper whose been watching my house," I said nervously.

"Well, I wouldn't go associating Ronda's killer with your parking lot crook just yet, Sam." Maureen replied as she stood up and walked back over to the big picture window to have another look around outside. "Are you sure you saw someone in the same field as earlier, Sam?"

"Absolutely!" I responded. "As soon as that flickering light came back on, I noticed someone there. You do believe me, don't you, Maureen?" I asked.

"Of course," she said. "Without question."

"It's not that, it's just..."

"Well, what is it?" I asked, before she could finish her thought.

"Well, Sam," Maureen said before taking a long pause. "I know you've been through a lot lately and you've had more than your fair share of bad luck. I'm just worried about how much more you can take before you have a breakdown," Maureen whispered softly.

She sounds exactly like Jack, I thought to myself. He'd always tell me I held everything inside for much too long, and he didn't want to be around on the day when it all came boiling to the surface. I gave Maureen a quick smile and told her not to worry, and that growing up in a house with four brothers made me a lot stronger than I looked. In that moment, thinking of my own family, I knew I couldn't stop until Ronda's killer was brought to justice.

As Maureen and I sat at my wobbly kitchen table talking, I insisted she stay the night since she'd be going with me in the morning to speak with Sheriff Hawkins. Shortly after, I went into the guest bedroom that Jack had decorated with antique furniture from the early 1900s. There was an old withered wooden vanity that sat in the corner. Jack said that it belonged to his adoptive mother's grandparents. Also, the walls were completely covered with old photos that told the complete story of his adopted family's heritage, and on the floor lay a real bear-skin rug that, from the looks of it, had been around since before George Washington was president.

Maureen walked in and said she wouldn't be able to sleep if she didn't at least go outside and check the premises to see if anything had been disturbed around the house. I was putting clean linens on the bed, so I asked her to wait a minute and Daphne and I would go with her. Maureen—ever the hothead—insisted she'd be fine and said that she could handle whoever was trying to scare me. She rushed out of the bedroom before I could tell her I didn't like the idea, then hurried and pulled the front door closed behind her as she walked out so the alarm wouldn't engage.

I ran over to the big picture window to make certain Maureen didn't stray too far from the house. As I approached the window and pulled back the curtains, I saw Maureen running towards the empty field across the street.

Oh no! I thought. Someone dangerous could be lying in wait just beyond the shadows. I snatched my black jacket from the front closet, then ran into the kitchen, and grabbed the first weapon I saw. Instinctively, I grabbed my house keys off the kitchen counter. Jack never liked the idea of me having to leave for work before the roosters got up. So, he insisted that I carry a small bottle of pepper spray on my key chain along with a key-sized folding knife. I put my keys in my jacket pocket and rushed over to the empty field to reach Maureen.

Once I got there, I saw Maureen who suddenly looked rather discombobulated checking the pockets of what appeared to be a man's coat.

"Why'd you run off by yourself, Maureen? You scared me half to death!" I said, frowning at her.

"S-Sorry, Sam," Maureen replied, barely able to get the words out while almost falling to the ground.

"Maureen, are you okay?" I asked. "You don't look so hot."

"I just need to lie down," Maureen responded.

Still slightly bewildered about the drastic change in Maureen's demeanor, I picked the coat up off the ground that I'd just seen Maureen holding and we hurried back to my house. As we walked up the stairs to the front porch, I checked the inside coat pocket and noticed the same candy wrappers that Maureen and I saw in the field earlier today. But other than the candy wrappers the pockets were empty. I had a nagging suspicion that this coat belonged to Sean, I just hoped he wasn't the crazed lunatic that was just watching my house.

We finally got back inside and I set the alarm again. Maureen looked exhausted. Being such an active woman, I had never seen her in such a feeble state. It took just about all my energy to help get her into bed. She'd jogged all over town today and now was barely able to walk. *Quite the turnabout,* I thought.

Shortly after, I went into my bedroom and tried to get some sleep but my mind was racing nonstop. I felt like I should be doing something but with no Sheriff at the station there wasn't much I could do, so I got out of bed and walked to the big picture window again just to see if someone—maybe the suspect— had come back looking for the coat, just in case I was wrong about it being Sean's. The streetlight was off when I glanced over towards the field, but when it flickered back on, I saw a man dressed in all black. He reached down and picked something up that was sitting on the ground near his feet.

Then suddenly a loud explosion shook the room and the entire window shattered into a million pieces. As I stood back up from instinctively crouching, I saw the person responsible running away like an Olympic track star. I soon realized someone had thrown a brick through my window with a note attached to it. My hands were shaking again as I gingerly unfolded the note, which read, *There are secrets that you shouldn't uncover, graves that you don't want to discover, and truths that will devastate and make you suffer, so leave now while you can!*

What a monster, I thought. And as afraid as I was, I chose to feel anger instead. *The nerve of some people thinking they could scare me out of the home that my husband and I built.* Well, I wasn't going anywhere. Now I was more determined than ever to get justice for those who couldn't get it for themselves.

I didn't want to touch the brick and leave my fingerprints on it, so I went into the bathroom and got a pair of medical gloves from the first aid kit, then I peeked inside the guest bedroom to check on Maureen. She appeared to be out like a light. I didn't want to wake her with any more shocking news, so I ran into the kitchen and got a couple of large trash bags along with some duct tape and then I covered the broken window and wrapped the brick in some of my fabric scraps, so I didn't accidentally touch it.

Boy, was I furious. *That brick could've hit Daphne*, I thought to myself. Not to mention the hundreds of dollars I would have to shell out to get that window replaced. I counted my blessings that no one was hurt. But if some lunatic thought they could scare me off that easily, they sure had another think coming.

I went to my bedroom to lay down again and by now it was after midnight. Surely, I'd be able to get some rest now. I lay there for the next twenty minutes with my eyes closed. I was trying to think of the most recent team who'd won the world series while simultaneously counting sheep—or anything I could think of to help me forget what just happened and doze off. However, nothing was working.

I seemed to be in a twilight sleep when I saw Ronda, and she was screaming just beyond the horizon. As I got closer, she motioned for me to turn around. Unfortunately, I was as frozen as a mouse who'd just seen a bobcat.

Just a few minutes later, I felt as if I was in a trance floating outside of my body when I heard Ronda whisper in a hushed tone, "If you're trying to solve my murder, the evidence may be right in front of you." Then I heard her giggle while saying, "As long as Daphne isn't blocking it."

I tried asking Ronda about the evidence she'd just alluded to. However, when I finally got close enough to her, like magic, she was gone. Immediately, Daphne came barging into my room and her barking snapped me back into reality. I had to pinch myself just to make sure I wasn't still hallucinating. I was unsure what that hypnotic state of mind I'd just experienced was all about, but it was more than enough to chill my blood. Now that I was petrified, I finally closed my eyes and mere seconds later, I was out like a light.

CHAPTER FOUR

The next morning, Daphne didn't get the chance to give me her infamous wet willy. I was up at 5:30 a.m. I had only slept a few hours because I knew I needed to be at the police station to see Sheriff Hawkins bright and early. I poured Daphne a bowl of granola and went into the guest bedroom to wake Maureen. I nudged her on the shoulder until she rolled over, but she didn't respond verbally so I decided to hop in the shower and let her rest for another five minutes.

Ten minutes later, I noticed Maureen was still asleep in bed, and until now I never knew she was such a sound sleeper. She slept well through the smashing of the window last night, and now she was sleeping through my attempt to wake her. I tried nudging Maureen a second time and got nothing for my effort, so I walked outside with Daphne to get some fresh air.

Five minutes later, Daphne and I came back inside and Maureen was still sound asleep. Well, this had been eating at me all night and I couldn't wait any longer. I wrote Maureen a note, explaining that I'd gone to the police station and not to worry about the broken window. Then I grabbed the biggest purse

I could find in my closet and placed the brick in it before I made my way to the police station.

It was 6:10 a.m. when I arrived and boy, did this place look different since Rodney Lucas retired as Sheriff just two months ago. I walked through the front doors with a sense of urgency, then ran through the lobby. I noticed that Charlie West was back at work sitting behind the front desk, so I asked that he get the Sheriff right away when suddenly someone tapped me on the shoulder. I turned around and to my surprise it was Sheriff Hawkins.

"Well, good morning, Mrs. Harris!" Sheriff Hawkins said. "You ran in here so fast I practically had to stop dead in my tracks so you didn't knock me down. What can I do you for?" he asked with that southern charm of his.

"Oh, pardon me, Sheriff, I didn't see you," I said. "However, I do need to speak with you, but it's somewhat of a private matter and I'd rather not do it here in the lobby."

"I know what it's about, sheriff," Charlie blurted out. "Can I come sit in on this one?" he asked.

"I'll call you if I need you, Charlie!" Sheriff Hawkins said firmly. "Now Mrs. Harris if it's privacy that you need, simply follow me. They've given me the biggest office in town since becoming Sheriff, so come on down to my fortress where we can chat for a while."

So many changes, I thought as I followed behind Sheriff Hawkins. Nothing looked familiar, and I saw no signs of the Lucas's presence anywhere throughout the police station. We continued to walk down a narrow yellow hall that I can only assume was inspired by the yellow brick road until we reached his office.

"What can I do you for, Mrs. Harris?" Sheriff Hawkins asked again.

"I have some disturbing details about the Jane Doe who was on the news last night," I said.

"Well, I just can't catch a break," Sheriff Hawkins muttered. "Those degenerates at that news station are running a complete crap show."

"I beg your pardon, Sheriff!" I exclaimed.

"Oh, I'm sorry, Mrs. Harris." Sheriff Hawkins replied. "I meant no harm. However, I've asked those folks down at that news station time and time again not to get the residents so riled up with their less than accurate reporting." Sheriff Hawkins said candidly. "It makes our job that much more difficult when I have every deranged soul in town coming in trying to solve police work. Don't get me wrong, Mrs. Harris..." Sheriff Hawkins said as we both glanced at the mess covering his desk. "You're not giving off Looney Tune vibes, so I wasn't referring to you personally."

"Gosh, Sheriff, you're too kind," I retorted.

"Well, now that we've exchanged pleasantries," Sheriff Hawkins said. "What kind of details do you have that pertain to my murder case Mrs. Harris?"

"Well, I ran into the victim yesterday morning while out exercising with a friend." I replied. "The girl who was murdered was not a Jane Doe; her name was Ronda Evans, and the two of us had a brief conversation yesterday."

"Let me stop you there, Mrs. Harris," Sheriff Hawkins interjected. "We're well aware of the victim's name, although that's the type of misinformed reporting I'm referring to concerning that news station. However, I need to know what you two spoke about, and where it took place." the Sheriff said, waiting with bated breath for my response. "You'd be surprised by the smallest details that could make a difference in my line of work, Mrs. Harris."

"Oh, of course, Sheriff," I whispered. "We were at the dog park, and I was explaining to Ronda how to get to the Steamy Brew Coffee Shop. She was going there to meet a friend, but she'd gotten turned around and needed directions."

"Who was the friend? And what time did this encounter take place between you and the victim, Mrs. Harris?"

"I didn't get the name of the friend she was meeting, but the time had to be a little after 7:30 a.m.," I said, softly. As I sat there motionless for the next few minutes, I watched as the Sheriff wrote everything down on extremely large Post-It notepads. *He certainly is very diligent about his work*, I thought to myself. With him in the lead, this case should be solved in no time and Ronda's family can have the closure they deserve.

"Well, this may prove to be helpful information," Mrs. Harris. "I'm glad you stopped in, Sheriff Hawkins said.

"Oh, but, Sheriff, there's so much more!" I exclaimed. I think I may be on the killer's radar!"

"Why on earth would you say that, Mrs. Harris?" Sheriff Hawkins yelled as he glanced deep into my eyes.

"You see this?" I responded as I pulled the well-wrapped brick out of my purse.

"Someone made sure I received this last night, and whosever responsible needs to be jailed," I shouted.

"Well, it's not the best wrap job in the world, Mrs. Harris. However, I can assure you we don't arrest folks around these parts for giving bad gifts."

"*Huh...Bad gifts...*" I repeated. "Oh, no, Sheriff, you misunderstood. This is a brick and it was thrown through my window last night. I only wrapped it in fabric, so I didn't get any fingerprints on it. I can assure you this was no gift!" I said firmly.

I casually stood up and handed Sheriff Hawkins the threatening note and rubber band that was originally attached to the brick. As he read, I explained about the shadowy figure lurking in the darkness outside of my house, and the helplessness I felt being surveilled by a possible murderer.

"Disturbing as this is, Mrs. Harris..." Sheriff Hawkins said. "I still don't see a real connection to my murder victim. We've had a rash of break-ins recently, and unfortunately, I think someone was just testing the waters and looking for their next smash and grab. You probably scared them off, so I wouldn't worry too much about being on anyone's radar."

"Hmm... You're probably right, Sheriff," I responded. "I initially dismissed it as runaways anyhow, but with everything that's happened recently and Ronda inadvertently leaving me that voicemail of her murder..."

"What?" Sheriff Hawkins shouted out. "Mrs. Harris, did I hear you say you have an audio recording of my murder victim while she's being attacked."

"I do," I replied. "Guess I should've led with that, huh? It's just that my last 24 hours have been a whirlwind and I'm not entirely sure what I'm doing at this point," I said, sheepishly.

"Well, all things considered, Mrs. Harris," Sheriff Hawkins said, "I think you're handling it better than most."

I saw my hand was shaking as I took my phone out of my back pocket to play that awful voicemail for the Sheriff. As I keyed in the passcode to my voicemail, I looked Sheriff Hawkins right in the eyes and told him to brace himself because this voicemail would probably be one of the more disturbing things he's heard since becoming Sheriff. However, before I could press play, we heard a loud commotion going on in the lobby area of the precinct.

The Sheriff got up and ran out of his office towards the front entrance, so I paused the voicemail and followed behind him. Most of the noise was coming from a woman with her back to us screaming to the heavens about something of hers that was missing. I hadn't heard the entire ordeal, but whatever was missing she was extremely distraught about it.

Sheriff Hawkins walked over to the woman, and placed his hand on her shoulder, then asked her to calm down and tell him why she was so upset. She turned around just as she was placing a flattened empty water bottle in her coat pocket and I only needed one glance at her. Other than a few wrinkles and the lack of pigtails in her hair, nothing had changed. The woman was my old childhood friend, Daphne Dee Benson.

She looked directly at me as she turned around. Even though thirty years had passed, she must've recognized me also because all of her hysteria immediately subsided.

"Samantha Riley!" the woman shouted out.

"Daphne Dee Benson," I whispered. I was so surprised to see her here in town that for a moment I forgot I was in a police station because a murder was committed.

"Well, as I live and breathe, Samantha Riley, that is you?" the woman asserted.

"Yes," I replied. "However, it's Samantha Harris now, although sadly I'm a widow because my husband Jack has since passed. But enough about me," I mumbled. Daphne Dee Benson, is that really you?" I asked, stunned and staring.

"In the flesh...well, sort of," Dee replied. "You're not the only one who no longer uses her maiden name," Dee quipped, as she raised her hand to show me her wedding band while blurting out. "It's Evans now, Daphne Dee Evans!" she proclaimed, "*Evans*—"

"Oh no," I thought to myself. Then I remembered we were in a police station. "Ma'am," Sheriff Hawkins blurted out while looking at Dee. "Is there anything I can do for you today?"

"I hope so, Mr. Hawkins," Dee said, while looking at the Sheriff's badge. "You see my name is Daphne Dee Evans, and I drove here overnight from out of state looking for my daughter. I've been trying to reach her for the past day to no avail. She would never go one night without calling me to check in when she's out of town, and I'm just worried sick," Dee whispered.

"I completely understand," Sheriff Hawkins said. "Do you know what business your daughter was tending to while here in St. Lux, Mrs. Evans?"

"Somewhat," Dee responded. "My daughter's a social media influencer, and I believe she came here under the pretense of meeting someone who wanted to advertise on her platform for a small fee. I had an eerie feeling from the beginning and I forbade Ronda from leaving town, but that sweet southern charm she possesses made me fold like a cheap tent," Dee said. "Subsequently, my mother's intuition kicked in, and I knew it was the wrong choice to let her go."

An influencer with the same last name. Now there was no way around this one. I knew for sure that my long-lost friend Dee was the mother of the recently deceased Ronda. Who just so happened to have left a voicemail of her murder on my phone. *But how could I explain all of this to her,* I thought to myself.

"Mrs. Evans, do you have a photo of your daughter on you by chance?" Sheriff Hawkins asked.

"Yes, of course," Dee replied as she pulled out her cellphone and began to scroll through her pictures. "I know I have at least one in here somewhere," Dee mumbled. "You see Ronda was very skeptical about taking photos, so much so that she hardly even let me take pictures of her anymore," Dee said.

"Hmm," I quietly sighed under my breath.

"Mrs. Evans, can you think of any reason why your daughter who's a public figure would go to such lengths to become so obscure?" Sheriff Hawkins asked.

"Yes!" Dee responded. "I know exactly when it started. You see," Mr. Hawkins, "my daughter lost everything last year because a disturbed fan used her likeness on some less than honorable sites. Afterwards, she fought tooth and nail to build her brand back and restore her image, and she refused to let anything or anyone cause her that kind of grief again," Dee exclaimed. "However, outside of her business endeavors she became somewhat of a loner, and she only recently started showing signs of her old self again. Good golly here she is!" Dee shouted, "Here's a picture of my beautiful daughter Ronda." Dee sighed as she waved her phone in the air.

Sheriff Hawkins gave me a quick glance, seemingly saying what we both had already confirmed. My old friend's daughter was dead.

"Mrs. Evans, can I talk to you in the privacy of my office?" Sheriff Hawkins asked, while looking very enigmatic.

"Certainly," Dee replied. However, as she turned to walk away, she grabbed my hand and asked me to come with her.

"Yes, of course," I responded. As we made the trip back down the Yellow Brick Road, all I could think about was the awful news we were getting ready to tell my old childhood friend. For the entire walk, Dee didn't dare let go of my hand and I think it was because she sensed something was terribly wrong.

Once we got to the Sheriff's office, I sat down and Dee sat in the chair next to mine, still holding my hand. As gently as he could, the Sheriff took the lead in explaining what had occurred last night. At first, Dee visibly froze at the reality of the situation. But once she realized Ronda had been shot, that Ronda's death was real, and that she was now responsible for identifying her body at the morgue, all the strength of her body seemed to leave her and she fell onto the floor.

An emotional Dee, overcome with grief, just rocked back and forth on the floor still clenching my hand. I tried, but there was little in that moment I could do to provide any sort of comfort. So, I just sat there on the floor with my old friend and hugged her as she called out her daughter's name. A stone-faced Sheriff Hawkins knelt and promised Dee he'd catch the monster responsible for her daughter's death.

Once she was fully able to grasp the situation, I asked Dee if she had anywhere to stay while here in town.

"Umm, no," Dee shook her head like a small child. "I came straight to the police station from Nashville last night. I didn't even try and find Ronda's hotel, I guess because deep down I already knew something sinister had taken place," she whispered.

"Okay, well I'm going to take care of you now," I replied. "I have plenty of room at my house."

After picking Dee up off the floor and sitting her back upwards in her chair, I walked over and explained to Sheriff Hawkins that I needed to get her home and that I'd be back momentarily to finish what we started. He, of course, shook his head in approval, then held Dee's hand as he told her he was sorry for her loss. As Dee and I walked out the police station, I wasn't sure if I made the right choice but I decided not to mention the voicemail to her. Without question, she'd heard more than her fair share of sad news for the day.

I'd thought about taking her to the morgue at the hospital, so she could view Ronda's body. However, once we got to my car in the parking lot, I found that I had to help an extremely unbalanced Dee into my passenger seat. She was starting to look so incapacitated, and I figured if she still had that heart condition like when we were kids, then she was in no shape for any added stress at this particular moment. So, after putting her in my car we drove the short distance back to my house. I figured we'd come back later for her car; right now, I just wanted her to rest for a while considering she hadn't stopped crying for twenty minutes straight.

It was shortly after 8:00 a.m. when we pulled into my driveway, and I noticed my front door was ajar when we arrived. I assumed Maureen hadn't seen the note I'd left and was on her way to meet me at the police station and forgot to close the door. So, I decided to phone her to keep her updated with all that had occurred this morning once I got Dee settled into bed.

Unfortunately, that took longer than expected since I was now dragging Dee throughout my house because she was almost passed out on her feet. With my bedroom closest to the front door, I decided to put her in there and I placed her purse on my nightstand where she'd be able to see it once she woke up.

However, as I sat the purse down, my hand got caught on the strap, causing it to fall over while knocking her cellphone to the floor. So, not wanting to wake her, I quietly picked both the cellphone and the purse back up and placed them on the nightstand next to one another, then I hurried out of my bedroom closing the door behind me. Afterwards, I began calling out Maureen's name to see if she was anywhere in the house. I walked into the kitchen and noticed my back patio doors were ajar. "This was very strange," I thought to myself. I hadn't used those doors since Jack's death and Maureen would never leave out the back way since she only had the key to the front door.

I walked over to close the doors, and from outside in the distance I heard Daphne start to whimper. As she got closer, she ran up the patio stairs, so that I didn't lock her out. "Daphne, what are you doing outside all alone!" I shouted. I had never really liked her to go outside by herself as we had coyotes and foxes in the area that wreaked havoc on livestock, and some personal pets as well.

"You get inside this instant!" I declared. As I closed the patio doors after Daphne ran inside, I noticed she had something in her mouth. After trying to pry it from her well-clenched teeth for five minutes, I was finally able to bribe her with a doggy biscuit. She dropped whatever she had in her teeth and I heard it clank on the tile floor. It was a small key, much too small for any kind of dead-bolt lock. It looked as though it would open a small lock on a diary, *perhaps*.

I put the key in my pocket and tried phoning Maureen, but she didn't pick up. Strange, I thought. But I had such an abundance of different misadventures on my plate already that I decided not to look too much further into this one right then. I thought instead to make Dee some breakfast since I knew she hadn't eaten anything all morning. But once I walked over to the refrigerator I noticed as Maureen so eloquently puts it, "that all the food in your house was inedible." I understood being on my current health kick meant a lot of dinner reservations for one, but I tried not to shove my eating habits down anyone else's throat. So, I peeked inside my bedroom to make sure Dee was still asleep.

Poor thing, I thought to myself. *She must be heartbroken; parents aren't supposed to bury their children. That's the worst thing that could happen to anyone.* I saw she hadn't moved since I helped her into bed, so I closed the bedroom door and decided to go and get Dee some breakfast from one of the best restaurants in town, Felix's Diner. The food there was so good I'd been tempted several times within the past month to do away with my diet.

Furthermore, it was right next door to the Steamy Brew Coffee Shop, one of the last places Ronda would've been seen alive. If I was going to get answers for my friend, I was going to start there.

I walked into the living room, turned on the TV, and searched for the current events channel in our local area. Luckily, I found it just as another story on Ronda's murder was getting ready to air, so I paused the television as the same photo of Ronda appeared on the screen that Channel 18 aired last night. However, while looking at the photo this time, I noticed Ronda didn't have the small butterfly tattoo on her neck that I so vividly remember seeing on her yesterday at the dog park. *Was this a dated photo?* I asked myself. I quickly took a picture of Ronda while she was on the TV screen, then hurried, and turned it off. I was planning on using her photo to ask the locals if they'd recently seen her around. With knowing everyone in town, I figured the killer could only keep up their masquerade for so long.

I grabbed my purse and Daphne's leash and we both headed out the front door and made our way into town. I had never been so nervous in my life. A nearly forty-year-old woman with just a fifteen-pound dog for protection was planning on going rogue and solving a murder. I didn't know what questions to ask, let alone know how anyone would react to my interrogation over such damaging claims. I was completely winging it; I had never even seen a single episode of *Law & Order* for goodness' sake.

I had no idea what was to come. However, the one thing I did know was an innocent girl who happened to be my childhood friend's daughter was dead. So, I wasn't going to stop until the person responsible was apprehended, prosecuted, and behind bars for life.

Daphne and I got into town around 8:45 a.m. We walked into the Steamy Brew Coffee Shop first to see if I could get any leads concerning Ronda's whereabouts yesterday when in my peripheral vision, I spotted Crystal Miller.

Crystal was probably around Ronda's age and an extremely sweet but very timid girl. She had a slight speech disorder and was a barista here at the coffee shop, and she usually waited on me whenever I'd come in for a cappuccino. We made eye contact and I waved her over towards the couch in the back, so no one could hear our conversation.

"H-Hey there, Sam, can I get you your usual?" Crystal asked.

"To tell the truth, I just came in to talk with you for a bit," I replied.

"Uh-oh, w-well, that doesn't sound too good," Crystal said. "W-What's up, is anything the m-matter?"

"I just want to ask you a couple of questions about someone who may have stopped in here yesterday."

"W-Well, unless they tipped a hefty amount I probably won't remember them," Crystal replied.

"Typically, that may be the case," I said. "But this girl was without question unforgettable. I pulled out my phone and showed Crystal the photo of Ronda that I'd taken off the news before leaving home. Did you see this girl in here at any time yesterday?" I asked Crystal as I held up Ronda's photo.

"Umm no..." Crystal responded. "I d-don't recall seeing her. Is she a f-friend of yours?" Crystal asked.

"Something like that," I replied. I didn't have the courage to let Crystal in on the reason why I was actually there, but if I wanted to figure out what happened I knew I was going to have to somehow become impassive throughout my inquisitions. "You do open the coffee shop on weekends, right, Crystal?" I asked. "Are you certain you didn't see this girl? She would've stuck out like a sore thumb yesterday as she was certainly overdressed for a coffee shop," I added.

"I-It's possible I did see her." Crystal responded. "I just can't give a definitive yes. With all the customers from the time we open and trying to finish up my online c-classes, the weekends tend to be a blur. I'm sorry, Sam. I wish I could be more useful," Crystal whispered.

"You and me both," I muttered.

Soon after, Daphne and I left the coffee shop and walked next door to Felix's Diner. Felix became a dear friend years ago when Jack and I would frequent his diner for his Friday Night Fish Dinners. I didn't see Felix today, but through the window I saw his wife Betty working the counter. If Crystal was timid, Betty was anything but.

"Hello there, Samantha!" Betty blared out as I walked inside. "I haven't seen you since the last time I seen you. Could I get you some breakfast, honey?" Betty asked.

"Oh, hi, Betty," I responded with a smile. "I actually will have your breakfast special with a blueberry muffin to go," I said cheerfully.

"Blueberries!" Betty repeated. "I thought you were allergic."

"Deathly," I responded. "However, this order is for a friend who I haven't seen in a while, but I distinctly remember she used to love blueberry muffins," I said.

"Well, that's good enough for me," Betty chirped.

"Hey, since I've got you, can I ask you a serious question?" I whispered, as I leaned into the counter.

"As long as it's dirty," Betty said with a smirk. After a quick laugh, I asked Betty if she'd seen anything strange going on around here yesterday.

"Well, this is, St. Lux, honey, so I'm gonna need you to define strange," Betty replied. "Well, actually come to think of it, Samantha, I've been out sick for the past two days. Felix would've been at the diner by himself yesterday."

Well, there goes my lead! I thought to myself.

Betty soon placed my order in a paper bag that read 'Felix Diner' across the front and handed it to me from over the counter. I thanked her then headed towards the dog park with Daphne. I figured I could kill two birds with one stone by taking Daphne for her walk while searching for clues where I'd originally seen Ronda.

Upon reaching the dog park, Daphne let out a ferocious bark that quite frankly startled me. I had never heard her sound so distressed. Then I realized we were standing in the very spot where she flopped on Ronda's shoe. *This is my chance,* I thought to myself. I just had to know who was responsible for Ronda's death. So, I grabbed my bottle of Bare Witness perfume from my purse and told Daphne to follow the scent, since I knew it was the same fragrance Ronda wore yesterday. Daphne stayed the course until she hit some very thick brush and, unfortunately, got turned around in some tall unkept bushes just behind the trail.

Just my luck, I thought to myself. After I grabbed Daphne's tennis ball from my purse, I took her over to the fenced in section of the park. As I let her off her leash so she could get her exercise, I noticed someone coming out from the bushes that we had just checked a little while ago. As they got closer, I realized it was Charlie West, the wannabe cop. So, I latched the fence where Daphne was playing and walked over towards Charlie.

"Hello, there, what were you doing in the bushes?" I asked.

"Oh, umm. Hi, Sam," Charlie said. "I'm just following some leads from work and I thought I'd come by and check them out."

"Well, do you need a fresh pair of eyes to help you look?" I asked.

"No that's okay," Charlie said firmly. "Looks like someone was pulling my chain, I'll catch you later, Samantha," Charlie shouted out as he ran off in the other direction.

I've always thought Charlie was a bit eccentric, but this was strange behavior even for him. After Daphne was done playing with her tennis ball, I put her leash back on, then placed Charlie at the top of my suspect list. He claimed that he was following a lead; however, I got the feeling that he was rummaging around after potentially losing incriminating evidence. *Maybe there was a struggle that occurred with Ronda in this very dog park while on her way back to the Pelican Hotel after meeting her friend,* I thought. A few minutes later, Daphne and I started to make our way home. We got about half a block from my house when I heard someone calling out my name. I turned and noticed a bear of a man on what looked like a ten-year-old little girl's bike. It was Felix Presto, the owner of Felix diner. *What are the odds?* I thought.

"Hey, Samantha," Felix yelled as he did the most amazing trick on a bike I'd ever seen—stopping just short of Daphne and I while simultaneously jumping over the handlebars, then putting the kickstand down all before his right foot ever touched the ground.

"Impressive!" I blurted out.

"Stop it, you flatter me," Felix boasted. "Can't say that I blame you, but I see you've come back to the dark side to enjoy some cuisine with flavor," he laughed, while looking at the bag in my hand from his restaurant.

"Boy, you sure can tease me, Felix," I said with a smile. "You know, I wish I was able to indulge in some of your good home-cooked food; aside from Jack I've never known a man who was such a wizard in the kitchen," I said, flattering him.

"Now that's a second-place ribbon I'll take any day of the week," Felix said, grinning from ear to ear.

"Listen, since I've got you here, Felix, can I have a moment of your time?" I asked.

"Of course," he replied. "Anything for my favorite customer. What's on your mind, Samantha?"

"Well, Betty was just telling me that you worked alone yesterday," I said, scrambling for the right thing to ask.

"Yeah, I did," Felix replied. "It was a complete drag, but Betty's been out sick and the show must go on."

"Well, did you happen to notice anyone lurking around the diner by chance?" I asked. "Or did you see anything out of the ordinary?"

"Hmm, I can't say that I did," Felix replied. "However, I did see a young lady sitting by herself for a while who looked completely disheveled." Playing back yesterday's events in his head, he remembered this specific girl. "I would've thought she was royalty aside from the fact that she was holding the heel to her broken shoe in her hand while mumbling to herself," Felix claimed.

"Was this her?" I pulled up Ronda's photo on my phone and, in my repressed excitement, thrust it close to his face.

"Yup, that's her!" Felix replied. "She in some sort of trouble?"

She's long past trouble, I whispered to myself. "Did you see anyone with her?"

"No, she ate alone," Felix replied. "However, I do remember going outside for a smoke break about half an hour after I served her, and I saw her sitting on the curb having a heated exchange with Crystal from the coffee shop next door."

"Crystal Miller, the quiet girl with the stutter?" I murmured.

"That'd be her," Felix said curiously. "Is everything okay?"

"No," I responded. "Not by a long shot. But I'll catch up with you later, Felix. I've got to make a call," I said in disbelief.

"No problem," Felix shouted out as he pedaled away.

After I went inside I called Sheriff Hawkins and told him what I'd discovered about Crystal. How she was less than honest about knowing the victim, and how she was seen with Ronda right before she would've disappeared. He asked me to come back down to the police station so he could get a listen to that voicemail Ronda left, along with taking my statement regarding Crystal being a person of interest. I agreed, and said I'd be there in half an hour, then we disconnected. Part of me didn't want to believe Crystal could've been involved in such a heinous crime. *I mean she was so shy, and even somewhat gullible*, I thought to myself.

None of it really made sense, but she clearly had something to hide because she certainly fooled me. I'm not sure if Crystal had a role in Ronda's death, but I was going to make certain that I was the last person who was bamboozled by her bashfulness.

CHAPTER FIVE

After I ended my phone call with the Sheriff, I ran back over to my front door and engaged the alarm. Suddenly, I noticed Daphne was hot on my trail, and I soon realized why she was watching me like a hawk. I still had Dee's breakfast in my hands and the aroma coming from the bag was enough to send her into a frenzy. I placed Dee's food on the kitchen counter and peeked my head inside my bedroom to check on her. I couldn't believe she was still sound asleep. But I didn't try waking her because there was little I could say that would be of any comfort at this time.

I closed the bedroom door and stood there for a while until I got my composure, then I walked back into the kitchen and sat at the breakfast nook area that overlooked the pond full of Koi fish in my backyard. Jack and I used to love sitting here every morning, watching the fish come to the surface while eating breakfast.

While sitting and taking a breather, I pulled my phone out of my back pocket and decided to give Maureen a call. However, now instead of ringing it went straight to her voicemail. *Her battery must've been dead*, I thought to myself. Well, now this was getting extremely weird! Maureen letting her battery die was like me getting on stage at a bar and performing "Single Ladies." I mean sure it could happen, but it was very unlikely.

As I sat there enjoying the pond, I felt a cold gust of wind that made my entire body shiver. Then I remembered some lunatic decided to go target practicing on my living room window. I got up to inspect the damage in the morning light and knew right away who I'd have to call to fix it—my good friend Tom Miller.

Although Tom's day job was standing in front of a green screen telling most of Michigan to prepare for rain or snow, he was definitely no slouch when it came to home repairs. So, I figured I'd give him a call to see if he had time later today to replace my shattered window.

I phoned him and he picked up on the first ring. "Hello, Samantha, it's good to hear from you," Tom said, while breathing like he'd just run a marathon.

"Hi, Tom, did I catch you at an inconvenient time?" I replied. "You sound a bit out of breath."

"Oh, no, you're fine! Tom insisted. "I'm just finishing up at the gym and my trainer's not happy unless I'm gasping for air. What's on your mind, Samantha? You calling about me replacing that busted window in your living room?" Tom asked.

"Yeah, actually, I am," I said after a brief pause.

I started to ask Tom how he knew about my broken window. However, before I could finish the question, he interrupted me and said that he'd noticed the window this morning on his way to the gym and was planning to call me afterwards to see if I needed it fixed.

"Okay, that sounds good to me," I said, completely astonished by his generosity. "I just have one thing I have to do now and we can meet back at my house around noon."

"That works for me." Tom replied.

"Okay, great!" I yelled cheerfully. "Make sure to text me a list of the supplies you'll need to replace the window and I'll stop at the hardware store on my way home," I said.

"Don't you worry about that, little lady. Anything you need I should already have in my van," Tom said flirtatiously. I thanked Tom for his kindness and we disconnected.

Before I left home, I disengaged the security alarm, waved goodbye to Daphne, and made my way back to the police station. I got there in less than five minutes and parked next to Sheriff Hawkins's patrol vehicle on the side of the building around 10:30 a.m. I walked towards the front entrance and noticed the Sheriff talking to his Deputy, Randall Hicks, in the lobby.

"Good morning again, Sheriff," I said as I playfully tapped him on his shoulder, mimicking what he'd done to me just a few hours earlier.

"We've got to stop meeting like this!" Sheriff Hawkins said facetiously. I waved hello to Deputy Hicks before Sheriff Hawkins suggested we go back to his office for privacy. So, I followed him back down the Yellow Brick Road until we reached his office. Then after he asked about Dee's state of mind, I informed the Sheriff of the new information I'd solicited while asking around town.

"Mrs. Harris, I'm not even going to ask how you obtained this information," Sheriff Hawkins said, as he buried his face in his hands. "However, just between us," Sheriff Hawkins whispered as he pulled his hands away from his face, "if you weren't deriving these useful tidbits of information by hook or by crook, I'd surely ask you if you wanted to be my new deputy."

"Oh, I didn't mean to overstep." I replied. "I guess I just have a personal investment in seeing Ronda's murderer brought to justice. However, I could never do what you guys do day after day."

"Well, I'm glad you feel that way, Mrs. Harris," Sheriff Hawkins said. "Because I am gonna have to ask you to leave the police work to the actual police officers. I don't need you going around town interrogating folks and this becoming a case within a case. I like simplicity," Sheriff Hawkins said firmly.

"Duly noted," I responded.

Suddenly, as Sheriff Hawkins sat silently writing everything down again on his over-sized Post-It notepads, a blaring alarm throughout the entire police station began ringing. Almost instantly I could hear officers outside the Sheriff's door yelling out, "10-45, we have a 10-45 at SafeLoan Bank."

I wasn't exactly aware of what 10-45 was code for, but I did know there was only one SafeLoan Bank in all of St. Lux, and my good friend Maureen Smith worked there.

Although it was Sunday Morning and Maureen typically worked as a personal trainer on the weekends, she was also a Branch Manager at this particular bank. So, it wasn't much of a stretch that she'd have to go in for any number of things on the weekend. I started to feel nauseous as I pondered if this was the reason I hadn't heard from Maureen. Had she received a phone call from work this morning and gone there?"

By now Sheriff Hawkins was up out of his chair and halfway out the door when I heard him yell out, "Sorry, Mrs. Harris, but duty calls. I'll give you a call later because I'll need to hear that voicemail and I'll also need to get your formal statement."

However, at that moment I was less concerned with giving a statement and more concerned about my dear friend Maureen's whereabouts. I sat there in the Sheriff's office for another five minutes trying to reach Maureen, but her phone was as dead as a doornail. I found a confused looking officer still on the premises as I was leaving and asked her what code 10-45 stood for.

She must've been a rookie because she ran to the front desk and got a book to look it up. "Ma'am, I found it," the young woman said as she waved me over towards her. "I found what a 10-45 is!" she shouted.

"Well, what is it?" I asked frantically.

"It's a bomb threat," she replied.

My heart started to race and my legs felt as if I were a rhinoceros on ice. Maureen had always been there for me. However, if she was in that bank, there was nothing I could do for her but pray. And I did just that as I walked back to my car, where I saw an unopened Post-It notepad laying on the ground. Well, I knew it belonged to Sheriff Hawkins, so with him getting in touch with me momentarily to finish up my statement I put it in my pocket and planned on returning it later that evening. Then I drove to Maureen's apartment to see if she was home. I must've rung her buzzer for ten minutes straight, but there was no answer. I tried opening the entryway door with the key Maureen had given me for emergencies, but it didn't work! Now I was worried sick about one of my dearest friends and full of regret that I'd left her alone this morning without so much as a goodbye.

Afterwards, I got back in my car and prayed again for Maureen's safety the whole ride home. Then as I pulled in my driveway a few minutes later, I tried to center myself before going inside just in case Dee was awake because I knew I needed to be a rock for her. Finally, after ten minutes of sitting in my car, I walked up the stairs and opened my front door. However, I still didn't see any signs that Dee had been up, so I peeked into my bedroom and noticed she was still asleep in bed. "With the horrific news she just received she'd probably be in bed the entire day," I thought. So, still worried about Maureen's safety I closed my bedroom door and went into the living room to see if the bomb threat was grave enough to make breaking news.

I turned on the television and noticed it was deathly silent throughout the entire house. *This isn't normal*, I thought to myself. Daphne was usually running around like a Tasmanian Devil until she got her mid-morning treat, so I walked through the house calling out for her, but she never responded. I looked under every bed and in every single closet throughout the house but she was nowhere to be found. Instinctively, I pulled out my phone and opened the, track your dog app, that I had linked to Daphne's GPS tracker on her collar.

Once I spotted her, I ran and opened the front door and there she was, across the street in the empty field, but she wasn't there alone. She was sitting quietly with someone as if she were familiar with this person.

Daphne, sitting quietly! *These were things she seldom did even for treats.* I thought to myself. *Who was this stranger?* I ran towards the empty field across the street calling out Daphne's name when the person beside her finally stood up. I got a few feet away before I noticed it was Sean. The young teen from the news yesterday morning.

"The nerve of you!" I yelled at the boy as I stood between him and Daphne. "Who do you think you are taking a poor defenseless animal from their home? Causing hundreds of dollars' worth of damage by breaking windows, and not to mention the fact that I found your coat last night. So, I know you've been spying on me for days. I should call the police and have you jailed!"

"You've got it all wrong, ma'am," the boy insisted. "My name is Sean Griffin. I'm fifteen years old and I didn't come to St. Lux to dognap this mutt. She comes out every once in a while and I give her half my lunch, then she usually goes back to wherever she lives. I would never hurt an animal. I just want to know the truth!" Sean exclaimed.

"Oh, and by the way," Sean said, "I didn't break your window but I saw who did, and as far as me spying on you, you're like a hundred years old."

"Ahhh," I gasped from the lack of subtleness he exhibited. "I beg your pardon, you little rug rat," I retorted. "I'm barely forty, but go on, what truth are you looking for here in St. Lux?" I asked.

"I'm just trying to get justice for my mother," Sean said, with his eyes starting to water. "She was killed over a year ago when I was fourteen. I snuck out of my bedroom window after she grounded me one day and later that night when I was climbing back in my window, I heard a gunshot. I ran towards the living room and saw someone running away dressed from head to toe in all black. The person responsible lived here in St. Lux, and even though he's now deceased, I'm going to prove his guilt if it's the last thing I do!" Sean proclaimed.

"Sean, have you gone to the Sheriff with this information?" I asked.

"The police won't help me," Sean said firmly. "I've already talked to some idiot Sheriff named Lucas a week after my mother's death."

'Rodney Lucas is a close friend," I interjected. "Although he's no longer Sheriff, I was referring to Sheriff Philip Hawkins," I said softly.

"I don't know who that is," Sean replied. "However, if he was friends with the murderer who lived in that house, then I'll pass," Sean said as he pointed at my house.

"Murderer who lived in that house!" I repeated. "Just where do you get the gall, young man?" I shouted out. "The man who lived in that house would never hurt a fly!" I exclaimed.

"Wow, so I won't be able to count on you for help," Sean said. "You sound just as bad as that brainwashed Sheriff Lucas. That joke of a cop referred to me as a confused child, then threw me out of his office once I accused his good friend Jack Harris of murder."

"A word to the wise," Sean said, "Defending someone who died after they've committed a murder doesn't make them a saint; it just makes them a dead murderer!" Sean said emotionally.

What? I thought to myself. My heart just about stopped. *Why on God's Green Earth would anyone say such a thing about Jack?*

"Let me guess from your reaction, I take it you were Jack's friend too," Sean said.

"I'm his wife!" I blurted out. Unfortunately, Sean looked completely dejected once I spilled the beans. However, once he was able to digest the news his entire demeanor changed. He got very agitated then started screaming bloody murder. "You're all in this together!" Sean cried out. "Silly me, I can't believe I ever talked to you. Everyone in this town is corrupt, *and not just a little bit, but a lot*!" Sean yelled out, echoing what I assumed was his favorite saying as it was also printed on his t-shirt.

"I can help you, Sean!" I shouted. "I'll make sure you and your mother get the justice you deserve," I said.

"I don't need your help," Sean yelled, "I want nothing to do with you, lady!"

Realizing I couldn't get through to Sean at this time, I asked him to give me a call if he ever changed his mind. Next, I reached for the Post-It notepad that I'd placed in my pocket earlier at the police station, then grabbed the ink pen that I kept in my phone case and wrote my name and number down before sticking it on Sean's sleeve as he ran off.

What just happened? I thought as I stood in the same empty field that was wreaking so much havoc on my life. I felt terrible that Sean was out there all by himself, but I refused to even entertain the notion that Jack was in some way responsible for his mother's death.

As I walked back across the street towards my house with my phone still in my hands, I decided to give Maureen a call again. But she still didn't answer. *Where could she be?* I thought to myself. I felt as though I was being pulled from every direction with everything that was going on and I had no idea which way to go or who to help first. I stood there in the middle of the road in a daze before a car turned onto my street and blew the horn at me while speeding by at fifty mph. *What was going to become of me if I couldn't clear Jack's name?* I thought. Would I turn back into the depressed alarmist I was after his death, or better yet some incompetent feeble old woman who can't even cross the street on her own accord? I chose neither.

After I made it across the street while standing on the sidewalk in front of my house, I decided to call Rodney Lucas and give the former Sheriff a piece of my mind. Rodney picked up the phone on the first ring.

"Hey, Samantha, is everything alright?" he asked.

"Well, I'm not entirely sure," I replied. "I hate to call you now, I know you and Kathleen are vacationing in Florida, but I..."

"Well, that's the thing," Rodney said as he cut me off. "We're actually at the airport about to board our plane coming back home. We decided after five consecutive days of non-stop rain we'd had enough. So, what's on your mind, kiddo?" Rodney asked.

"Umm, I probably should wait until you get back into town," I replied. "I guess I let my emotions get the better of me because it's really not the kind of conversation you have over the phone," I said.

"Okay, sounds good to me," Rodney responded. "We're boarding shortly, so how about you come over to the house around six tonight and I'll have Kathleen cook us up some dinner."

"You don't need to go through all of the trouble," I responded.

"Nonsense!" Rodney shouted. "It's no trouble at all. We'll see you at six."

"Okay, see you then," I said hesitantly as we disconnected.

As I finally started to reach a state of calm, I entered my house and began to shut the front door, when I noticed Tom Miller pulling into my driveway.

"Your wicked friend, Maureen, isn't here, is she?" Tom shouted from his car.

"I don't know what you two have against one another," I said as I walked back outside to greet Tom. "However, I actually haven't been able to reach Maureen all day and I'm starting to get worried," I added.

"Maybe the villagers made their way here from Salem and she couldn't use trickery to escape this time," Tom said with a smirk.

"People are dead, Tom, and it's no laughing matter. Maureen could be anywhere out there needing our help. I know you two haven't always seen eye to eye, but as a courtesy to me, I could really use your help finding her."

"Of course." Tom said, "I was just messing around, Sam. You know I never really disliked Maureen," Tom claimed. "She just rubbed me the wrong way when she made that scene at Jack's funeral, and in front of everyone accused me of making a pass at you. Well, I was kind of taken aback by it and she's been pretty standoffish ever since then," Tom said.

I was shocked that Tom even remembered that day. After all, he was pretty drunk when he arrived at the wake. "Water under the bridge now," I said to Tom. "As long as you two are cordial to one another, that's all I can ask for. But to be honest I never understood why you two had all of those blow-ups over a misunderstanding to begin with."

"Well, it wasn't entirely a misunderstanding," Tom said as he pulled my new picture window from the glass rack on his van.

"What do you mean?" I asked, as I grabbed his tool chest from the van's back hatch area.

"Well, while I stand on my morals that I wasn't hitting on you that day, I have developed a slight crush since then," Tom said.

Oh my. I thought to myself. "I had no idea," I whispered. "I guess I never really thought about that part of my life after I lost Jack," I said. "I just figured I'd grow a mustache, then get eight to ten cats, and become the crazy cat lady who scared the neighborhood children," I laughed while also drawing a laugh out of Tom.

"It's okay if you need more time to think about it," Tom said. "I'll ask you out on a proper date in the future, if and when you're ready."

Was I crazy? I thought to myself, *turning down one of the most eligible bachelors in all of St. Lux. Tom had everything. He was tall, dark, and handsome with short black hair and a killer smile. The only problem was he wasn't Jack.*

I was one of the lucky ones who'd met the love of my life in high school, and I couldn't just forget about him because he was gone. I knew I shouldn't limit my life to just my past experiences and I guess subconsciously I knew Jack wouldn't want me to. However, how could I be happy with someone else when I was so furious with Jack for leaving me?

I walked onto the porch as I watched Tom work from his van, then I offered him a sandwich and a glass of iced tea. "I just ate a protein bar on the drive over, but the iced tea sounds good," Tom said.

"Okie Dokie Macaroni, I'll be right back," I shouted out as I simultaneously ran inside to the bathroom convinced I was going to puke from embarrassment from having just uttered the phrase "Okie Dokie Macaroni." However, as I knelt by the toilet, the feeling soon subsided, and I began to hear footsteps getting closer behind me.

"Dee!" I yelled out. Are you finally awake?" I walked towards the living room and as the footsteps got closer, I realized it was just Tom. He was asking to use the restroom.

"Oh, of course Tom." I said. "I'll just be in the kitchen fixing myself a sandwich. Meet me in there when you're done, and I'll have a nice tall glass of iced tea waiting for you."

"Okie Dokie Macaroni," Tom said with a smile that made me smile back.

As I walked into the kitchen, I saw Daphne was hanging out by the back patio doors, keeping an eye on the squirrels as usual. I made myself a turkey sandwich and poured Tom a glass of iced tea, then sat at my wobbly kitchen table. Tom joined me shortly after and for the next hour or so, we talked about everything under the sun. I'd never had such an in-depth conversation with Tom quite like this before. He seemed so open and so vulnerable.

He even opened up about his rumored suicide attempt a little over a year ago. At that point he'd lost everything due to his uncontrollable drinking— his wife, children, house, and even his career in law enforcement. Everything Tom loved was in his rearview and he blamed Rodney Lucas, who was Sheriff at the time, for the downward trajectory his life took after his firing from the police station.

Tom thought he was next in line to become Sheriff of St. Lux. However, once those dreams fell by the wayside, so did the Tom we had all grown to know and love. He thought he couldn't start over again. But because he was such a beloved officer here in St. Lux, at that time, all I had to do was ask the community to come together to help save one of our own. Shortly after everyone jumped aboard and rallied together to pay for one of the best alcohol treatment facilities that money could buy, Tom, now still a regular who went to the meetings, has been nothing but grateful ever since. I knew I could trust Tom with my life, but I didn't want to burden him with all that had been going on. Aside from that, I still hadn't fully accepted that unbelievable story Sean had just thrust upon me. So, I made a conscious decision to omit certain details in order to spare Tom from some of the horror that was now my life.

After all, the transgression I was currently working up the nerve to inform Tom about would probably be enough on its own to send him spiraling. However, I finally worked up the courage fifteen minutes later to tell Tom about Ronda's death. Unfortunately, I had to mention how he was indirectly tied to it. So, I walked back outside where Tom had since gone to finish up my window and blurted out— "Tom, I need to talk to you about something rather serious."

I saw Tom peek his head from around his van where he had been putting his tools away, then he asked me if everything was okay.

I sat down on my porch swing and whispered the words, "Not this time, Tom."

Tom closed his van door, walked over towards the porch, and joined me on the swing, then asked me directly, "What is bothering you?"

"Well, I don't want to get you upset and have you turn into that old Tom you're trying so hard not to be," I said. "However, you've got to understand this is something I've been debating whether or not to tell you since you pulled into my driveway a few hours ago."

"What is it, Sam?" Tom asked in a concerned tone. "You have my word I won't hulk out."

"Okay, but it's about your niece, your niece Crystal," I said.

You see Crystal wasn't just Tom's niece but she was more like one of his daughters. Crystal came to live with Tom when she was around five years old after Tom's brother and his wife (Crystal's parents) tragically died on a cruise ship that sank. Tom was awarded guardianship and he and Crystal have been inseparable ever since. Even after Tom's wife Rebecca left with their two children, Crystal stayed by her uncle's side.

"Crystal," Tom muttered. "What about her?" he asked softly.

"Well, I don't know if she's involved or if she has any knowledge about the murder that recently occurred," I said, barely finishing my statement before Tom yelled out.

"Murder? What murder, Sam?" Tom looked at me with the most confused look on his face. "Is my niece in some sort of trouble? Is she okay?" Tom asked frantically.

"She's fine," I assured Tom. "But I'm not sure why she felt the need to fib when I asked her if she knew the victim." I pulled out my phone showing Tom Ronda's photo. "However, let's assume she's got a good reason for hiding the truth," I continued, as I put my phone back in my pocket. "Unfortunately, that lie, coupled with the fact that she was one of the last persons seen with Ronda, is not going to bode well for her. As tragic as it is, we both know once the gossip starts to spread, it usually never stops, and that damning information will lead the cops to believe Crystal not only had motive but also opportunity," I said to a despondent Tom.

I went on to tell Tom about how I met Ronda in the park and how it was sheer happenstance that she asked for my number. Then I mentioned how Ronda ordered a ton of scrunchies and the next thing I knew I had a voicemail of her murder on my phone. I went into detail about how I tried retracing Ronda's footsteps by questioning a few locals around town, starting at the Steamy Brew Coffee Shop, one of the last places she would've been seen alive.

Furthermore, I mentioned to Tom that Crystal was seen arguing with Ronda on the very afternoon she was brutally murdered.

It's a bad look for sure, I thought. *Not to mention the fact that Crystal told so many lies today that she was well on her way to becoming a functioning sociopath.*

Then I told Tom exactly what Crystal had divulged to me, and I reiterated the vastly different story I got from Felix about how he saw the two girls in a heated exchange in front of the coffee shop.

Tom agreed it didn't paint Crystal in the best light, but said he couldn't imagine her being responsible for the death of a bug, let alone a human being.

I concurred, agreeing with Tom one hundred percent, but warned him we should find out what Crystal was hiding before she got herself entangled in a situation where she'd need the jaws of life to break her free.

CHAPTER SIX

Tom and I both got into his van and rushed over to the Steamy Brew Coffee Shop to talk with Crystal. I spent the entire ride over explaining to a distraught Tom every little detail I knew about Ronda's murder. I could see he was holding back tears and I wasn't quite sure if they were for Ronda or if deep down somewhere he was actually tearing up for a guilty Crystal.

We finally arrived at the coffee shop a little after 1:30 p.m. Tom parked and ran inside, and I followed quickly behind him as I knew he had an uncontrollable wild side. Tom rushed to the front of the line demanding to speak with Crystal.

"Where's my niece?" Tom shouted out. "Is she in the back? Tell her to get out here!" he yelled.

"Hello, Mr. Miller," Chuck, the store manager, said as he walked from the back room. "Crystal's not here," Chuck claimed.

"What do you mean she's not here, Chuck?" Tom yelled. "Where the hell could she be? She left home this morning to go to work," Tom said.

Well, trying to defuse the situation before it ignited, I asked Chuck politely, if he was absolutely sure Crystal wasn't there. "It's very important that we speak with her," I said.

"Yeah, so where is she?" a furious Tom interjected. "Sam already came in this morning and spoke with Crystal around the time when she would've been starting her shift at this dump. So we know she's here," Tom said with anger.

"That may very well be true," a now-agitated Chuck replied. "However, Crystal insisted she had an emergency with her dog Sparky around ten this morning, and she was adamant about taking him to the vet herself," he said. "Since Crystal is a dear friend, she knew the way I felt about animals and that I wasn't going to let any dog suffer on my watch. So, I dismissed her, and now if you'll excuse me, I have customers waiting," Chuck said forcefully.

Since we were unable to reach Crystal by phone, Tom and I walked back outside and I noticed he looked completely out of sorts. Anxiety started to replace the anger Tom displayed less than five minutes ago in the coffee shop. It was almost as if he believed Crystal somehow could be responsible.

"Don't worry, Tom!" I said. "We'll find your niece and I'm sure she'll have a good explanation for all of this."

"Well, unfortunately, I don't think there's going to be a good enough excuse to explain this one away," Tom said dejectedly.

"What do you mean, Tom?" I asked.

"I mean I may have to take off my rose-colored glasses pretty soon because my niece no longer has a dog," Tom replied. "My niece's dog Sparky died a few weeks ago," he said, holding back tears again. "Crystal didn't want to talk about it, so I buried my feelings with the dog, but for her to be so dishonest at the drop of a hat... Honestly, I can't fathom what kind of trouble she's gotten herself into this time," a now disconsolate Tom said.

"I-I-I..." Tom tried to talk but was barely able to get the words out. He finally went on to say that Crystal just wasn't in the right mindset.

Well, she certainly knew how to string more than a few lies together, I thought to myself.

Suddenly, I noticed the look on Tom's face and I intuitively knew he wasn't far from turning back into his old self again. And if he fell off the wagon, there was no telling what could happen. I knew this news about Crystal would be difficult for him to digest, but he looked as if he was desperately trying to withhold information that clearly pointed to her guilt.

Out of the blue, Tom asked me if I could drive myself home as he handed me the keys to his van.

"Sam, I just have a few things I need to do and I won't be able to bring you along," Tom said.

"Are you worried about Crystal?" I asked. "I'm not sure if you going off on your own is such a good idea, Tom," I whispered.

"I'll be fine," Tom replied. I'll meet you back at your house after I'm done," he said as he walked off after giving me one of the tightest hugs I'd ever received.

After getting in Tom's van and thinking about all of the stress I've been dealing with lately, I have to admit that I gave into temptation and drove to Susie's Sweets just around the corner. I suddenly wanted the biggest jelly donut that money could buy.

I didn't see Susie's electric Batmobile parked out front when I pulled up, so I thought maybe I could get in and out without being verbally assaulted for once, but, boy, was I wrong.

I walked through the door and noticed a guy in his early twenties behind the counter, and although I wasn't a fan of all the changes Susie had recently done to her father's business, the ensemble she had chosen for her staff to wear was simply adorable. Their uniforms were blue polo shirts and khakis that had pink stitching on every seam, and black trim on every cuff. However, the uniforms were mostly covered up by aprons her employees wore that bore the company's name—aprons that I had graciously bedazzled to help a fellow businesswoman in her time of need.

I walked to the front counter and ordered a jelly donut from the cashier, and no sooner had I paid for my order than I heard Susie yelling from the back. "Those donuts are for hardworking, compassionate, townsfolk Chad, and she's a wolf in sheep's clothing who doesn't like to honor her contracts. I'll handle her," Susie said emphatically.

"Well, hello, Susie," I said as she approached the counter.

"Please, Samantha," Susie said snidely. "Let's not do small talk again, huh. It's not becoming for either of us."

"However, I am glad you're here," Susie continued. "I heard through the grapevine you're running around town interrogating the fine citizens of St. Lux, as if you're some modern-day cat woman or something. So, I have just one question for you—Where's my product?" Susie yelled, referring to her scrunchie order.

"It's not at all what you think, Susie," I responded.

"Not what I think?" Susie repeated. "Well, then I guess I'm just confused. Although, if I recall, yesterday I heard you complaining that you didn't have enough time to complete orders because of this full-time job that was so arduous. Now from the looks of it you've got more than enough time to commit to this new Barney Fife thing you've got going on. So, when do my scrunchies come into play?" Susie screamed.

"Well, I have to admit I haven't had much time to work on anyone's back orders lately," I said. "However, there is a good excuse for the delay."

"Save it!" Susie shouted. "Excuses are for the confessional, or when you accidentally stab your fourth husband because you noticed him trying to secretly gawk at your hot mail lady, but I digress. Last I checked, you worked for me and I paid you in advance, so I expect to get what I paid for. Is that understood?" Susie screamed as if I was one of her employees.

"Well, I've honestly been in quite the whirlwind lately," I said. "Believe it or not, Susie, I've been in some pretty compromising predicaments the past few days. I'm currently trying to retrace someone's footsteps in an attempt to find out what establishments they could've patronized yesterday. Have you seen this woman?" I asked as I flashed Ronda's photo at Susie.

"No, I haven't seen the Jezebel!" Susie shouted out as she pushed my hand away. "You mean to tell me you haven't even *started* my scrunchie order because you're too busy running around town playing some fun for dummies' version of a scavenger hunt!?"

"I can assure you, Susie, this is no game," I said firmly. "Someone in St. Lux has this poor girl's blood on their hands and I intend to do everything in my power to make sure their reign of terror ends with her," I shouted back.

"Well, why don't you just leave the police work to the police?" Susie sneered. "Or are you just trying to get close to that disgraced ex-cop, Tom Miller? He sure is one hunk of a man," Susie stated, as the heat from her body nearly set off the smoke alarms. "I'd certainly wait in line for a ride on that roller coaster."

"Gross," I whispered under my breath. "I'll have you know, Susie, I'm still a married woman," I said with pride.

"No Samantha, you're a widow," Susie crassly retorted back. "With that being said, for the life of me, I can't figure out why the most eligible bachelor in town is lusting over you. I mean you're clearly a woman who doesn't care about the finer things in life," Susie shouted.

"I think I'll take my donut to go," I said before Susie could get out another insult.

"Well, Chad, you heard her!" Susie shouted. "Don't just stand there like I pay you to model aprons. Get the woman a donut."

A very nonplussed Chad looked at me with a smile on his face, as if he was immune to Susie's crudeness, then he handed me the biggest jelly donut on the shelf and told me to have a great day.

Does he know the secret to becoming completely Zen I wasn't aware of? I thought to myself. It seemed as of late Susie was the only demonic entity that could take me out of my comfort zone. But whatever this was Chad was doing, I wanted to give it a try.

Before I could get out the door, an unrelenting Susie yelled after me, "So, will this new vigilante thing you've got going on now take precedence over me getting my scrunchies on Wednesday?"

I calmly channeled my inner Chad, then turned around, appearing completely unbothered and smiled at Susie, telling her, "It's a possibility." Unfortunately, Susie, as the perfect nuisance that she is, waved me off with a flick of her wrist, while simultaneously rolling her eyes and shouting out, "Simpleton!"

After her latest insult, my inner Chad left the conversation and that spunky, clandestine mean girl persona was front and center, when I abruptly shouted back, "You know sometimes these scavenger hunts can last for days. So how about I press mute on you until then and I won't have to dish out any vigilante justice, okay?"

Zinger, I thought to myself as I heard Chad laugh out loud.

"Well, some people just have no manners!" Susie shouted as I walked out the door.

The nerve of her, I thought to myself as I stood outside. If I wasn't busy trying to solve a murder, I'd probably be committing one dealing with that woman. I got back in Tom's van and was ready to head home to check on Dee, when I had the strangest thought. It was a long shot but my intuition had been right all day today. And now I had a slight suspicion where Ronda could've acquired that fancy fur she had on. If I was her age with the body of a goddess and the fashion style to match, there'd only be one place here in St. Lux that would get my motor running. *Simona's Style & Grace Fashion Boutique*, I thought to myself. It was just five minutes across town and it was the only place nearby that sold the high-quality clothing that Ronda clearly preferred. If she got that beautiful fur while here in St. Lux, then Simona definitely would've sold it to her.

I took off for the boutique and arrived there around 2:00 p.m. I walked inside and saw Simona standing at the front register. Her boutique was thriving as I could barely make my way over to her through the crowd.

"Hey, Simona!" I yelled out as I made my way over towards the register.

"Samantha, is that you?" Simona blurted out. "What a nice surprise. To what do I owe the pleasure?"

"Well, I wish I could say this was just a friendly visit," I replied. However, I just feel like I'm going crazy, Simona."

"Say no more," Simona whispered. "You just give me fifteen minutes and I'll have this place cleared out," she said. True to her word, her shop was completely empty in exactly fifteen minutes. How she took care of everyone so professionally in that amount of time is still a mystery to me.

"What's on your mind, Samantha?" Simona asked as we walked towards the fitting room and sat down in two plush leather chairs.

"W-Well," I stuttered, barely able to muster the courage to speak. Finally, after gathering myself, I told Simona that I had a voicemail recording on my phone of someone being murdered.

"Oh, my goodness, Samantha," Simona muttered as she placed both hands on her cheeks reminding me of the movie *Home Alone* that Dee and I used to watch as kids.

"I'm sorry to hear that," Simona said. "Was it anyone close to you?" she asked.

"That's the thing, I didn't know her personally. I had just met her yesterday," I said. I gave her my phone number because she wanted to purchase a few of my scrunchies, and the next thing I know I woke up from a nap and I had a voicemail notification chirping on my phone."

"Wait a second!" Simona shouted. "Are you pulling my leg, Samantha? You know you almost got me the last time with that scary story about the woman who stabbed her husband over twenty times, only for me to find out it never took place and the deranged woman was just a villain you were testing out for your next novel."

"No hidden agenda this time," I said firmly. "I apologize for scaring you then, but now I just need to get answers for my inconsolable friend."

"An inconsolable friend..." Simona repeated. "Well, who's the friend?" she asked.

"Well, her name is Dee but she no longer lives in St. Lux," I replied. "However, we were best friends as little girls until her family moved out of state. And it just so happens the deceased is her daughter. But I had no knowledge of any of this until after her murder. Now Dee's at my house and if she's not crying, she's asleep, and I just don't know what to do in this situation," I whispered as a flurry of sadness rushed over me. Before I lost the courage, I showed Simona Ronda's photo and asked if she recalled seeing her around the boutique.

"No, I can't say that I've seen her," Simona said. "What a beautiful young girl though, it's such a tragedy."

"Well, I figured it was a long shot but I had to follow my intuition," I said. "Oddly enough, when I ran into her yesterday, she was wearing a designer fur coat, so I assumed if she got it while visiting St. Lux then it would've come from here."

"Wait!" Simona shouted as she walked back over to the register. "Was this a black fur coat that closes with a thin black belt at the waist?" She asked.

"Yes!" I yelled out as I followed behind her. "Do you recall seeing her now?" I asked.

"No, but I remember selling that coat last week," Simona said. "It was the only fur that I'd sold in two months. However, the girl from your photo isn't the one I sold it to," she added as she opened her laptop to check her receipt logs.

The suspense nearly killed me as I stood there patiently waiting for Simona's computer to go through a software update. After it rebooted, she told me that the fur coat in question was sold a week ago yesterday. "Did the person pay with a credit card?" I asked frantically.

"They certainly did!" Simona replied. "Looks like Crystal Miller purchased that coat last Saturday at 5:03 p.m."

I stood there utterly stunned. Crystal was such a sweetheart when I would frequent the coffee shop. *What would drive such a shy sweet person to kill?* I thought to myself. *Furthermore, if she actually was guilty, would she be willing to kill again to escape her inevitable fate?* I pondered.

"Oh wow, I truly don't know what to do with this information," I moaned to Simona. "On the one hand, I don't want to hurt the Millers because I consider both Tom and Crystal good friends. However, on the other hand, I have a responsibility to do what's morally right, and above all else, Dee deserves justice for her daughter's callous murder."

"Whatever you do, Samantha, just promise me you'll be safe," Simona whispered in a mother-like tone.

"Always!" I said firmly as we shared a smile.

"Well, you know if you need anything you can just say the word," Simona said as she leaned in and hugged me. "You may not know what to do just yet, Sam, but knowing you the way that I do, I know whatever you decide, your morals will never be in question," Simona candidly complimented me.

"Thank you, Simona, I needed to hear that," I responded, as I wiped a tear from my eye.

"Well, of course, sweetie, but did I hear you say that you didn't want to hurt Tom," Simona gleefully said. "Is this the infamous Tom Miller, you know, the one who's more than a little smitten with you?" Simona yelled.

"Well, did everyone in town besides me know about this crush?" I blurted out.

"I'm afraid so," Simona laughed. Then she suddenly said, "Wait a second!" And while seemingly having the most inopportune epiphany of all time, she asked, "Isn't this Crystal girl Tom's adoptive daughter?"

"Yes." I responded. "Thank you for finally showing up to the party," I chuckled. "Biologically, she's his niece but when Tom was granted custody, he went the extra mile and adopted her. That's why I'm torn," I said.

"Oh, geez," Simona whispered. "Now I see your dilemma. "You either get to start a new life with one of the most eligible guys in all of St. Lux or destroy his daughter/niece. Well, I can't say that I envy you," Simona said affectionately. "Which way are you leaning?" she asked as we walked towards the front door.

"Unfortunately, there's no doubt in my mind about what I have to do," I said. "I just hope Tom understands one day."

I gave Simona a hug goodbye then ran out of the boutique and hopped into Tom's van. I thought I'd better go check on Dee before I did anything else. She could be awake by now and I'm sure she'd want to hear about this preponderance of evidence that's overwhelmingly pointing to Crystal. So, I started the van and headed towards home, which was only about five minutes away.

I was only around the corner from the boutique when I spotted Crystal walking on the sidewalk. Not wanting to lose her, I pulled over to the side of the two-lane highway and turned my hazards on. I yelled Crystal's name at the top of my lungs, but I didn't get so much as a glance in return, eventually I noticed she had a set of headphones on. So, after taking off my seatbelt, I put the van in park and ran across the street and tapped Crystal on the shoulder.

"Oh, hello, S-Sam," Crystal said lethargically, not even noticing her uncle's van parked across the street. The look on her face was as if she was completely mesmerized with whatever it was she was listening to on her earphones, as she had them strategically draped over her head because of her fashionable updo. However, due to her runny makeup, I could tell that she'd been crying for some reason.

"What's the matter, sweetie?" I asked.

"Well, n-nothing you'd understand," Crystal said, as she started to walk away.

"Honey, I deal with second-graders all day," I retorted. "I don't think there's a problem in existence that I wouldn't understand. "

"I j-just want to go back in time so I can erase what I've become," Crystal shouted.

Oh my, was this an admission of guilt? Could she be responsible for Ronda's death? I thought to myself. "Well, what is it that you've become, Crystal?" I asked calmly while secretly hoping that she didn't say a murderer.

"It d-doesn't matter, Sam," Crystal replied. "You could never understand my p-plight in life and the things I go through with being as beautiful as you are," Crystal griped.

"Well, you need to make me understand; Is this about Ronda Evans?" I asked.

"H-How do you know about R-Ronda?" Crystal asked as I noticed Ronda's name made her visibly uncomfortable.

"Well, looks can be deceiving," I responded. "I know a lot more than people give me credit for. What I don't know is why Ronda had a coat on that you purchased?" I asked as I stood in front of Crystal to block her from leaving.

"Grandma, you t-tracked me down to find out why someone had on a coat I p-purchased?" Crystal asked while insulting me at the same time. "Well, you can tell that f-fraud she can either give back the coat willingly, or I'll see her in c-court!" Crystal shouted out.

While being called old twice in one day would've been enough to break the spirit of most women my age, thanks to Susie, I'd fortunately built up quite the tolerance for unjust insults. I thought to myself. However, barely able to speak now, I asked Crystal, "Are you telling me that you don't know?"

"I don't know w-what?" Crystal asked.

"Well, I'm afraid Ronda's been murdered," I said emotionally.

"W-WHAT?" Crystal shouted. "*Murdered!* How could that be I just saw her y-yesterday?" Crystal said while looking as confused as a pig eating a ham sandwich.

"She was shot, but sadly we don't know who fired the shot," I said. "You need to go home, Crystal; your uncle is worried sick about you," I said.

"How dare you?" Crystal yelled in my face. "You t-told my uncle about this?"

"I told him about the murder and where the evidence led me," I replied. "Anyone with half a brain would've come up with this same conclusion, and, Crystal, this doesn't look good for you," I said caringly.

"W-Where do you get off?" a now-angry Crystal shouted. "You seem to be going around town following clues that s-somehow led you back to me and now you assume I'm a murderer?" Crystal screamed.

"Well, in my defense, the evidence looks pretty damning. However, I'm just trying to find out what happened," I said in a calm voice.

"You know the one t-thing my uncle doesn't need right now is to be involved in another s-scandal, and now you've all but branded his niece as some crazed murderer," Crystal shouted.

"I'm trying to help, Crystal," I said calmly, trying to put a lid on her anger. "I never wanted this responsibility. However, I now feel like I owe it to my old friend Dee, and I certainly owe it to Ronda, seeing as how I heard this awful tragedy that's now ingrained in my memory."

"Heard w-what?" Crystal asked.

"Well, I heard her murder take place." I said, "I have a voicemail recording of it on my phone."

"Oh, my goodness, that's terrible," Crystal said as she placed her hand over her heart.

"Who died?" she asked with care.

I stood there completely dumbfounded, trying to take in Crystal's last question.

"Ronda died," I said a few seconds later, as I looked into Crystal's eyes, which all of a sudden appeared glossy and childlike. "She was shot last night," I said.

"Well, I'll get my uncle on t-this right away," Crystal shouted out. "He's a cop, and although he doesn't handle bad news very gracefully, if there's a monster out there, he'll find out who it is and put them behind bars."

As I stood there completely confounded, I couldn't help but think if her uncle was looking for monsters, then he may just be looking for her. Although Tom hadn't been a police officer in quite some time, it was more than apparent to anyone with eyes that every shred of evidence I'd gathered thus far pointed solely to Crystal.

Still slightly bewildered, Crystal caught me off-guard by hugging me before she ran off yelling that she was going to find Tom. I didn't know whether to stop her or use her as bait to lure Tom out of this state of depression he was now in. By the time I came to my senses, she was gone, and I was standing on the sidewalk alone staring at the traffic going by.

I walked back to Tom's van, thinking to myself the whole time, *What just happened here?* Of course, I wasn't sure if Crystal had just pulled the wool over my eyes. But if she had, then she definitely deserved an Oscar.

In my heart I just wasn't convinced she was guilty. She was—for sure—hiding something, but I don't think it was a murder. I knew I was getting pretty close to figuring out who was responsible for Ronda's death; I just needed a little more time. As I hopped into Tom's van, I started it back up and decided to continue on my journey home.

I arrived at my house five minutes later and Daphne greeted me at the front door. I walked into my bedroom and saw Dee was still sound asleep, so I closed the door again and phoned Maureen, but she still didn't pick up my call. I wasn't sure what I should do next. Between getting indirectly involved in Ronda's murder, and that kid Sean accusing my deceased husband of murdering his mother, I didn't know which way to turn. So, I walked into the living room and instantly thought of the story Channel 18 reported last night about Ronda's death. I stared for twenty seconds at a blank television screen before I realized I had been asking the wrong people about Ronda's whereabouts. If I wanted answers, I needed to start asking some uncomfortable questions to get them, beginning with Tom's Channel 18 coworkers and how they were able to obtain a photo of the usually guarded Ronda so effortlessly. A photo that was clearly taken well before her death.

The list of suspects was growing faster than Pinocchio's nose. Fortunately for me, my guard had somewhat come down and I was learning to see beyond everyone's little white lies. Someone in St. Lux was a stone-cold murderer and, for some reason or another, they had access to photos of the victim throughout different stages of her life. And as photogenic as Ronda was, that was a liberty even her own mother wasn't permitted.

CHAPTER SEVEN

I stood there in my living room still confused by all that had transpired over the past few days. I looked at the clock above the television and noticed it was a little after 3:00 p.m. I knew I had a few hours before I went to the Lucas's for dinner and I figured Sheriff Hawkins would contact me when he was back in his office, so I decided now was the perfect time to go and confront Talia Wren.

Talia was the Executive Producer for all Channel 18 News programming that aired. She was also Tom's boss and a handful, or so he claimed. What's more, she would've been the one who okayed Ronda's photo to air on last night's broadcast, so she surely would've known where it came from. I poured Daphne another bowl of granola, then grabbed my purse, and ran out the front door to Tom's van. I was on my way to the Channel 18 News station that was located in the center of downtown St. Lux to finally get to the bottom of this. I got there in less than five minutes and parked out front by the meter. Luckily, Tom had six quarters in his coin holder, so I grabbed them all and fed the meter because downtown was infamous for ticketing cars that didn't pay for parking.

It was a November day in Michigan, but the weather couldn't have been nicer. Tom was spot-on yesterday when he said today would be sixty-five and sunny out. I loved Tom, but our local journalists getting anything right lately was a rarity. Everyone in town knew about the financial trouble that the network was going through. So, I fully expected to walk into the crap show that Sheriff Hawkins had depicted the news station to be. I walked inside and although it wasn't as bad as Tom and Sheriff Hawkins would lead you to believe, they weren't that far off. Tom had complained on several occasions about the working conditions at Channel 18. I usually just shook my head and agreed because Tom suffered from a touch of obsessive-compulsive disorder and would complain if a restaurant didn't have an even number of chairs at a table.

I walked through the bug-infested building and from the moment I took my first step, I felt like I was in the twilight zone. The security guard had his feet propped up on the desk in front of him while sleeping on a toilet bowl that he was using as a chair. Next, a random girl walked by with the word "juicy" conspicuously planted across her backside while she shouted obscenities into her cellphone. Finally, an extremely tall man came over and threw his cup of coffee which just barely missed me. Then he demanded that I get him a cup that was worth drinking.

Where was Tom to flaunt his weatherman position when you needed him? I thought to myself. Suddenly, as I stood there in utter disbelief that anyone could possibly behave in this way, a very thin, young man ran over towards the kerfuffle and tried to explain to the giraffe of a man that I wasn't his assistant. The man stood there unimpressed with both of us, then shouted at the young boy, "COFFEE NOW" as he walked away. Visibly shaken, the boy said that he'd been the tall man's assistant for about four weeks now, so he wasn't exactly sure why I had to take the brunt of that coffee fiasco. But he thanked me, nonetheless, for not losing my cool and making a scene. Then he apologized for his boss's behavior and said he was leaving right away to go on another coffee run.

I told him that he wasn't responsible for someone else's behavior and that he had no reason to apologize. A few seconds later, the young man introduced himself as Mike Bell and asked me if today was my first day working there. I introduced myself also, as I silently thanked God that I wasn't employed here. Then I mentioned to the young man that I was only looking for Talia Wren.

Mike's anxiety level seemed to go up a couple notches after I mentioned Talia, so I asked him if everything was okay and could he take me to her office?

"Oh, I'm fine," Mike replied, "I'm simply curious about why a seemingly normal human would deliberately be looking for Talia. Do you have a death wish or something because no one ever seeks her out on purpose?"

"It's a long story, Mike," I said, while shaking my head.

"Well, I won't ask for details," Mike answered. "However, just know that Talia is ten times worse than that scary behemoth who just threw the cup of coffee at you. I mean, she's a completely different breed of nasty, and she makes Stretch over there look like Mary Poppins," Mike said, referring to his boss's height. "However, if you really like being in the vicinity of lions, I guess, I could take you to her lair. She's a creature of habit, so she's probably still eating Linner and if we hurry we can catch her." With that, he grabbed my arm and took off, almost dragging me behind.

"Sounds great—" I said while fixing my shirt sleeve that Mike had just about pulled off. "However, did you just pronounce it—"

Before I could finish my question. Mike shouted back at me, "Yes, I did indeed mean to say *Linner.* Talia likes to eat lunch and dinner at the same time. Couple that with the fact that she has the tendency to combine words and you get a whole new dialect. Please don't ask!" Mike yelled. "She does it nonstop and I get headaches just thinking about it," he griped.

Although I had so many more questions, I threw my hands up and hurried after him. As Mike walked me through the back hallway to meet with Talia, I couldn't help but harp on the fact that Mike was actually Stretch's assistant, which meant to some degree, Stretch thought I was Mike. A twenty-something male for goodness' sake. I mean I knew I could stand a little lipstick here, and a little blush there, but to be mistaken for a guy (albeit he's very thin) was truly disheartening.

As we got closer to Talia's door, everyone we passed had a strained look on their face. I figured it was all the stress from working at the news station and having such demanding bosses. Even Mike started taking baby steps and his demeanor changed the further we got from the news floor. He stood behind me, shaking after we heard Talia yell out, "Who's there?" once she'd spotted our silhouettes outside of her frosted glass door.

Mike then pointed towards Talia's office while saying, "You asked for it—*Voila, there it is!*" He went on to say that if I didn't make it out alive it was really nice meeting me. I smiled and waved goodbye at Mike while thinking to myself that this was just what I needed to be dealing with right now, Susie's evil doppelganger.

I walked into Talia's office fully expecting a cat fight to the death, and what I got was anything but. Talia was extremely charming and very forthcoming. *Could she have a split personality?* I thought to myself. How could everyone else see this woman as abrasive and contemptible, yet I saw a kind and beautiful soul.

I formerly introduced myself to Talia because although we had seen one another around town in the past, I wasn't sure if she'd remembered me. She offered me a seat and I got right into the reason for my visit. I didn't get a bad vibe from Talia, but I didn't want another interaction with someone that would be full of lies like what I'd experienced with Crystal earlier today. Even though Talia had been nothing but nice to me up until this point, I wasn't going to be pulling any punches. Someone in this station had to know something and it was up to me to figure out what that something was.

"I'm sure you're aware of this girl's tragic murder that took place last night," I said while holding up Ronda's picture. "However, I need to know where this photo originated and how someone who works at your news station got possession of it."

"She sure was a stunningly beautiful girl, wasn't she?" Talia said. "I sure hope the police catch the monster responsible for her death."

"So, you do recognize her. Well, do you know anything about what happened?" I asked.

"Oh, heavens no!" Talia blurted out. "I try and avoid those ghastly murder stories like the plague. You know despite what you may have heard about me, I don't really have the stomach for it," Talia said.

"Well, aren't you the Executive Producer of this show?" I asked with the most perplexed look on my face. Are you telling me you have no involvement in over half the stories that this broadcast disseminates?"

"I'm telling you exactly that," Talia replied swiftly, looking away from me and straightening some papers on her desk.

"Do you know how I got this job, Mrs. Harris?" Talia asked.

However, before I could tell her I didn't have time for a guessing game, she cut me off and informed me of how certain things weren't always as they seemed. "Most people are on the outside looking in," Talia said while still straightening the pile of paperwork on her desk. "So, it might appear that I'm living high on the hog with a car for every day of the week, since my father's the head of the network and all. However, I got my current position despite my father being head of the network and I'm here because of my own merit and work ethic. Truth be told..." Talia said, tucking her long jet-black hair behind her ear. "My own father bribed every single executive that was around at the time just to sabotage my chance of working here. He's extremely misogynistic, and his male chauvinistic superiority complex didn't stop on the day that I was born."

I knew that Talia's father, Michael Wren, was an important man who made a lot of different people a lot of disposable money. It would've been a tall ask to take someone like him down if he was somehow involved in a cover-up of Ronda's murder. Talia went on to say that for years, up until recently, her father used every trick in the book to get her to leave the company. "Although when he saw it wasn't working, he resorted to undermining everything I said and made a point to do it in front of our subordinates," she claimed. "Soon enough, they all followed suit and I became the evil witch lady everyone loved to hate, and the entire news station imploded."

"Are you saying that even though your name is on everything around here, you don't really call the shots?" I asked.

"There you go, Mrs. Harris," Talia scoffed. "Now you're getting it. I do the best I can with what little authority I'm given. But at the end of the day, I just feel like an overpaid intern," Talia stated bluntly. "Those people out there loathe me because of my father's influence," Talia said, gesturing at her office door. "So, I spend the better part of my day running around screaming like a banshee because it's the only thing they'll respond to."

In that moment, I was beginning to see a much softer side of Talia, a side her employees weren't the least bit aware of.

"Well, maybe 'loathe' is a strong word," I said. "Maybe there's just a disconnect and if you figure out what that is, then you solve the problem."

"Well, aren't you an encyclopedia," Talia said with a smile. "Full of knowledge and an answer for everything. Where do you get the strength?" Talia asked.

"Funnily enough, I get it from those who like to tear me down," I responded. "However, as far as having all the answers, boy, do I wish that were true. Unfortunately, I don't have one for the predicament I find myself in right now," I muttered.

"Well, I wish I could help you with your problem, Talia replied. "However, if your boy toy Tom couldn't be of any service..."

"MY BOY TOY!" I shouted out, interrupting Talia.

"Oh, I'm sorry, Talia said. "Did I overstep? I mean, you see a girl out eating lunch at a fancy restaurant with a guy and you just assume. I thought you two were an item, my mistake," Talia sneered.

"Are you referring to the time when Tom and I were sitting outside at the Medium Well Steakhouse having lunch and you walked by?" I asked. "Well, that was completely innocent. We were out celebrating Rodney Lucas's retirement and he and his wife just so happened to have gone to the restroom seconds before you walked by."

Just before I let Talia give some weak excuse for seemingly being the responsible party who told all of St. Lux that Tom and I were an item, I had an epiphany. "Wow! Wait," I shouted out. "Did you just say you couldn't help me if my boy toy couldn't?" I asked. Well, putting aside the fact that she thought Tom was my so-called "boy toy," I asked her if she was insinuating that he knew something about the details of Ronda's murder?

"Well, didn't Tom tell you?" Talia said. "He's also an executive producer. My father made sure of that a few months back," she griped. "He wanted a man to be in charge and he essentially got his way because Tom oversees pretty much everything, and that's why I assumed if he couldn't help you, then I surely wouldn't be able to. I figured you two already talked," Talia said sincerely.

"So, you had nothing to do with the story that aired last night about Ronda's death? Are you saying it was all Tom's production?" I asked, confused.

"Are you sure you two aren't an item?" Talia asked. "You sound like a woman in denial. As I mentioned before, I tend to stay away from those awful murder stories. And aside from that, I have a difficult enough time getting my staff motivated as it is. If I had told them to air the story, they would've found a way around it out of spite," Talia said, finally putting the paperwork in a neat pile on her desk.

"That's where Tom comes in," Talia said with a smirk. "I'll let him boss the staff around, and I figured he's likable enough, so why fight my father on making him my equal? Fortunately, I've learned to pick my battles around here," she insisted.

"He didn't tell me any of this today," I muttered.

"Oh, that's why you look like you just lost your best friend," Talia said with some empathy. "Well, the way he talks about you around the station, I thought you two would've been closer than Siamese twins."

"Well, I thought we were close...but what do I know, I also thought he was just a meteorologist," I responded.

"Honey, if my father wasn't such a pig, a meteorologist would be Tom's only title," Talia retorted. "However, now I kind of refer to him as a jack-of-all-trades around here. He gets to wear many different hats."

As I sat there taking in more unsolicited news about Tom, all I could think was if one of those metaphorical hats he wore was covering a well-acted out façade.

"I'm not sure if this news ruined any romantic feelings you may have had for Tom," Talia said. "If so, that was not my intention. I'm fully aware I can come on a bit strong, and I know I can be something of an acquired taste, Mrs. Harris. I'm not for everybody. And I'm fairly certain you yourself came in here ready to rip me a new one based on some preconceived notion about me," Talia asserted.

"Well, I-I—" I was completely speechless because not only was she right but she had also just enlightened me at the advanced age of thirty-nine to never judge a book by its cover.

"Don't worry about it," Talia said as I tried to apologize for misjudging her. "I'd be a fool to still be working for this broadcasting company and not have thick skin," she said. "Can I tell you something though, Mrs. Harris?"

"Of course, but only if you call me Samantha," I responded while drawing a smile out of her.

"You betcha," Talia replied. "Well, Samantha, you seem like a very sweet but very sheltered woman. I—on the other hand—like to keep a healthy balance of good and wicked in my life, so here's my good deed for the day," Talia said firmly. "Being a woman of a certain age I'm sure I don't have to tell you everything that glitters isn't gold, and as bad as I said my father was, some days I come in here and I can't tell the difference between him and Tom. So, unless you're looking for a lifetime of heartache, whatever feelings you may have had for Tom, I'd recommend locking them up and maybe misplacing the key."

Talia stood with her arms crossed and candidly looked at me like an authority figure. She then handed me her business card with her direct number on it and informed me that she'd have a chat with Tom once he returned to work in two days.

Two days! I thought to myself. I hope I can find Tom before then. As I stood up to put my phone in my back pocket, I noticed Talia reaching out her arms to give me a hug goodbye. *This behavior is a complete 180 from the monster she was painted out to be,* I thought.

Talia then said if there was anything that she could do to assist with putting a killer behind bars to just say the word. Well, I wasn't exactly sure who was responsible for Ronda's death at this point, but there was something else that was driving me crazy that Talia could assist me with. So, I blurted it right out and asked Talia about her fascination with combining words and told her I was only curious because portmanteau words were a huge pet peeve of mine. I knew I wouldn't be able to sleep if I'd left even one stone unturned, and since Mike had just informed me about Talia's play on words quirk, I couldn't help but wonder if she had a thing for showing sides of her personality that benefited the situation. *Was that too farfetched?* I thought to myself. After all, she showed her staff a completely different version of herself than the one I was getting here today. Furthermore, I was well aware of the fact that she used the correct pronunciation for the word "lunch" less than ten minutes ago, when she described seeing Tom and I out eating lunch at a fancy restaurant. I wasn't sure if any of this meant anything but as far as lies and half-truths go, I was no longer glossing over them. As far as I was concerned, everyone was a suspect.

"Oh, geez, you got me!" Talia said, as she flung her head back while she laughed. "Typically, I don't break character while at work but I guess when you're good, you're good, and Samantha, as inquisitive and endearing as you are, well, that's the right combination that makes you pretty darn good. I'll bet you could get a dying man to gift you his last wish," Talia joked.

"Well, my staff is right if they told you about tanguage," Talia said intensely.

"Tanguage." I repeated. "Is that some form of Talia's language?" I asked.

"Yes," Talia said. "It's me combining my name with the word language to come up with my own form of communicating. You see, initially, when I first arrived here, I would get tongue-tied in meetings because of my nerves and I would just butcher every presentation. Finally, I decided to turn a negative into a positive and have a little fun while doing it," Talia said candidly.

"Tanguage freaks the new employees out while keeping the old not-so-bright ones far away from me; it's a win-win." Talia said with a smirk. "Lucky for you, you're an encyclopedia and no one can pull the wool over your eyes."

"Oh, how I wish that were true," I said. "Unfortunately, not only has someone been able to pull the wool over my eyes but now I also feel like I've been blinded by the entire flock of sheep," I whispered softly. Talia had one more hearty laugh at my expense, then we said goodbye to one another once I realized it was almost 4:00 p.m.

"I made my way back home and called Maureen once I got in my driveway, but still the call went nowhere. So, then I gave Tom a call and of all the days his phone battery was now somehow dead as well.

After getting out of the van, I went inside to check on Dee and saw she was still asleep in my bedroom. So, I decided to check her to make sure she was still breathing. Once I heard her start to snore, I was able to let out a sigh of relief. Then I walked into the kitchen and gave the hyper Daphne a fresh bowl of water. Once she was finished drinking, I took her out back so she could run around. As I stood there on the back patio watching Daphne run in circles, I noticed a huge white spot on my otherwise green lawn. Thinking it was just trash I went to dispose of it. But the closer I got; I realized it was a clump of pills. It looked like someone had strategically placed them in my yard. It appeared as though someone just stood on my lawn and poured half their prescription out. I was mortified because each morning this was the exact spot where Daphne would abandon her plan of chasing squirrels once she realized they were too fast. *Could someone have dumped these pills here on purpose?* I thought to myself. I reached down to see exactly what kind of pills they were and if they were dangerous for dogs to ingest, since I had no real concept of how long they were out there. I picked up one of the pills and instantly knew what they were for. Jack had had a really bad bout with insomnia for a while and I knew without a doubt that these pills were for insomniacs. I stood up after I put the last pill that was on the ground into my coat pocket and turned towards my house. Then I noticed one of the windows in my spare bedroom was cracked open. This was weird because it was too chilly yesterday to open a window and I hadn't been in that particular bedroom all day today.

Then I had a chilling suspicion. I ran towards my house with Daphne hot on my heels and I saw the patio stairs in my peripheral vision. Then I took a nosedive because Daphne was certain she needed to be a guard dog at this point and check the premises before I entered. She cut me off right as we got to the stairs and I decided to take the tumble in order to not step on her. Once I got up, we went inside and I ran straight into the bathroom. As silly as it may sound, I hadn't been able to get rid of anything that belonged to Jack. Even his medication was still in the medicine cabinet, so I opened the door to the cabinet and was shocked by what I saw—or I should say—rather by what I didn't see.

Jack's insomnia medication was gone. However, it couldn't have been missing for very long as I recall going into this very cabinet two days ago and seeing those pills as I got cough syrup out for a lingering cough I had. As I stood there in utter disbelief, I realized those were Jack's pills that had been poured out onto the lawn.

My intuition was on high alert and I assumed that this was the work of the killer. I figured if someone was brazen enough to break into my house for some more than likely expired prescription medication, then they certainly knew I was hot on their trail and wasn't above framing me for whatever illegal activity they needed those pills for—and not to mention *murder.*

CHAPTER EIGHT

I rushed into the spare bedroom to close the window and noticed Maureen hadn't taken her keys when she left this morning. They were still sitting on the nightstand beside the bed. *She couldn't have gone home,* I thought to myself. I figured she would've had no way of getting in and she most certainly wasn't at work because she left her wallet that contained her bank entry card as well. Things just weren't adding up, but I wasn't going to slow down until I knew everyone was safe and sound.

I walked back into the living room and noticed on the television that the bomb scare at Maureen's bank finally made breaking news. So, I turned up the volume and, boy, was I relieved to hear that it was all just a hoax. I could finally breathe again. I still didn't know where Maureen was, but at least I knew she wasn't in imminent danger.

I turned off the television and sat in Jack's favorite recliner chair. It was funny because on so many occasions, I pretended to hate this thing when he was alive, although I would often sneak and sit in it myself, whenever he was away from home for the evening. It was an old, lumpy, white reclining chair with black polka dots that didn't match any other furniture in the house, and it was big enough to sit an entire family of four at the same time. It was for sure an eyesore. But Jack simply loved it and he always looked as if he were in deep thought whenever he sat in it. Figuring I could use some guidance, I thought I'd give it a try.

I sat down and it felt as if I were sitting for the first time in a week. I was finally able to turn my brain off and simply relax. Jack had always warned me that I didn't have an off switch and now I was starting to think that's why he was so adamant about keeping this chair; I think he knew I secretly loved it. As I sat there, I felt as though I was sitting on clouds and for a brief moment, I felt problem-free.

That is until I heard Dee moan from my bedroom. I soon realized I had the kind of problems that even the most comfortable of chairs couldn't alleviate. I instantly got up and ran towards my bedroom, thinking Dee would soon be needing some comfort. I slowly opened the bedroom door and looked inside only to find Dee still sleeping peacefully. It looked as if she'd barely moved since earlier today, so I closed the door while thinking to myself, *maybe that was Daphne that I'd heard.*

I walked back into the living room and noticed it was barely 4:30 p.m., and I didn't have to be at Rodney and Kathleen's until 6:00 p.m. I knew sitting around on my hands wasn't going to get me any closer to figuring out what happened to Ronda, so I decided to head over to Tom's condo.

I realized I wasn't going to reach Tom by phone and I certainly wasn't waiting two days until he was scheduled to go back to work. Tom may have had his share of problems in the past, but as far as I was concerned, he'd always been a good friend to me. His past behavior didn't speak to the Tom I knew, and the last thing I wanted was for him to lose his way and start to self-destruct again.

I took Tom's van again since I had blocked my car in when I came back home from the news station. As I was backing out of my driveway, I looked down the road and noticed everyone's favorite Grey-Haired Crackling Hens sitting on the main meddler's porch. As long as it was someone else's business, I knew the Grey Cougars definitely had their noses in it. So, I figured this would be my chance to elicit some answers for the many aberrant questions that had taken over my psyche.

I pulled over to the shoulder and walked down to Eleanor's front porch. Eleanor was the eldest of the Grey Cougars and by far the feistiest. She was short in stature and had a head full of grey hair, hence the name Grey Cougars. For one reason or another, Eleanor always wore the skimpiest of miniskirts with white knee-high socks. It didn't take a psychic to see the look she was going for, even nearing her eighty-fifth birthday. But sadly, I knew if she got one more wrinkle around her midriff, her future was going to be twisting those skirts up as opposed to pulling them up.

"Hello, ladies!" I shouted out as I approached the stairs that were littered in beer cans.

"Hey there, Lucille!" a seemingly intoxicated Margaret yelled back. "It looks like you've lost some weight. What's your secret?" she asked.

"Oh, I'm Samantha," I said. "Lucille's the travelling nurse who lives across the street, but no worries we get mistaken for one another all the time."

"Umm yeah, we don't correct her anymore," a very subdued Eleanor said. "Frankly, it's a waste of time and as you can see no one on this porch can spare much of that. So, what brings you by, Samantha?" Eleanor asked.

"I know why she's here," a slightly less inebriated Alice blurted out. "She wants to join our club because these young kids hate for us grandmas to have all of the fun," Alice added while gawking at me.

"Well, I doubt that's why she's here," Eleanor responded before I ever had the chance to say anything. "I've never seen her indulge with the bottle long enough to join a club with the three amigos. Besides, her bosom is far too perky to be one of us, so there's got to be another reason for her visit," Eleanor said aggressively.

"Busted!" I blurted out. "Silly me, trying to get one over on you ladies. What was I thinking?" I asked.

"The problem is you weren't!" Eleanor retorted. "Now, kiddo, cut the charades and tell us why you're here. "

"Yeah, Lucille, you're as bad as my husband, Paul," Margaret shouted out. "With that awful forty-five-minute foreplay hogwash he continues to do, and now whatever new form of fondling this is, it seem like both of you drive me to the park but never really let me play on any of the swings, if you know what I mean."

Oh, my, I thought to myself. *I knew these ladies were tough, but today for some reason they were just brutal.*

"Well, on that note," I said. "I'll cut the small talk and get straight to the point. Have any of you seen anything bizarre going on in the neighborhood lately, or have you heard anything unusual late at night?" I asked.

"Well, I heard a window get broken out last night," Margaret said. "Then once I looked out my front window, I saw someone running into the empty field across the street from your house, Lucille."

If calling myself Lucille would somehow help me find answers, then I didn't mind playing the part for the day. "I saw someone as well," I said. "Do you know who it was? Could you see their face?" I asked frantically.

"Honey, I've got glaucoma and cataracts, I can't even see your face," Margaret replied.

"Well, what about you, Eleanor?" I asked. "Have you seen anyone lurking around my house lately?"

"Do your ex-cop boyfriend count?" Eleanor asked.

"My ex-cop boyfriend?" I repeated.

"That's right. He's now St. Lux's good-looking weatherman," Eleanor said, as if she'd just read *Boyfriends for Dummies.*

"So, Tom Miller!" I screamed. "Well, for the umpteenth time today, Tom Miller is not my boyfriend and he is certainly not my boy toy," I said firmly. "However, why would you suggest he's been lurking around my house?"

"Well, contrary to popular belief, not all of us old bats have cataracts," Eleanor said. "I can actually still see. No offense, Margaret," Eleanor laughed.

"None taken, you denture-wearing gazelle," Margaret retorted.

"Oh, dear," I whispered. "I certainly didn't mean to get anyone angry or start a shouting match between friends," I said in a panic.

"Who's angry?" Eleanor asked. "Did you not just hear Margaret refer to me as a beautiful gazelle? Well, if that's not a heavenly friendship filled with love, then I don't know what is."

"Umm, okay," I muttered while simultaneously wishing I was anywhere but there. "So, you're positive you've seen Tom hanging around my house?" I asked.

"I sure am," Eleanor said. "I'm as positive about that as I am that Margaret will fall off that stump reaching for her fifth beer today. Unfortunately, I've seen him multiple times driving that fancy white sports car. But on occasion he'll sometimes drive that same van that you just parked on the shoulder there," Eleanor said convincingly.

I was completely taken aback. Eleanor had just named off two of Tom's three vehicles. So, there was no doubt in my mind that she had seen him. "He just circles the block," Eleanor went on to say. "It seems as though he's casing your house. Well, at least that's the conclusion me and the old Grey Cougars came up with," she said in a teasing tone.

"Oh, you know about that name!" I responded with a little embarrassment.

"I know *everything*," Eleanor replied.

"Well, do you happen to know anything about the Jane Doe who was on last night's news?" I asked. "Her name was Ronda Evans and I was close friends with her mother when we were kids. So, anything you may have seen or heard could essentially help get a killer off the streets," I said emotionally.

"Well, I'm not one to gossip," Eleanor said, as I turned to look at the nearest tree to make sure it wasn't currently struck by lightning.

"However, all the Grey Cougars have a theory about what happened to Ronda," Eleanor said passionately. "We think whoever killed that young girl had a real disdain for women, and unfortunately, it was personal because someone walked that poor girl into that old, abandoned house, and right into an ambush," Eleanor added, as she stood from her rocking chair.

Oh no, I thought to myself as my knees started to buckle. Had I inadvertently given Ronda directions to meet the friend who eventually shot and killed her?

"Why do you assume that Ronda's killer had a problem with women?" I asked, thinking of Talia Wren's chauvinistic father, Michael.

"Just from what was done to the body after the fact," Eleanor said as she cracked open another beer. "The police found her in—well—let's just say a very subservient position. Not to mention the fact that the killer took the time to fix her runny makeup and even put her hair up in one of those fancy modern ponytails. Now if that doesn't shout *call my therapist because I hate women,* then I don't know what does," Eleanor said emphatically.

"Wait what?!" I shouted out. "They found Ronda with her hair in an updo?" I asked.

"They sure did, Lucille," Margaret yelled out. "What's it to you?"

"Well, it might mean you ladies are onto something," I responded. "You see all of Ronda's luggage was stolen on her flight here to St. Lux earlier this week. She told me this just yesterday and said she hadn't replaced any of her missing hair accessories."

"Oh, okay, but I'm still lost, Lucille," Margaret blurted out as I was making my point.

"Don't you see, ladies?" I said, as eagerly as a kid running unsupervised through a candy store. "I saw Ronda just a few hours before her death when she told me this. We had a conversation about her purchasing some of my scrunchies, so there's no way she could've put her hair in an updo of her own accord!" I shouted.

"Well, I'll be... Eleanor, you may have just helped me get one step closer to cracking this case!" I yelled out in excitement. "Someone must've fixed Ronda's makeup and hair after the fact, and I have an idea of who that someone could've been. But how did you know about all of this?" I asked. "It wasn't on the news."

"I told you earlier, I *know* everything," Eleanor said.

"That's good enough for me," I replied. "But now I have to hurry and inform the Sheriff about this new information," I said enthusiastically.

"Well, just one more thing before you go, Samantha," Eleanor said in a more serious tone.

"Yes, what is it?" I asked.

"Just be careful around your weatherman," Eleanor said.

"Yeah, unfortunately, these days everything that glitters isn't gold," Alice chimed in while quoting the same phrase Talia used when warning me about Tom.

"I know we give you young folks a hard time," Eleanor went on to say. "However, these Grey Cougars see more than you could ever imagine, and the verdict is still out on him."

I had lost count of the times today that I'd been warned to stay away from Tom, and from the Grey Cougars of all people. Well, they saw things that happened in the neighborhood to which even the police weren't privy. Suffice it to say, just like the intel that I'd received from them concerning Ronda, they were usually pretty spot on with their little tidbits of information regarding any gossip floating around St. Lux.

Although I have to admit, I wasn't overly convinced at this point that it was some deranged monster that hated women who was responsible. I mean just a few hours ago, I myself was debating whether or not I would get into a cat fight with a woman who I presumed to be a she devil. And not a day goes by where I don't daydream about dropping a piano on Susie's head, as if she was Sylvester the Cat. So, fortunately, I knew a woman could have bouts of rage as well, and I wasn't overlooking anyone. Especially since I learned the killer took the time to put Ronda's hair in an updo, which just so happens to be a style that Crystal faithfully wore.

After my little epiphany, I told all the ladies goodbye and thanked them for their help. Then I started to walk over towards Tom's van when I heard the loudest thump behind me. I turned around and saw that Margaret had fallen face first onto the stairs, presumably reaching for another beer. Suddenly, I heard Eleanor yell to Alice, "It's like were friends with Moe from the three stooges. This girl never learns!"

"Oh, dear God!" I shouted as I ran back. "Is she okay?"

"She'll be fine," Eleanor said as she plopped down into her rocking chair. "Leave her down there and let her see what her life has become. This isn't her first rodeo! Everyone knows it's her scaring all the young men away by getting so sloppy drunk because Lord knows back in my day these legs would've stopped traffic," Eleanor added, as she raised her right leg, blinding me momentarily with her lack of undergarments. As I turned back around, now running towards Tom's van, I also realized that I was simultaneously running from the mental image Eleanor had seemingly just scarred me with. After reaching the van, I continued on my way to Tom's condo, and I got there just in time because Crystal pulled into the spot right next to me seconds after I parked.

"Crystal—Hi! Were you able to reach your uncle?" I asked as we both walked from our vehicles and met at the sidewalk.

"I haven't been able to get in c-contact with him," Crystal said. "It worries me because the only other t-time he's ever taken off and was unreachable was when Aunt Becca left with the kids. But when he finally c-came back home he just wasn't himself," Crystal claimed.

"What do you mean?" I asked.

"He just was no longer the s-sweet guy who raised me," Crystal responded. "Something in him changed, but I guess that happens when p-people go around town spreading false rumors about you," Crystal said, as she gave me a chilling death stare.

Trying to break the tension, I told Crystal that I came over to see if her uncle was there. However, looking at their windows with all the shades drawn I concluded that I'd probably already missed him. "Do you mind if I come inside for a bit?" I asked.

"Is there any p-particular reason why you need to?" Crystal asked.

"Well, I thought maybe if we looked around, we could find a clue as to where Tom could have gone," I replied.

"Okay, you have five minutes," Crystal said. "After that, I'm heading b-back out the door."

"Well, I'll be done in three," I responded. We both walked into the condo and, just as I expected, everything was in order. Tom was pretty particular about everything being in its place when it wasn't being used. I checked the bathroom and Tom's bedroom and didn't see anything unusual. Then I looked inside the refrigerator to grab a bottle of water and noticed I wasn't the only one who didn't have anything edible in my house. Besides baking soda, old guacamole dip, and water bottles, the fridge was completely bare.

Next, I made my way into Crystal's bedroom while she was in the restroom, and I saw luggage tucked away in the corner. I let out an extremely loud gasp, but quickly composed myself because I was afraid that Crystal would come running in and throw me out if she saw me in her bedroom. I walked over towards the closet where the luggage sat, then spun it around on its wheels, and got the shock of my life.

The name Ronda was encrusted with jewels on the other side of the suitcase. I hurried and opened it and instantly knew that it didn't belong to Crystal. There was just no way a barista could afford the items that were inside. I checked the smaller compartment and saw numerous hair accessories— and if I had any doubt before— I certainly had none now.

At the very least Crystal was a lying kleptomaniac but could she really have made the huge jump to murder? I thought to myself.

I decided to take one of the headbands that looked familiar, but I couldn't quite put my finger on why. It was pink with diamonds all around it, and I was certain I'd seen it before. As I stood up while placing the headband in my jacket pocket. Crystal came barging in and said no one was allowed in her bedroom. Well, I could no longer keep the mountain of evidence I'd discovered against her a secret anymore.

"Where did you get this luggage, Crystal?" I asked with fear in my voice.

"W-What business is it of yours, Sam?" Crystal replied.

"Well, it's my business because Ronda's dead and you have her luggage!" I shouted out. "However, it'll be the cops' business pretty soon unless you start telling me what's going on," I said firmly.

Crystal walked over to her bed and sat down in disbelief. "I don't for one second b-believe she's dead," she cried out. "She's probably just d-doing a skit for her followers, and I honestly can't believe she'd stoop to such levels just to embarrass me," Crystal whispered.

Is she having a mental breakdown? I thought to myself. Or was this some form of remorse on display. Whatever it was, it had her completely out of touch with reality. So, I walked over, sat next to Crystal on her bed, and held her hand. Then I told her this wasn't a skit and Ronda was, in fact, dead.

"This is not a game, Crystal," I said firmly while still clenching her per-spiring hand. "Ronda has been murdered and, unfortunately, more than one road leads back to you as being the person responsible. At this point, you need to help me help you," I said, gently.

"The n-nerve of you!" Crystal yelled as she jumped up off the bed. "The lengths Ronda will go to f-for a few likes online, and now you're here looking for her next meme. If you wanted me out of the way so bad so you c-could have my uncle all to yourself, then all you had to d-do was ask," Crystal shouted.

"What?" I yelled as I stood up. "That's not what I want at all," I said.

"I see it all so c-clearly now," Crystal said. "You and Ronda cooked up this elaborate scheme to remove me from the mix. Well, if she thinks I'm going quietly, you'd better tell her she d-doesn't know who she's dealing with," Crystal said, her anger intensifying the air in the room and I suddenly wanted to be far away from the complexity of the whole situation. But I knew this may be my only opportunity to get more information, so I tried to defuse Crystal's tension.

"I'm not exactly sure how many cups of coffee you had before leaving work this morning, but you're not making much sense," I said, reaching to pat her on the shoulder. "Ronda was *murdered*," I paused to let it sink in, "...and whether or not you want to believe it, that's not going to change. However, just as I found out, the police will find out that you didn't leave work this morning to care for a sick dog. On top of that, you're now hiding luggage that belongs to a dead woman in your bedroom." I tried not to raise my voice, but I did out of frustration.

Crystal pushed my hand off her shoulder. "Are you s-spying on me now?" she said.

"Honestly, I'm trying to help you," I replied. "Crystal, this isn't a game, and the fact that you were seen with Ronda shortly before her murder automatically makes you a suspect," I said, just as Crystal was interjecting another crazy unfounded allegation—

"Oh, so you and Ronda p-planned on seeing this lie all the way through, huh?" Crystal snorted.

I had never seen this side of her before. I was completely appalled by her nonchalant attitude toward a young girl's murder and her casual ability to turn everything around and make herself the victim. Well, at this point I'd had enough, and I thought it was the perfect time to bring out my bad cop persona.

"I don't think you want to talk about lies," I blurted out. "Seems like you've hoodwinked every soul in town today."

"The audacity of you g-getting so self-righteous with me," Crystal screamed. "Aren't you the same S-Samantha that made my uncle's marriage implode by constantly playing the damsel in distress?" a very misinformed Crystal confidently said. "Now you want to come in here and t-tell me about my shortcomings, all the while t-trying to turn not only my friends against me but also my favorite uncle!"

"I told him the facts, and he saw them for what they were," I responded. "The same as everyone else will see them unless you start telling the truth," I said carefully.

Right then, Crystal's phone began to ring. When she answered, I couldn't hear what the person on the other end was saying, but without warning Crystal's whole attitude changed. It was as if she hadn't been arguing with me for the past few minutes. She had, in an instant, morphed back into the sweet Crystal I'd always seen at the coffee shop, and I felt as though I no longer needed to be a bad cop. A very subdued Crystal, now off her seemingly life-altering phone call, informed me that she needed to head out.

"I don't think that's such a good idea," I whispered softly, unsure of what her response might be.

"I'll be f-fine," Crystal replied. "I'll check back in with you in a c-couple of hours and I'll tell you everything you want to know, starting with why I have that s-suitcase," Crystal whispered. "It's bad, but it's definitely not murder-related," she said with her familiar shy smile.

I'd felt in my heart Crystal was telling me the truth and for whatever reason it seemed like maybe she was now willing to accept Ronda's death. Maybe it was the love I had for her, but it was just something gnawing at me, something in my soul saying she couldn't have been responsible. However, that didn't mean I was just going to overlook all of the overwhelming evidence that pointed to her.

I walked over towards Crystal and gave her the biggest hug I could muster. "It may seem like I'm against you now," I said. "However, for what it's worth I don't think you did anything wrong. But I do think you're afraid of something. Call me once that fear becomes too much of a burden," I gently gave her another affectionate squeeze.

I let myself out and walked over towards Tom's van. I was beyond tired of everyone seemingly disappearing on me, so before I left home, I took Daphne's GPS tracker off of her neck and placed it in my purse. I stuck double-sided tape on it that I found lying on Tom's back seat and placed it under the back bumper of Crystal's car. I didn't exactly think of Crystal as a suspect at this point but whatever she was up to, I was going to have firsthand knowledge this time.

I got back into Tom's van and took off to meet the Lucas' for dinner as it was almost 6:00 p.m. I just couldn't believe Crystal thought I was the reason for her uncle's marriage falling apart. I certainly hadn't been sending Tom any signals that I was interested, so I'm not sure why all of St. Lux assumed we were anything more than friends, and I certainly didn't know why Crystal had been harboring resentful feelings towards me. However, I didn't have time to think about it now. I was on a mission for the truth and that's exactly what I was going to get.

I pulled up at the Lucas's at 6:00 p.m. sharp and saw Kathleen sweeping her driveway. Someone must've thought it was still Halloween because they completely trashed the Lucas' house with silly childish pranks. Eggs had been thrown at every window and door, and trees that were thirty feet tall were covered in toilet paper.

Kathleen was one of the sweetest people I knew, but as I got out of Tom's van to help her clean, I heard her yell, "Don't you dare touch that broom. You're a guest here. Besides, I'm almost done."

"What happened here? Do you guys have any idea who could've done this?" I asked.

"Well, obviously I don't have any concrete proof," Kathleen said. "However, I have a feeling it's the same person from a year or so ago that vandalized Rodney's car. It just feels like someone's holding a very personal grudge against Rodney from his Sheriff days, but we haven't the slightest idea who it is," Kathleen explained.

A light bulb instantly went off in my head. It had to be Sean who vandalized their home. He probably damaged Rodney's car over a year ago also because he felt slighted by him during his mother's murder investigation. Well, questioning Sean today somehow must've stirred up old feelings and he came back for round two on their home. I didn't know if I should say anything to Kathleen about my suspicions. After all, this was the same Sean who'd just accused my deceased husband of murder. If I sent a former Sheriff after him and scared him away, I'd never get to the bottom of this. So, I decided to keep this to myself for now and, when given the opportunity, confront Sean myself about his reckless behavior.

After about fifteen minutes of chatting with Kathleen and letting her steer where the conversation went—because I didn't have the heart to tell her why I was actually there— Rodney came outside.

"Welcome to the party, you need any toilet paper?" he yelled from the front porch while pointing at all the trees that were covered in it.

"I've actually already been funneling it through my back window for the past ten minutes," I joked. Rodney laughed as he met Kathleen and I at the edge of the driveway.

"Sorry about the mess, Samantha," Kathleen said as she filled her trash bag with more toilet paper. "Unfortunately, everything's completely falling behind schedule since getting home and seeing the shenanigans people are willing to pull for a laugh. Thank God, I've already started dinner, but it could be another hour or so before it's done," Kathleen said.

"No worries," I replied. "Chaos has been my weekend summed up in a nutshell."

"On days like this, I just want to go to my favorite little hole in the wall and get sloshed!" Rodney screamed.

"Sloshed," I whispered back to myself. *Oh, no.* I thought. *What have I done?* I told Rodney and Kathleen that I had to make a quick run, but assured them that I'd be back in time for dinner. After all, I still had more than a few allegations that I needed Rodney to shed some light on.

I hopped in Tom's van and headed across town; I was more than certain that I'd find Tom here as I made it to the Tunnel Funnel Bar in less than five minutes. I walked inside and wished I could say I was surprised to see Tom. However, once he was aware of the mountain of evidence that surrounded his niece, something in me knew that he'd go spiraling. *Over a year of sobriety down the drain,* I thought to myself.

Standing in the entryway of the bar, I thought about how sick and tired I was of everyone always being there for me. But when it came time to help my friends, I was always a step behind. Now, in a way, I felt responsible for Tom falling off the wagon again. After all, he was only at this bar because of information he'd discovered about Crystal. Information I'd felt responsible for putting out in the universe.

However, the Grey Cougars weren't the only ones with a plausible theory. I couldn't prove it just yet, but I suspected that the mysterious abundance of evidence that basically fell into my lap about Crystal was nothing more than a deterrent. A deterrent to keep me off the real killer's trail, and subsequently leave pandemonium in its wake. Well, between playing with people's lives, framing innocent girls, and, not to mention, murder, I wasn't sure if there was a crime this monster wasn't willing to commit. I'm uncertain if the person responsible thought this form of deceit would keep them in the clear. However, messing with everyone in my life whose friendship I cherished was definitely going to prove to be this maniac's undoing.

CHAPTER NINE

I anxiously walked inside and sat down at the bar next to Tom. "Get your things!" I said firmly, "I've come to take you home." Tom was beyond impaired and he looked as if he was in a bottomless pit of despair. Instinctively, I tapped on the counter to get the bartender's attention to see if I could get Tom a glass of water, only to realize that the barkeep was on their makeshift stage because it was karaoke night.

As I tugged on Tom's shirt to try and get him to stand up, I saw a young lady walking onto the stage to sing her karaoke song and I just couldn't believe it. *Was this some sort of sign?* I thought to myself. "This is not really happening," I muttered to Tom as the lady started to sing what appeared to be her go to number "Single Ladies." The exact song I'd always reference myself doing on stage at a bar when I knew something had a very low probability of happening.

I sat there transfixed as she motioned for people in the audience to join her as her back-up dancers. I thought to myself, *Should I, could I? It just might help me shake the stress out of my system.* After all, I did hit this one happening right on the nail even down to the song choice, and it wasn't like Tom was going anywhere. However, before I could muster up the courage, I heard someone behind me shouting out my name.

"Mrs. Harris Mrs. Harris!" The woman shouted out. As I slowly turned around, I saw a woman with bright orange hair whose face was covered in freckles walking over towards Tom and me. I didn't recognize her, but she obviously knew me from somewhere.

"Aren't you Mrs. Harris from Holcomb Elementary?" the very intoxicated woman yelled out.

Oh, dear God, not another inebriated person, I thought to myself.

"Yes, that's my place of employment. Do I know you?" I asked.

"Well, I would hope so," the woman said with a sarcastic twist. "You got my husband fired from teaching because you and the rest of those overzealous mean girls didn't like the competition. I'm Allison, Reggie Cooper's wife," the woman said as I gasped from shock. Until I'd just met this woman, I didn't know Reggie Cooper was married. The word "marriage" certainly never flew from his lips when he aggressively harassed every woman who worked at Holcomb Elementary. Truth be told, everyone at school felt as if that's why he resigned; legally he was never fired. However, we all believed Reggie knew there was a strong sexual harassment case building against him, and he wanted to get out in front of it.

Well, maybe he didn't want the accusation all over town, I thought to myself. Sadly, with his own wife completely oblivious to what actually happened, it looked like his plan was working. However, for the life of me I couldn't figure out why everyone in St. Lux was telling half-truths and outright lies?

Even though it seemed as if I knew a little bit more about her husband's after school activities than she did, it really wasn't my place to tell her, especially since she was so worked up already. "Listen, Mrs. Cooper," I said with sincerity, "maybe this is a conversation you should have with Reggie."

"No!" Allison shouted out. "This is a conversation I'm going to have with you," she said as she repeatedly poked my upper arm with her finger.

"Well, I don't wanna hang with Mrs. Cooper," I retorted. Referencing the television show from the early 1990s with a similar name called *Hangin' with Mr. Cooper*, but I'm sure she was too inebriated to even enjoy the pun.

By now the bartender was walking over towards us, so I yelled for a bottle of water to try and sober Tom up. But just as the bartender walked away to get the water, Allison whispered in my ear, "Wait until the school board hears about how you're shacking up with this murderer!"

Well, after that, I pulled away, wondering how Tom got on anyone's radar for murder. Allison, in a drunken rage, shouted out, "Don't look so surprised, sweetie. I know a few overzealous mean girls myself and the streets are talking about your little ex-cop-turned-criminal."

The nerve of some people, I thought before lashing out at the woman. "Who do you think you are?" I screamed. "This man has nothing to do with whatever it is you think I did to your husband, and purposely trying to ruin someone's life is utterly despicable. How dare you be so thoughtless," I shouted.

"I love the passion," Allison said sarcastically. "That heartfelt speech lets me know that he's someone you deeply care about. However, come hell or high water I'm going to make sure you pay for the grievance you've perpetrated upon my family," Allison squinted her eyes into slits and growled.

Tom, finally able to stand on his own accord, stood with the bottle of water in his hand, turned around, then wagged his finger at Allison before shouting out. "Listen here, you carrot-top reject! I still have pull at the Sheriff's Department and I'm going to be on you like white on rice unless the next thing out of your mouth is an apology."

Tom was barely standing on his own, but he certainly still had a knack for intimidation.

"Well, sorry," Allison spat out.

"No worries," I responded. "I'm sure you're going through a tough time right now but I can assure you no one at that school was responsible for your husband's departure."

"Well, I'm going to find out who was!" Allison shouted as she stormed out of the bar.

"Oh my—thanks for saving me," I said, looking directly at Tom.

"It's what I do best," he said with a smile.

We left the bar and got into Tom's van. Then I told him I could drive him home and just walk the short distance back to my house since we didn't live that far from one another. However, he said unless Crystal was home that wouldn't work because not only had he lost his sobriety today but he'd also lost his cellphone and house keys.

Instead of telling Tom what he'd done wrong like he was one of my students, I asked him what brought all of this on.

"It's a long story, and the details are a bit fuzzy to me at the moment," Tom said, while holding his head. "However, I promise I'll tell you everything later. But for now, would it be okay if I just crashed in your guest bedroom?" Tom asked.

"Of course," I replied. "However, after I drop you off I'll be heading back out to the Lucas' for dinner. So, I should warn you that I have a good friend currently sleeping in my bedroom, please don't be alarmed if you two cross paths. Her name is Dee, and she's actually Ronda's mother," I whispered.

Tom looked genuinely shocked as he blurted out. "Well, I didn't know you were friends with the victim's parents. I just thought you met her once and she wanted to buy some girly rubber bands from you."

"Okay, first off, they're called scrunchies!" I sniped. "Furthermore, while you're correct in believing Ronda and I only met once, there are parts to the story that I purposely omitted to avoid anyone else becoming involved in this tragedy. I'll fill you in later also, but right now you need to rest."

As we pulled into my driveway, Tom started sobbing while muttering, "If Crystal's responsible for this, I'm not sure I could ever forgive her."

Well, it seemed like the aftermath of Ronda's death was trickling down and wreaking havoc on more lives than anyone could've imagined. A real domino effect was happening right before my eyes.

"Let's go inside, Tom," I said. "I'll help you into bed." As we opened the front door, Daphne came running towards Tom and tried jumping into his arms before falling back down onto the floor. He knelt and wrestled with her for a while until kneeling became too much effort for someone who had God knows how many drinks. So, I helped him up and walked him into the guest bedroom.

Tom fell onto the bed face first, and in a hushed tone told me I was the best friend he'd ever had. In a slurred voice, he went on to say how sorry he was for telling me about his romantic feelings earlier and that he didn't want that lapse in judgement to ruin our friendship. As I walked over towards the bed from the doorway to reassure Tom nothing could ever ruin our friendship, I heard snoring and saw that he'd fallen asleep in the middle of our conversation. So, I grabbed the blanket and covered him up before closing the bedroom door.

Before leaving to head back over to the Lucas' for dinner, I tried calling Crystal to let her know Tom was with me, so she wouldn't have to worry about his whereabouts. But she didn't answer. I also tried calling the police station to try and get ahold of the Sheriff. However, in such a small town I guess the entire department was still dealing with the aftermath of the bomb hoax, and there was no one available to answer my phone call. So, I decided to peek into my bedroom to check in on Dee. But she was still asleep and I was starting to get worried. I wasn't sure if this behavior was normal grief or something else altogether.

Although I was confused by Dee's abnormal grieving process, I didn't want to read too much into it. So, I closed the bedroom door, yelled goodbye to Daphne, and headed out the front door. I started the short trip back to

Rodney and Kathleen's, and the whole ride there all I could think about was Reggie Cooper and his wife Allison. *Could those two be involved in a murder?* I thought to myself.

Well, at the very least, they could be the ones responsible for surveilling my home and breaking my window. After all, Allison wasn't exactly subtle when she said she's going to make me pay for the hardship her family was going through. Granted, I didn't exactly see a stone-cold killer when I looked at her, but there was definitely something dark behind those eyes.

I pulled back up at the Lucas' and this time I saw Rodney sitting outside by himself on the front porch. I got partway up the stairs and noticed he was halfway through a six pack of beer. "Rodney, we need to talk now!" I said firmly as I reached the top stair. "So, I'm going to need you to be very sober, and very honest. Can you do that for me?" I asked.

"Of course, anything for my best guy's girl," Rodney shouted out. "What do you need to know?"

"I need to know about a kid named Sean Griffin," I replied. "He said his mother was murdered over a year ago and he came to St. Lux to talk with you at that time because he suspected he knew who the killer was," I said with urgency.

"None of this is ringing a bell," Rodney responded apathetically.

"Well, how about this...?" I said. "The person who Sean suspected was Jack, and he claims you tossed him out of your office once he made you aware of this. Rodney, I need to know what he's talking about, and what's more, I need to know if my husband is actually resting in peace!" I shouted.

"Samantha, it's not how it seems. As Sheriff, I had to think quick on my feet to help a friend," Rodney claimed.

"So, then you are familiar with this kid, Sean? "I blurted out. "Well, does this mean it's true, Rodney? W-was Jack somehow involved in his mother's murder?" I asked, barely able to speak.

"Absolutely not!" Rodney said adamantly. "However, with that being said, I can tell you I remember this Sean kid vaguely," Rodney whispered as he motioned for me to sit next to him on the hard concrete porch.

"Well, what happened to Sean's mother?" I asked. "Why would this boy be so unyielding about Jack being his mother's murderer?"

"I can't really tell you much, Samantha," Rodney said, while hanging his head. "Unfortunately, I never really looked into it because for one, I didn't believe for a second that Jack was involved, and two, the murder happened in the neighboring county, so I turned it over to their local police," Rodney said this as casually as if he was talking about the weather.

"How convenient, and I'll presume you had them completely ignore the fact that Sean accused Jack of murder?" I snapped.

Then only a few seconds later, it hit me. "Oh, dear God!" I cried out. "This is why he vandalized your house. What did you do to this kid?" I asked. "What are you hiding?"

"I did what I had to do as Sheriff to protect my friend!" Rodney shouted out. "I wasn't going to let some pimple-faced boy ruin Jack's life with some unsubstantiated accusation."

"Did Jack know about this?" I asked, beginning to feel sick.

"Jack had nothing to do with any of this," Rodney asserted. "I was Sheriff at the time and I handled everything in-house."

"I have to go!" I said to Rodney as I stood up from the hard concrete.

"But aren't you going to stay for dinner?" Rodney asked. "Kathleen cooked up a feast!" he shouted.

"I'm sorry, but I don't have much of an appetite now," I retorted. "You can think of something cool and tell Kathleen I said it. I'm more than certain that you're still capable of thinking quick on your feet when someone comes asking for the truth, Sheriff," I said sharply as I ran to Tom's van.

Everything is unraveling all at once, I thought to myself, as I drove to Jack's favorite park about five minutes from downtown St. Lux. Once I got there, I got out of the van and walked towards a huge boulder that sat in the middle of the park. This was where Jack brought me when he initially purposed and I'd said no because we were only fifteen years old. Subsequently, this park became a running gag for us. Anytime he'd ask me a question, no matter the subject, if we were in close proximity to this park I'd tease him, and my answer to his question would always be "No."

However, this time around I needed Jack to be the one saying *No*, to the one question that I so desperately needed to ask him. I sat down on the boulder and asked Jack the most difficult question in his death that I wouldn't have had the strength to ask him in life.

"Hi, Jack," I said as I looked up at the sky. "You know I love you and I'm sure you're well aware of what's going on down here. However, I just need to know if you were you involved in any way," I whispered. But as soon as the words left my mouth a heavy downpour started.

It was almost as if Jack was crying, and as strange as it may sound, that was all the answer I needed. I knew my husband wasn't guilty of this crime, but I guess with Ronda's murder and everything I'd been through these past few days, the situation just started to get a bit unhinged, and everyone looked capable of anything. I sat there for a while in the rain having a one-sided conversation with Jack, although the calm before the storm or some other supernatural entity made the conversation seem like it was anything but. However, as the rain began to cease, I stood up next to the boulder feeling as if it was the day when Jack first dragged me to this park. Fortunately, nothing had changed from that day to this one because in a pinch Jack was still showing me that he'd always be there.

I blew Jack a kiss and hurried to Tom's van, so I could get home and change out of my wet clothes. As I pulled into my driveway, I saw my next-door neighbor, Mr. Black, peeking through his blinds.

Oh, dear God, I thought to myself. I hadn't been over to check on Mr. Black in days. Mr. Black was an extremely frail, old man. He was around my height covered in liver spots and somewhat of a recluse. If you didn't catch him looking through his blinds, then you were likely to miss him. I cut across his lawn and ran to his front porch.

"Mr. Black, Mr. Black!" I yelled out. "Are you okay? Have you eaten today?" I asked. Even if you were lucky enough to share companionship with Mr. Black on a daily basis, it was a coin toss whether or not he'd remember you the next time he saw you. I'd had several talks with his daughter, Sandra Black, about putting him in a retirement home, but she always came across as if she could care less.

"Mr. Black!" I called out again before I grabbed the spare key he kept behind his flowerpot. Strangely, only a few months earlier he requested that I use this very same key if he was having a dementia episode. He said he started having trouble remembering things but affirmed he lived by one philosophy given his advanced age. "If I don't know you, then I'm not opening my door for you."

A truism for sure, I thought to myself. However, given the past few days I'd had, those were words to live by.

"Mr. Black, are you okay?" I asked again once I gained entry into his home.

"You're the one who was outside playing with flowerpots in the rain," Mr. Black retorted. "The better question is, Are *you* okay?" he asked with a smirk.

"You were pulling my chain this whole time, weren't you?" I asked as I laughed, despite myself.

"Well, honestly, there's nothing good on TV at this hour," Mr. Black said. "So, of course I wanted a front-row seat for whatever one woman show you were putting on. And what's more, if I'm being frank, the door was unlocked ages ago."

"You sure know how to give a girl a hard time," I said with a smile.

"Well, most of my senses aren't working," Mr. Black replied. "So, I like a prank that'll just linger in the air for a while. I'm a hoot and a half when I can remember who you are," he laughed. "However, now that I've had my fun, I don't want you to catch your death in those wet clothes, Samantha. Let me get you a towel," Mr. Black said as he walked towards his linen closet.

Given the circumstances, I was pleasantly surprised by Mr. Black. For someone who often forgot his cat died thirty years ago, he sure seemed to have a grasp on all his faculties today. As he walked back into the living room with the towel, I apologized for being so scarce lately.

"Well, there's no need to apologize, Samantha," Mr. Black said. "I don't expect a young, vibrant woman to babysit an old man for the rest of his days. You have to go out and live," he said with affection.

"Unfortunately, that's my problem!" I said as I sighed. "Anytime I try and live by stepping out of my comfort zone, I'm either doing something wrong or nothing at all. There just seems to be no balance in my life. I go out of my way to give and give and give, and no matter the circumstance there's always someone there to take and take and take, and it just makes me feel like a door-mat at times," I said, suddenly feeling despondent. "Why can't I be more like you Mr. Black, and stop setting myself on fire just so other people can shine?"

"Well, being an old man," Mr. Black said, "you'd think I'd have some deep philosophical answer for that, but here's the advice I'd give my own daughter. While there's absolutely nothing wrong with loving to love, on those days when you're trekking down treacherous roads just glance over to make sure that same love is standing beside you, and not running ten miles ahead of you."

"Well, gee, golly, Mr. Black!" I responded with emphasis. "You know, I do cherish our time together."

"As do I," Mr. Black said with a grin on his face.

"Before I go home to change out of these wet clothes, have you been listening to your police scanner lately?" I asked.

"As a matter of fact, I had it on earlier today," Mr. Black replied. "They were going on and on about the bomb threat that turned out to be nothing more than a hoax," he added.

"Well, have you heard anything about the girl who was murdered last night?" I asked.

"No, I can't say that I have," Mr. Black responded. "It seems everyone from that precinct has been running around like chickens with their heads cut off today from the bit of chatter I heard. Unfortunately, as it pertains to that young girl, I don't know any more than what I saw on the news last night," Mr. Black said.

"Oh, well, okay!" I unconsciously blurted out before taking a deep breath. "Well, one last thing before I go, Mr. Black..."

"Of course, anything, Samantha," he replied.

"Have you seen anyone hanging around my house lately?" I asked. "Someone broke my front window out last night, and worse than that they've been inside my home rummaging through my medicine cabinet," I said as a bit of fear crept into my voice.

"Well, I did see a young man earlier today—" Mr. Black responded.

"I'll bet it was Sean," I blurted out before Mr. Black could finish his statement.

"Well, I obviously don't know his name," Mr. Black said. "However, if Sean is the young man who you chased out of the field earlier today, then it's not him who I'm referring to."

What? I thought to myself. "Well, who else could it have been?" I asked.

"This fella was much taller than the kid you chased away," Mr. Black said. "He also had long curly brown hair."

Oh, dear! I thought. *Was he describing Charlie?* I hurried and pulled out my phone to scroll through my pictures, hoping to come across one of Charlie.

I had taken a few photos this past summer when our church held a barbeque for the congregation, and I was well aware of Charlie's hidden talent for photo bombing, so I was sure I had one of him somewhere.

"Is this him?" I asked Mr. Black as I held up Charlie's picture. "Is this the boy you saw?"

"That's him, alright," Mr. Black said confidently.

"Are you absolutely positive, Mr. Black?"

"Unfortunately, the only thing I've ever been more positive about is that I'll need to wear a diaper if I drink too much before bed," Mr. Black casually replied. Then he asked, "What does he want with you?"

"I wish I knew," I said in a hushed tone. Now, more confused than ever, I knew I needed to figure this whole thing out, for everyone's sake. Before leaving out to go home, I told Mr. Black not to worry about cooking in the morning because I'd bring his usual breakfast tomorrow.

"What would I ever do without you, Samantha?" Mr. Black asked.

"Well, luckily, you'll never know," I said as I gave him a kiss on the forehead, then made my way home.

I walked through my front door and could tell everyone inside, including Daphne, was sound asleep. I went into my bedroom as quietly as a mouse, so not to wake Dee, and grabbed a change of clothes from my dresser. Once I was done changing, I noticed my phone vibrating on the bathroom sink where I'd left it. After I picked it up, I saw that it was Crystal calling me back.

"Hey, Crystal," I whispered so not to wake anyone. "Are you feeling any better?"

"No!" Crystal shouted. "I d-don't know if it's my subconscious or what but I feel responsible. I feel like everyone's w-watching me, like they're judging me," Crystal whined. "Can I come over and explain w-what happened?" she asked.

"Yeah, of course," I responded. "I have a friend over and your uncle's here also but they're both asleep if you need privacy."

"No!" Crystal aggressively chimed in and cut me off before I could finish my statement. "I don't w-want him to know. Can you meet me at Stepping Stone Park in f-fifteen minutes instead?"

All I could think in that moment was that prayers really do come true, and Jack was definitely the guardian angel who was watching over me. Stepping Stone Park was the park I'd just left. It was Jack's favorite place in all of St. Lux and I knew it was no coincidence that Crystal was now asking me to meet her there, especially since I'd just asked the heavens above if I'd ever be able to remedy a problem when I didn't have a propitious solution.

"Of course, Crystal," I said. "I'll be there in fifteen minutes."

"Okay, see you soon," Crystal replied, then we disconnected. I pulled into the parking lot of Stepping Stone Park a bit sooner than fifteen minutes, so I sat in Tom's van and waited for Crystal. Fortunately, the sun was back out and it was now painting a beautiful rainbow in the sky. I must've sat there daydreaming for five minutes because the next thing I knew Crystal was honking her horn at me.

I got out of the van, and Crystal and I walked over to the benches that sat just off to the side of the barbeque grills. "Well, what's troubling you, Sweetie?" I asked as we sat down.

"I-I just don't know where to start," an obviously distressed Crystal said as her eyes began to fill with tears. "I've just done so m-much wrong recently. I've told this lie to c-cover up that lie and that lie to cover up this lie, and sadly I no longer recognize m-myself," Crystal cried out.

Seeing her so broken and beaten down, I knew I had to think fast to take some of the load off of her shoulders. So, I did what any self-respecting woman who was pushing forty would do. With no music, I got up from that bench and I single-handedly "Single Ladied" all throughout Stepping Stone Park.

With Crystal now laughing—albeit at my expense—I finished up the last twirl in my routine and sat back down next to her. Then I said, "You can tell me anything your heart desires." Then I started to laugh before blurting out, "It's obvious after my little dance number that this is a judgement-free zone."

Well, it must've worked because for the next half hour Crystal told me everything she'd been holding inside. While most of it was bad, nothing pointed toward her being a murderer. She explained how she had been having romantic feelings for girls for the past year, and how she didn't want her stern, unyielding uncle to know. She then said after winning an online contest and hanging out with Ronda once, she really took a liking to the Instagram star. Subsequently, after becoming one of Ronda's followers online, her infatuation grew. However, with Ronda being an online sensation, her time was limited, and the spark in their friendship slowly dwindled out.

Crystal went on to say that she was the one who put the very compromising photos of Ronda online. I was in a state of shock, but I also had my listening ears on. I didn't flinch an inch as she told me her version of events because I didn't want to scare her away.

Crystal then said she never wanted to ruin Ronda's life by putting those images online. Instead, she thought she could swoop in and save her from the unmerciful bullying that would surely arise because of them. However, once that didn't work, Crystal said she was aware Ronda was coming to town and decided to steal her luggage in an attempt to make one last plea for her affection.

"How did you get your hands on Ronda's luggage?" I asked.

"It w-was surprisingly easy," Crystal said. "I knew Ronda's schedule like the b-back of my hand all the way down to the f-flight she'd be on coming here to St. Lux. So, I flew to Tennessee and c-caught her same flight back. I knew she'd be so oblivious to w-what was going on around her that I would go unnoticed," Crystal said with a devilish smirk.

Ronda's death was a tragedy for sure, I thought to myself. However, Crystal's obsession is downright fascinating. *Who would go to such lengths for a date and what psychosis was Crystal now exhibiting?* I wondered. Furthermore, could it be a family trait? Was this the vibe everyone was picking up from Tom? This was like a car wreck and I couldn't look away. Unfortunately, the more Crystal's story played out, the more she seemed like a villain in one of my books, rather than the sweet innocent girl I knew from the coffee shop. "Well, inquiring minds want to know," I said anxiously. "How'd you get Ronda's luggage?" I repeated.

"Well, I knew s-she had the attention span of a hamster because there was once a time when she put every aspect of her life online," Crystal said. "I also knew if she didn't have an audience, then it was just a m-matter of time on a one-and-a-half-hour flight to Michigan that she'd be falling asleep from boredom," she said.

Crystal then revealed that after she noticed Ronda catching up on some sleep, she walked into first class undetected and grabbed her carry-on.

"The same c-carry-on—by the way—that should've been c-checked at the gate," Crystal shouted out. "However, little Miss Gets-her-way yelled at the flight attendant that she was a huge star, and said she wasn't checking her bag because she didn't want anyone handling her things. I was furious," Crystal said, as she started to turn beet red just from recounting her story. "The sad truth is I adore Ronda. However, part of me was t-tired of the wealthy flaunting their status and making all of their problems disappear. I wanted to t-teach her a lesson," Crystal shouted out.

"What kind of lesson? Did you hurt Ronda in any way?" I asked.

"No!" A now confused-looking Crystal blurted out.

Sitting there, I realized all I had to do was take one glance into Crystal's eyes to know that this wasn't the same girl from the coffee shop. Truth be told, this wasn't the same girl I was talking to five minutes ago. The dramatic shift in attitude was like chalk and cheese.

"Well, do you know who could've killed her?" I asked.

"No, I'm sorry." Crystal said as tears began to cover her flushing cheeks. "Are you truly certain t-that it's her?" she asked. "I'm confused as to why you w-would say Ronda's dead," she cried out.

Well, I wasn't sure what was going on with Crystal mentally but I knew she wasn't all together there, and I honestly suspected it had nothing to do with Ronda's death. Crystal was starting to exhibit erratic behavior and depending on what time of the day you talked to her, it seemed like she wasn't Crystal at all. Now she was claiming she didn't recall the conversation we'd had only a few hours earlier about Ronda's death.

Either she was the world's best actress, I thought to myself, *or she had some form of selective amnesia going on that was off the charts.*

"Ronda's been murdered, Crystal, and unfortunately a lot of the evidence points to you as the prime suspect," I boldly stated. "However," I added, "I think someone's trying to frame you, so can you think of anyone who would want to do such a thing?"

Unable to physically speak due to the shocking news of Ronda's death, Crystal shook her head no. It was as if I hadn't told her any of this before; she was behaving as if this was breaking news.

All of a sudden Crystal looked at me with glassy eyes and shouted angrily, "Why w-would I be a suspect when my uncle's the one with the motive and the gun?"

"Shocked by the accusation, but also curious. I asked Crystal if she thought her uncle could've done this?"

"Absolutely not, I misspoke!" Crystal said fiercely once she realized she'd just incriminated her favorite uncle. "I g-guess I lost my head," Crystal whispered. "I think I'm just going to go h-home and lie down for a while; it's been a long day." She stumbled as she walked frantically towards her car.

"Wait!" I yelled as I followed closely behind her. "I have a million more questions. Why were you and Ronda arguing in front of the coffee shop, and why would you make such an accusation about Tom? What is his motive and are you protecting him?" I asked.

"I h-have to go," Crystal shouted out. "However, that was just a slip of the t-tongue and there's really no need to read anything into it," Crystal added.

"Why would I read anything into it?" I asked.

"You just seem like the glass-half-empty t-type," Crystal retorted. "Like now, despite me never having a-asked for your help, you look at me and you see a lost girl in need of a savior," she said passionately.

"You may have had your fair share of troubles lately," I said as I stood with my back at Crystal's car door, momentarily blocking her from leaving. "But appearances can be deceptive, and I do believe there's more to you than meets the eye. I'm no savior, but I can be a friend," I said with just as much passion.

"Crystal, you were clearly in love with Ronda," I said intensely. "Don't you want to see her killer brought to justice? Whoever that may be," I whispered, holding back tears.

"I also love m-my uncle," Crystal blurted out. "Bringing to the forefront anything he may or may not have done won't c-change that. Besides, why would you believe a hoodwinker whose duped every soul in town?" Crystal said sarcastically using my words against me while referencing our earlier conversation.

There she goes again, I thought to myself. She sounded like a completely different person and while staring into her eyes again, I realized there was nothing there. Then I noticed a physical change in her demeanor as she brushed me aside and got into her Mini Cooper. It seemed as though she had transformed back into the cold, calculating girl whom I never really noticed before, and quite frankly I was starting not to care for this version of her.

"Don't be a stranger, Crystal," I shouted as she started her car. "I know you're going through a tough time, but if you ever need anything give me a call and I'll be there in a heartbeat," I said in a caring voice.

"Get r-real, grandma!" Crystal shouted crassly. "I'm living my b-best life, so now I've just got to go f-find Ronda. Catch you later," Crystal shouted out as she drove off.

Suddenly, I wasn't sure if I should ignore her or have her committed. On multiple occasions, we'd discussed Ronda's death but somehow it still wasn't registering with Crystal. *She's in some state of deep denial for sure,* I thought to myself.

At this point, I didn't know what to believe. Half the town told me to be careful around Tom, and now his own niece slipped up and inadvertently accused him of murder, although she was about as reliable as a convertible on a rainy day.

Still, I wondered, was some truth coming to the forefront with Crystal's slip of the tongue? *Was Tom's nice guy act just a ruse?* I thought to myself. *Did I somehow lose my astute ability to unbiasedly use discernment when it came to him? Or was he just guilty by association for being so close with Crystal?*

Unfortunately, whoever was responsible for Ronda's death was definitely pulling all the strings. A criminal mastermind, if you will. They had the whole town going left when they went right, and the manipulation level seemed to be off the charts. I didn't see that as either Tom or Crystal. Fortunately, I've never been good at playing the puppet role, and while everyone else remained affixed to a string, doing as they were told, I was about to break loose from the puppet master and carve out my own path.

CHAPTER TEN

I got back into Tom's van and realized it was a quarter after 8:00 p.m. I hadn't noticed until now but the sun must've gone down shortly after I arrived at the park. Now I was all alone at this dark playground with a killer on the loose, and the sound those rusty old swings were emitting with every blustery gust of wind was enough to scare the dickens out of me.

I started the van to remove myself from this creepy situation. Then, while looking in my rearview mirror after I backed out of my parking spot, I noticed around six police cars speeding towards Main Street. Aside from the fact that I never knew St. Lux had that many patrol vehicles, I didn't think too much of it at the time. I just figured Sheriff Hawkins's day was just as busy as mine, especially since I wasn't able to reach him nor had anyone from the police station called yet to finish my statement after the bomb hoax pulled them away earlier. I put the van in drive and decided to head home and let Tom know that Crystal was okay, well, okay physically anyway.

I pulled into my driveway a few minutes later and saw Daphne perched on the back of Jack's humongous polka dot chair. After getting inside, I closed all the curtains that Tom had opened when he was replacing my window. Then I went into the laundry room right off the kitchen and poured Daphne a bowl of granola.

I checked both bedrooms and noticed that Tom and Dee were still asleep. I was really starting to worry about Dee at this point. If for no other reason, I thought she should at least get up and put something on her stomach. However, there definitely was no handbook for helping a friend who was in this kind of pain, and the first thing to go is the appetite.

Next, I walked into the kitchen and fixed myself a turkey sandwich for dinner with a side of pita chips and a tall glass of iced tea to wash it down. After I sat down at the wobbly kitchen table and finished about half of my sandwich, I started to hear the outside patio stairs creak just behind me. Well, it was a cool gusty night but I'd yet to encounter a strong enough wind that could make old stairs creak.

Completely fed up with people lurking outside of my home, I threw caution to the wind and pulled open my sliding glass doors. "Maureen!" I shouted out as my jaw nearly hit the floor from disbelief. "What are you doing out here?" I asked. "Get inside you must be freezing out there."

The temperature had dropped several degrees since the sun went down and the night air was starting to feel much more like November again. I noticed as she came inside that she looked completely disheveled. She even still had on her running attire that she wore last night when she stopped over. "Maureen, are you okay?" I asked. "Where have you been? I've been trying to reach you all day," I yelled in a worried tone. However, instead of responding, Maureen just stared vacantly at her reflection in the sliding glass doors. "Were you at work when the bomb threat happened?" I asked. "Are you hurt in any way?" I whispered. Unfortunately, Maureen still didn't answer, but at least this time I heard a faint groan as she put her hand on her forehead.

Having dealt with more than a few friends in the past that didn't know their drinking limit, I said to Maureen disapprovingly, "I hope you haven't been drinking again. I don't need two of my dearest friends falling off the wagon on the same day." "Drinking," I whispered underneath my breath. It was the only reasonable explanation for her behavior. She was so incoherent that she couldn't even form a complete sentence. Suddenly, as I walked Maureen to the other spare bedroom and helped her into bed, I started to feel like the world's unluckiest babysitter. Not only did I have a grieving mother to look after but now I also had two intoxicated friends to keep an eye on.

After making sure Maureen was safe in bed, I walked back into the kitchen to finish my sandwich. I wasn't quite sure what made Maureen give up her sobriety today, but I knew I was going to be there to help her through her recovery. However, I also knew the amount of emotion running through me was taking its toll with each passing hour. After I finished eating, I walked into the living room and noticed through a small gap in the curtains that the same broken street light from yesterday was starting to flicker again today. I pulled the curtain back and saw Mr. Black standing in the empty field across the street.

Whatever is he doing? I thought to myself. The weirdness that St. Lux has brought to the forefront lately, well, if it wasn't my actual life, I'd write about it.

"Mr. Black, Mr. Black!" I yelled out as I ran across the street to get him out of the cold and back inside. "What are you doing out here?" I asked. "Has everyone gone mad? Why are you out here in the cold and with a killer on the loose no less?" I shouted.

"I saw him!" Mr. Black screamed. "I saw that boy from your photo earlier."

"You saw Charlie?" I asked hesitantly. "Is he somewhere here now?" I whispered.

"No, I saw that little prick run off," Mr. Black said angrily, while holding his recently replaced hip. "I watched him as he came out of this field and ran across the street to your front porch. He peeked through your windows. That's when I came outside and scared him off," Mr. Black said.

"Oh, dear," I muttered. "I don't know how to thank you, Mr. Black," I said with gratitude.

"Well, both you and Jack have done plenty for me," Mr. Black replied. "So, it's my honor to be able to return the favor."

"You should be safe for now, but if you hear anything out of the ordinary you be sure to call the cops," Mr. Black said passionately.

"The cops!" I repeated with a smile as I grabbed his arm to help hold him up. "I thought you were going to say that you'd be my knight in shining armor, and I could call you," I joked.

"Well, you can," Mr. Black replied. "Just know that I'm an old man and as much as I love you, Samantha, unfortunately running over to this field has exhausted all of the energy the good Lord was going to bless me with tomorrow."

I caught myself laughing out loud at Mr. Black. He was definitely a mood setter, and nothing if not charismatic. "Well, before Charlie makes you run an entire marathon, let me get you back inside." I muttered. As I walked Mr. Black to his front door, I thanked him for always being there for me in my time of need. After I heard him lock up, I walked back home and did the same.

I thought of going downstairs and finishing Susie's scrunchie order. However, my mind was racing at a rate where it would've been impossible to concentrate on all those little intricate details. So, being fully aware of this crippling tunnel vision I suffered from, I knew my type A personality was starting to emerge and I was going to be like a dog with a bone until I figured out what happened to Ronda.

Unfortunately, I knew it would also be just as difficult for me to focus while in class tomorrow with my students, so I called my boss, Principal Williams, and let her know I needed to use a few vacation days starting tomorrow. She said it was about time I decided to use a personal day for myself and assured me that she'd be okay if I decided to take the entire week. Seeing as how I had more than seventy unused vacation days, Principal Williams said I might as well make a week of it. I told her that wouldn't be necessary, but if I needed more than a few days I'd let her know.

I didn't tell her I was actively trying to solve a murder case because it seemed like everyone I told either became involved in some way, or a suspect of some kind. I felt like the killer was two steps ahead of me at every turn, and I refused to get anyone else entangled in this unfortunate web of lies. After chatting for a few more minutes with Principal Williams, we disconnected. I sat down in Jack's recliner in the living room, then clicked on the TV and noticed I had two Channel 18 News recordings that were unwatched on the DVR. *How very strange*, I thought to myself. I loved watching the news, but I never had it set to be recorded.

Then I thought back to this morning. While trying to secure the copy of Ronda's photo that Channel 18 News was broadcasting to the entire world, I must've somehow inadvertently hit the record button after turning on the television set before leaving. Nevertheless, I turned the volume up, then hit the play button. On the recording, I saw David Holtz interviewing Sheriff Hawkins in real time about the bomb threat. Afterwards, David interviewed wannabe cop Charlie West about the same thing. However, Charlie wasn't quite as impassive as the Sheriff was, and it was obvious that he most certainly wasn't his carefree, blow-with-the-wind self, and he soon explained why.

Charlie claimed he had just left work and stopped by the bank to withdraw some money, so he could take his little brother Chris out to celebrate his birthday tomorrow. He then stated about five minutes after arriving at SafeLoan Bank, and while waiting in line, a swarm of cops pulled up and accused him of planting a bomb on the bank's premises. From there, Charlie said everything went haywire. As I sat there trying to get a good read off of him, I can't say that I was swayed in one direction or the other in that moment. However, as Charlie continued to tell his story to David, I had to rewind the DVR to make sure I heard him right.

A now sniffling Charlie said he "was thrown into the back of a police car and treated like a common criminal." He then mentioned that he'd never been so scared in all of his life, and he couldn't understand why he was being treated so poorly by his co-workers and friends. David wrapped up the interview by giving Charlie his condolences and informing him that the bomb threat was just a hoax.

Charlie, visibly stunned by the revelation, instantly changed his tune, and then took full responsibility for the bomb scare. Being almost forty years old, I knew bad acting when I saw it and Charlie stepping up and taking responsibility for the bomb hoax was bad acting at its finest. Still, it made me wonder what horrific act Charlie could've been privy to that would make him take the blame for something like this.

After vowing to never watch Channel 18 News again because their stories only seem to disrupt my life lately, I clicked off the television set. I felt like so many lives seemed to be intertwined because of the original news segment that I'd watched about Sean yesterday, but I couldn't seem to figure out why.

Needless to say, I felt like I was letting everyone down. With so many lives at stake, and time not on my side, I knew I had to get to the bottom of this tragedy, and soon. So, unfortunately, I decided maybe Susie was right; I mean I wouldn't call myself Barney Fife the way she so rudely described me. *However*, I thought, *maybe I could think outside the box and try to look at things from a criminal's perspective for a change. Maybe that way I could bring the suspect out of hiding.* I knew I'd never hear the end of it if I used a plan inspired by Susie, but if it meant getting a killer off the streets then so be it.

As I sat there thinking of an elaborate scheme to set into motion, my phone began to ring, and I noticed it was Rodney Lucas calling. Well, I was still pretty upset with him, but the unanswered questions from Jack's past that only Rodney knew the answers to wouldn't allow me to sever ties.

"Hello, Rodney!" I said as eloquently as I could through gritted teeth. "What can I help you with?"

"Well, I just delved a little deeper into that case after you scolded me, and from what I gather Sean mother's name was Nina Griffin," Rodney said. "Sam, I wish I'd warned you about all of this in the past, but I just wanted to protect you after Jack died because I knew he wouldn't have wanted you to be involved in any of this," Rodney said wholeheartedly.

"Jack was my husband and I loved him dearly," I said assertively. "However, the one thing I never needed him to do was to decide what was best for me. It wasn't Jack's call, and it's certainly not yours," I said emphatically. I wasn't sure what came over me in that moment. It felt as if I was standing up for all the women in the world who went unnoticed because of overbearing men like Rodney and Talia Wren's father, Michael Wren. Whatever it was, it felt good standing up for myself and not just sitting quietly agreeing with something that I knew was unequivocally wrong in my heart.

After talking for a few more minutes, Rodney apologized for his role in everything and assured me Jack had no knowledge of any of this. The former Sheriff then said he'd learned OF new information about the case and asked me to stop by tomorrow so I would be in the know. He continued by saying that he'd taken care of Sean and he wasn't going to let him skip town this time without answering a few questions.

Being Rodney's friend since high school, I knew him taking care of a situation couldn't mean anything good for Sean. "Rodney, what have you done?" I asked warily. "Where is Sean?" I shouted.

"Don't you worry, Samantha," Rodney responded. "I've got everything under control."

"Rodney, you've possibly kidnapped a teenaged boy and have him stashed away somewhere like your John Wayne Gacy!" I screamed. "This is far from under control. You can't torture information out of this poor kid. He's been through enough," I said angrily. He watched his own mother die for goodness' sake." Then it hit me. "Oh, dear God," I muttered. "Sean was right. You're trying to cover up his mother's murder. But why?" I whispered.

Before Rodney could get a word out, I yelled that I had to go and hung up the phone. I couldn't believe all of the skeletons that were seemingly falling out of various friends' closets. Could I be overly tired from the long strenuous day that I'd had, or were everyone's secrets finally starting to come to the surface? I never dreamt that things could get much worse, but, boy, did I ever test fate by thinking that.

Feeling numb, I sat in my living room in Jack's chair for a few more minutes until I was able to fully comprehend that Ronda's murderer could possibly be one of my dearest friends. I didn't know what would come next, but for an instant I wished I'd never heard that voicemail. *Then I would be none the wiser to any of this,* I thought to myself. I got over feeling sorry for myself rather fast once I looked down the hall towards my bedroom door, and realized that Dee, one of the true victims, was on the other side of it.

I walked into the kitchen and noticed Daphne scratching at the sliding glass doors, which typically meant she needed the bathroom. So, I grabbed my jacket and we walked outback. As I stood on the patio checking emails on my phone, I spotted Daphne doing her confusing, "I can't go there" bathroom bit.

After she finally went, I called her back towards the patio and I noticed a blinking red light that was flashing underneath my deck. I walked down the stairs and reached my hand between the wooden slats to pull up what I thought would be one of Daphne's forgotten toys. However, what emerged was a tape recorder. *Who could be so maladjusted?* I thought to myself. *First, they physically spy on me and now this.*

Then I thought back to when I decided to fall instead of trampling on Daphne only a few hours ago. It happened in the exact spot I was currently standing in, and if this tape recorder was here, then I would've noticed it. This meant someone had just planted this here recently, but if they thought they were getting away with it this time they'd better think again.

I had a friend named Michelle Lewis who was a fingerprint analyst, and she'd owed me a huge favor for tutoring her two sons a few months back free of charge. I called Michelle up in a panic and explained the whole Peeping Tom situation, and how I had just found a tape recorder underneath my deck that I needed her dactyloscopy expertise in. Well, it didn't take much convincing as Michelle said she was going stir crazy being off work. And just sitting around the house for the past two weeks due to a concussion she suffered from a nasty fall wasn't helping matters. She said she was so bored she actually thought about playing video games with her youngest boy, Max. Needless to say, she obviously relished in the possibility of doing anything other than killing zombies with her eleven-year-old.

She told me I could bring the tape recorder over right away, and she'd start to assess the prints to determine whether or not they could be compared to any others that may be on file. I told Michelle she was a lifesaver and let her know that I'd be there shortly, then we disconnected.

Michelle lived in the next town over, but it was just a fifteen-minute drive from my place. After I put my cellphone back in my pocket, I ran inside and got some medical gloves out of my first aid kit. I grabbed a plastic bag from the kitchen on my way back outside and placed the tape recorder in it. In that moment, I couldn't believe what I was doing. If I found out who was harassing me at my home, then there was a good chance that I'd also find out who was responsible for Ronda's murder, and more than likely I'd lose a friend. I instantly put all of that doubt in the back of my mind and made my way over to Michelle's extravagant mansion in the hills.

Once I arrived, I noticed her dog Herman, a one hundred and thirty-pound rottweiler, roaming inside the gated yard. I knew Michelle only let her dog out when she was gone. Unfortunately, I didn't have any treats to give Herman, but for my sake, I sure hoped she remembered me from my last visit.

I grabbed the bag with the tape recorder and walked over to the fence, then I rang the bell repeatedly. However, Michelle never answered. I knew her gate code, so I decided to let myself into the gated area to make sure everything was okay. After all, I had just spoken with her and she knew I was coming over, so I found it a bit weird that no one was answering the bell. I went inside the gate but, never having walked to Michelle's front door from the road before, I never realize how far back her house sat. It was at least three hundred feet from the gate until you reached her front door. I called Michelle's cellphone the entire time I was walking, while praying that Herman remembered my scent. She was a friendly dog, but, boy, was she intimidating. I stopped to pet her on her head, then she ran to the front door as if she wanted me to follow behind her.

I took off running behind Herman while simultaneously calling Michelle's cellphone for the fifth time. As I approached the door, I heard Michelle's cellphone ringing, and instantly thought maybe she'd experienced some sort of dizziness due to the concussion and subsequently fainted. Then suddenly I looked down and noticed a note sticking partially out from under a mat on her front porch.

I picked the note up and learned that Michelle had misplaced her phone and needed to rush her son Max to the hospital. Max was a sweet kid, but he had a temper that could rival the most ferocious lioness in the pride. The note said Max kicked his television set out of anger because he was in last place on his video game, and, unfortunately, made it fall off the shelf and onto his head. Michelle told me not to worry too much in the note, but also said that Max was going to be the proud owner of several stitches. Michelle ended the note by saying that she wasn't sure how long they'd be at the hospital, but I could just leave the tape recorder on the porch if I wanted.

As I put the bag down on Michelle's front porch I thought, *Boy, am I glad it wasn't anything more serious than a few stitches.* Then I jumped off the porch and Herman walked by my side until we reached the gate. Once there, I knelt and played with Herman for another five minutes or so. Then I told her I'd see her later before closing the gate behind me and heading back home.

I arrived home shortly before 10:30 p.m. and no sooner did I walk in my front door than I heard my cellphone rang. I was shocked to notice from caller I.D. that the call was from someone at the precinct.

"What could this be about?" I thought to myself. Could this be Sheriff Hawkins? Had he finally realized that he'd never called me this evening to finish my statement? I answered the phone and to my surprise it wasn't Sheriff Hawkins at all. It was the precinct alright, but it was the department that held petty criminals and someone was using their one phone call to call me. The recording went on to say that someone from St. Lux County Jail was trying to reach me and asked if I wanted to accept the charges. Well, I didn't know who it could've been, so as I stood there pondering which one of my bedrooms was now empty, because the person who should've been occupying that space was currently in jail, I yelled out. "Yes, I'll accept the charges."

I was then scolded for the next two minutes by a pre-recorded message about the dos and don'ts while talking to a St. Lux inmate. Finally, once I was transferred through to the person who called me, I was shocked to learn it was Sean Griffin, the young teen who'd accused Jack of being involved in his mother's murder.

"Mrs. Harris, is that you?" Sean cried out.

"Yes!" I responded. "What happened, Sean? Why are you in jail?" I asked frantically.

"I'm sure I don't have much time to explain," Sean said in a panicked tone. "But I didn't do anything, Mrs. Harris. However, now I'm being harassed about recanting the story I gave concerning my mother's murder," Sean exclaimed.

Oh, dear God, I thought to myself. This had Rodney Lucas written all over it, and I was partially to blame because I was the one who'd put Sean on his radar.

"Say no more, Sean," I said in an agitated tone. "I'll be there in less than five minutes. You won't have to stay the night in there, I promise you that," I shouted out in anger.

"Thank you, Mrs. Harris," Sean yelled out in relief before the call ended.

I didn't even have time to fully grasp the idea that Rodney played a part in putting an innocent child behind bars. *What was going on with him?* I thought to myself. I remembered a time when Rodney would go above and beyond to protect the citizens of St. Lux from petty criminals. Now it just seemed as though he was going out of his way to become one. As I stood there in my living room I was now more sure than ever that Sean possibly had damning information about his mother's murder—information that someone didn't want disclosed.

I didn't know whether Sean blocked certain details out of his mind or purposely kept things to himself because he thought no one would believe him. Whatever the truth was, it was now pertinent for me to find out what happened to his mother, even if that meant looking into his claims about Jack's past. As unfortunate as it was, Sean's young life could very well depend on it.

CHAPTER ELEVEN

It was now around 10:45 p.m. and I was heading out the front door on my way to the police station. I got into Tom's van and drove the short distance from home to the precinct. Upon arrival, I saw Charlie West out front talking to an ununiformed officer.

"Charlie, Charlie!" I shouted as I ran towards the front entrance. "I need to speak with you. Do you have a moment?" I asked assertively, thinking the whole time that he could possibly be to blame for all of this.

"Well, it's been a pretty busy night so far tonight," Charlie replied, as the ununiformed officer tossed his cigarette butt and walked towards his car. "However, I guess those criminals inside aren't going anywhere, so what's up, Sam?" Charlie said.

"Well, recently I've had a few strange occurrences happen around my house, and I have reason to believe that you're responsible for some of them," I said firmly. "What baffles me is why you would go to such lengths to spy on my home?" I said, looking up at him in bewilderment.

"Sam, I would never!" Charlie blurted out. "You're like a big sister to me, and you're also a good friend. I can assure you that I've never spied on you," Charlie said vehemently. I was blindsided. I never would've guessed that Charlie thought of me with such high regard, and I felt just awful for accusing him. Was I somehow unaware that I was bringing that same tunnel vision that made me a semi-successful writer into trying to figure out who murdered Ronda? More importantly, had I influenced Mr. Black's decision in any way by showing him Charlie's photo? I wasn't so sure anymore. It was starting to feel as though I was so focused on Charlie and Crystal that I was blinded from seeing other people for who or what they really were.

"Oh, dear, I'm so sorry," I whispered. "I didn't mean to accuse you, Charlie, and I'm sure all of this was a case of mistaken identity," I said in the most apologetic way. "I know you're a good kid and you just want to help in these police matters, but I guess being so closely intwined within a murder will bring out the wariness in a girl." Unable to look Charlie in the eye, I felt a lot of guilt in that moment. "Unfortunately, I'm not above speaking from pure emotion," I said, "which, as I tell my students every day in class, can be very detrimental to a healthy lifestyle." Feeling terrible as I watched the pain on Charlie's face after I accused him of surveilling my house, I asked if he could ever forgive me. I was fully aware that putting unfounded information out into the universe could have dire consequences. I couldn't live with that on my conscience if—in fact—I was wrong about Charlie.

"Of course, Sam," Charlie said, with a smile. "I know you have to ruffle a few feathers in order to get to the truth, so I don't blame you at all for questioning me. After all, you can never be too careful about who to trust nowadays. Some people love to watch you burn even if they're holding a fire extinguisher in their hands," Charlie said callously.

My sentiments exactly, I thought to myself.

But something about Charlie's statement reverberated just under the surface. Somewhat confused myself, I felt he may have played a bigger role than he let on. Unfortunately, I wasn't all together sure if he was even aware of it. It was a great displeasure of mine to have to use Charlie in this way, but I needed to get to the bottom of this tragedy once and for all. So, as Charlie started to walk up the stairs to the police station, I couldn't help but follow him as I blurted out, "I found a tape recorder someone hid underneath my deck!"

Charlie's reaction was sheer shock that soon turned into panic as he ran up the stairs and fumbled to get the door open. In that moment, I knew Charlie was privy to something, but I also felt in my heart that the story he had just told me was sincere. *How could both things be true at the same time?* I asked myself.

"Someone's spying on you to the extent that you found a tape recorder at your home?" Charlie asked.

Like a moth to a flame, I thought to myself. "Yeah, frightening, isn't it?" I responded.

"Luckily, I'll have the fingerprint analysis soon and I'll have a better understanding of why I'm being harassed."

"Well, would you happen to know the name brand of that tape recorder you found, Sam?"

"Not offhand." I replied. "Why do you ask?"

"Just tying a couple loose ends together. You can never be to careful," he said as he turned around and reached for my hand to help me up the last step. "I'll have a better understanding once I sort out a few things."

Hmm, sounds like he's also working on a plan, I thought to myself.

Charlie, always the gentleman, finally got the door open, then held it ajar as he politely gestured with a sweeping hand. "Ladies first," he said.

"Why thank you, kind sir," I replied, walking in. "Good to know chivalry isn't dead."

If I had learned anything in all my years of being a teacher, it was never to badger a child for information, particularly if you knew you already had them on the ropes. Chances were if you left them alone to stew, they'd always come back, especially once they realized you were a confidant and not a foe. After all, that's exactly why I was currently at the police station. Sean felt as though I was someone he could trust when he needed someone to trust the most.

I walked through the lobby and spotted the Sherriff's Deputy, Randall Hicks, sitting behind his desk. Randall's parents were sweethearts but, boy, was he feisty. Randall never had any ill-will towards anyone I knew, but he was certainly someone you didn't want to cross.

I walked over towards Deputy Hicks and as calmly as the night sky I whispered in a mellow tone, "I'm here to pick up Sean Griffin."

"Is that the kid or the drunk?" Deputy Hicks asked.

"The kid," I responded. "May I ask what was he booked for?" I said, confused as to why he was even being held.

"Vagrancy, I believe," Deputy Hicks casually said.

Boy, was I livid. *I'd never heard of anything quite as ridiculous in my life,* I thought to myself. My entire mood changed as I realized that Sean was just a pawn in someone's twisted game of "hide the witness." "So let me get this straight," I said sarcastically. "You guys had no real reason to bring him in, so you arrested him for homelessness?"

"Among other things!" Deputy Hicks shouted as he stood up from his desk. "Unfortunately, I can't go into the specifics, Samantha, but this kid is into some wicked stuff. And if I were you, I'd stay far away from him," he added, forcefully.

"Well, that source who gives you this intel about poor helpless kids—it wouldn't happen to be Former Sheriff Rodney Lucas, would it? I asked firmly.

"It'll do you a world of good to keep your nose out of police matters," Deputy Hicks retorted. "That kid has been wreaking havoc for more than a year now, and once we get enough evidence, hopefully he'll be the proud new owner of a nice comfortable suite in St. Lux's Children's Village."

Damn, I thought to myself. That's St. Lux's Juvenile Detention Center. I couldn't allow Sean to end up there when he did nothing wrong. He was just a lost child dealing with the death of his mother all on his own. And to be thrown inside a facility like that just because you refused to shut up about it, well, that was pretty low for sure. "I'd like to speak with Sheriff Hawkins, right away!" I demanded. "Is he still around?"

"He's gone for the night," Deputy Hicks replied. "Furthermore, I can't release the kid unless he has a place to stay." Deputy Hicks said with a smirk.

So, after taking a deep breath, I told Deputy Hicks that wouldn't be an issue because Sean would be staying with me. Then after secretly pinching myself on the thigh because I realized that I'd just taking full responsibility for a moody teenage boy, I looked Deputy Hicks square in his eyes before I shouted out, "I'd like to see Sean now, so we can go home."

However, before taking me to see Sean, Deputy Hicks blurted out, "There's only two types of people that I ever encounter doing this job: the guilty and the I-can't-believe-I-got-caught guilty! So, before you drive off into the sunset with your fairytale ending, Mrs. Harris, just know that your precious Sean falls into both of these categories."

Finally, as Deputy Hicks walked me towards the back of the police station, out the corner of my eye I could see the holding cells. Unfortunately, that image of the very first cell will probably haunt me forever because there was Sean, in a corner, balled up in a fetal position as if he had no more fight left in him. *This is a complete abomination*, I thought to myself. The humiliation Sean must've felt in that moment was almost too much for me to bear. Fortunately, Deputy Hicks allowed us to talk while he went back out to get the paperwork ready that I needed to sign.

I asked Sean if he was okay and if he'd had anything to eat today. He said he hadn't, then he begged me to get him out of prison. "Well, this isn't quite prison, Sean, but I'll definitely be getting you out of here," I said gently. "But

I can't say I'll be so gracious with the monsters responsible for putting you in here. So, what happened anyway Sean? How did this all come about?" I asked.

"Well, the police picked me up just as I was walking to Felix's Diner to get some dinner," Sean claimed. "They yelled at me to get on the ground, then they searched me for weapons. I told them I didn't do anything, but no one would listen," Sean said despondently.

"Can you think of any reason why they would be so gung-ho about putting you away?" I asked. "Is there anything else that you can think of that would warrant this type of behavior from the police?" I asked, feeling empathy for the young kid.

Sean hung his head and stared down at the floor before waving me closer to the bars that separated us. "I did do something, Mrs. Harris," Sean whispered softly.

"What is it, Sean?" I asked, "What did you do?"

"Well, the former Sheriff who botched my mom's murder investigation, the one who you called your friend earlier today, I trashed his house," Sean whimpered, with regret in his eyes. "However, no one saw me, Mrs. Harris!" he cried out. "The dumb cops have no clue who's responsible for the vandalism; they're just trying to strong-arm me into switching my initial statement about my mother's murder." As I stood there in awe that I was talking to a fifteen-year-old child, I came to the overwhelming realization that my dream of becoming a foster parent could soon be a reality. *Jack would've loved Sean*, I thought to myself. In many ways, Sean reminded me of my late husband, which boded well for me because that was something I could use to my advantage to get Sean to open up.

"Don't you worry about that, Sean; I'll get you out of here. Then we'll swing by the drive-thru at Felix's Diner and get you that dinner you wanted. I just need to go back up front and get you released into my custody and I'll be right back. Okay?" I said to the frightened young boy with reassurance

"Oh, thank you, Mrs. Harris," Sean whispered softly.

I walked back up front and filled out the paperwork to get Sean released into my custody. The whole time I could hear Deputy Hicks barking orders at everyone until he turned his venomous rant on me by telling me that I was making a huge mistake by trusting Sean. I couldn't believe what I was hearing. This was a fifteen-year-old child who had done nothing wrong but was somehow being treated like the scum of the earth.

"Shame on you, Deputy Hicks, shame on you all!" I shouted out, as I completed the forms and walked them towards his desk. "You know, Deputy Hicks," I said, as I leaned into his space. "I met a very peculiar lady today and I might even go as far as calling her a friend. Her name is Talia Wren; she works in a very prominent position over at Channel 18 News," I said casually. "Needless to say, it would be a shame to have your face plastered all over the television screen once Sean decides to tell his story to the media," I smirked. "Well, I can just hear the gossip now... A scared boy whose mother was murdered thrown into a juvenile center because he knew too much. Well, those are the kind of headlines that invented water coolers, don't ya think?" I added in my gotcha moment. "So, you need to ask yourself one question, Deputy Hicks—Just what kind of an officer are you? Because, unfortunately, that generalization of all the guilty people you run into while on duty applies to you as well. So, are you guilty or are you the type to do anything-to-cover-my-tracks-to-keep-from-looking guilty? Quite frankly, as far as I can see..." I slammed the paperwork on his desk "...you'll look guilty in the court of public opinion regardless, especially since you're actively using all of your resources to torment a fifteen-year-old boy, while letting a deranged killer roam free! I do believe this type of policing is frowned upon by the citizens of St. Lux," I scolded.

As I looked into Deputy Hicks's eyes, I thought I was finally getting through that tough do-or-die exterior he so often displayed. *His human side is finally at the forefront,* I thought to myself. All he needed was a gentle nudge.

"I can see you want to do the right thing, Deputy Hicks. So, what's stopping you?"

"Let's just say I don't go around looking for the good in people," Deputy Hicks callously answered. "Once someone shows me who they are, unfortunately I tend to believe them."

Wow, so much for reading his demeanor, I thought to myself. Deputy Hicks could outwardly show himself as a big lovable teddy bear, while secretly thinking about taking your head off in the back of his mind. He was a tough vault to crack for sure and dealing with him was certainly going to be no walk in the park. He was just the right amount of demented and professional in my opinion, and that combination could be disastrous for anyone in his path.

As I followed Deputy Hicks back to the holding cells, I heard him mutter, "The Sheriff is going to be furious!"

Trying to lighten the mood, I told the Deputy that he could have Sheriff Hawkins give me a call tomorrow morning, and I'd be more than happy to explain everything about Sean.

"Not Sheriff Hawkins!" Deputy Hicks shouted out. "The Former Sheriff, Rodney Lucas. He's the one who picked the boy up a couple of hours ago and instructed me to hold him here until morning when he got back," Deputy Hicks said candidly.

What type of shenanigans is Rodney up to? I thought to myself. Could he have wanted Sean to stew in this holding cell overnight, so he'd be ripe for the picking and confess to whatever was asked of him in the morning? I was starting to feel completely overwhelmed by it all and, unfortunately, I saw no signs of it being over anytime soon.

I reminded Deputy Hicks that technically they had no real reason to hold Sean, especially since they'd only charged him with vagrancy and I clearly wasn't going to allow him to be homeless. So, the next sentence out of my mouth was, "I'm going down to the family court in the morning to make this official."

Sean will have a good home where he can lay his head down every night and there will be no need for him to deal with trumped-up charges, such as this, I thought to myself.

I hadn't spoken to Sean about this yet. But I just couldn't stand the thought of this intelligent, young man being consumed by grief and ending up on the wrong path. I felt as though I not only had the opportunity to speak out for the precious lives we lost, but I also had the chance to speak out for those who were still with us but who lacked the wherewithal to speak out for themselves, even if that meant Sean throwing a teenage tantrum because he thought he could do this all on his own. No matter how bright Sean appeared to be, he was still a fifteen-year-old child and he didn't have the life experience to deal with this all on his own. More importantly, he shouldn't have to.

After Deputy Hicks unlocked the cell and told Sean he was free to go, he dashed right by the Deputy and the next thing I knew I was getting the biggest bear hug from a teenager who only a few hours ago accused my dead husband of murdering his mother. *It wouldn't sound any less strange if I repeated it,* I thought to myself.

"Thank you, Mrs. Harris!" Sean yelled out with joy as he continued hugging me for several more minutes.

"My pleasure," I responded. "Now let's go get you something to eat. Unfortunately, I don't think Felix's Diner is still open at this hour," I said as I looked at my watch and noticed it was 11:15 p.m.

"How about a burger from McClucky's?" Sean suggested.

"Well, you must've been reading my mind," I said with a smile.

As we drove to get food, Sean started to fire off a variety of questions in rapid succession, many of which required a more detailed response than a simple yes or no answer. Well, I figured if I was going to gain his trust completely,

I could let him be bad cop for a while. However, it did strike me as odd that he didn't bring up his mother nor did he mention how he thought Jack was involved in her murder. Nevertheless, he sure was pushing the envelope. After we got to McClucky's and I placed Sean's order, Sean told me that his mother used to bring him here as a child and he had nothing but fond memories of her every time he ate here.

"What about your father?" I asked. "Do you live with him? I'm sure he must be worried sick about you by now," I said.

"Your guess is as good as mine," Sean said in regard to his father.

"Well, what about any other family?" I asked. "Someone surely must be looking for you."

"I don't think so," Sean said wistfully. "It was just me and my mom."

Sensing I was bringing up a topic that this poor kid just couldn't handle in that moment, I bit my tongue to prevent any further affliction on Sean.

"It's okay, Mrs. Harris," Sean bravely said. "I'll be fine if you need to ask me questions about my past."

"I'll tell you what, Sean," I replied. "How about we get your food now, get you home and get you a good night's rest, and we'll see how you feel in the morning?"

"That works too, Mrs. Harris," Sean said, showing me a big smile.

"You don't have to call me 'Mrs. Harris,'" I said, as I handed Sean his food. "You can call me Samantha if you'd like."

"Okay, Mrs. Samantha, but that doesn't roll off the tongue as easily," Sean said as he took a big gulp of his purple splash.

"On the other hand, Mrs. Harris does have a nice ring to it," I retorted.

As we drove the short distance from McClucky's to my house, I watched as Sean gave Daphne a run for her money as the world's fastest devourer. I didn't know if I was making the right choice with Sean, but I knew I didn't believe in coincidences. It was more than just happenstance that he stumbled into my life, and unlike Deputy Hicks, I was more than willing to look for the good in people.

As we pulled into my driveway, I noticed my front door was ajar. *Now is not the time.* I thought to myself, as Sean and I walked towards the front porch. Suddenly, I heard Daphne begin to bark. *Oh good, she hasn't somehow made her Great Houdini escape just yet*, I thought, hoping that there was a good explanation for all of this.

As I looked over at Sean, who looked fearful of entering a house that may have just been broken into, I said to him, "I'm sorry that you have to come into all of this chaos."

Trying to put on a brave face, Sean stated, "Compared to being locked up in the joint, a breaking and entering scene should be a breeze."

Sensing he was hiding fear with humor—although I've never been a parent—my protective instincts kicked in and I told Sean to wait in the van.

"No way, Mrs. Harris!" Sean yelled out. "We can protect each other if we don't split up, and no offense...but I'll be a sitting duck in this van."

"Good point," I replied. "However, I want you to stay behind me. "

"No arguments here," Sean whispered.

As Sean followed behind me, we went from room to room and the only one that was currently occupied was the spare bedroom Maureen was sleeping in. Tom was gone and so was Dee. *Where could they be?* I thought to myself. Tom was still quite intoxicated when I left, and Dee hadn't moved from my bed since her arrival.

I don't like this. No, I don't like this one bit, I thought as every worst-case scenario filled my head.

As we continued throughout the house flipping up every possible light switch we could find, we finally made our way into the kitchen and I noticed that someone had written a note and left it on the counter. It was from Tom and it read, 'Took your friend to Oak Grace Hospital. Please come when you see this.'

After assuring Sean that no burglar was in the house, he opted to stay and rest rather than take another car ride and possibly sit up all night in a waiting room chair. I told him I'd be back as soon as possible, then set him up in the spare bedroom that Tom had left empty.

While driving to Oak Grace Hospital, I realized that I hadn't been back there since the day Jack died. I kept telling myself that no one else would suffer that same fate. However, if I'm being honest, wishful thinking just wasn't doing the trick nowadays.

Once I arrived, I parked in the visitors' parking area and rushed inside. *How lucky was I to not have to go through the hassle with the front desk?* I thought to myself. Tom, like a white knight, was standing right there when I needed him most.

"Tom, Tom!" I yelled as his back was turned to me. "Is everything okay?" I asked once he turned around. "Where is Dee?" I shouted.

"Sam!" Tom yelled out as he embraced me with a hug. "She's not okay, but I got her here just in the nick of time. It was looking pretty grim for her," Tom said.

"What was the matter?" I demanded. "She was fine when I left home," I said.

"Actually, she hasn't been fine all day," Tom responded. "She was drugged."

"Drugged!" I repeated. "How could this be? Who could've done such a thing?" I asked.

"Well, the doctors are running tests to see exactly what's in her system," Tom said. "They said it could take days for a conclusive result,"

Oh, my, I thought to myself, *First Ronda, now this.* "Do they have any inkling when this could've happened?" I asked.

"Well, they're not sure if she was self-medicating, or if something more sinister is to blame," Tom said. "However, she was in pretty bad shape when I found her."

As I stood there looking at Tom, I didn't want to believe it, and honestly my heart wouldn't allow me to believe it, that this was the Tom everyone had been warning me about. Dee was grief-stricken when I last saw her a few hours ago, but she certainly wasn't in need of hospitalization.

Could Tom be responsible? I thought to myself. He certainly wasn't above spying on my house, so was it a stretch to think maybe he was watching my every move? Maybe he saw me in the park with Ronda yesterday, and in his mind he thought that killing off my friends would somehow make me fall into his arms. I'd certainly seen this storyline on cable TV before.

Fortunately, for Tom, I just couldn't go beyond mere suspicion when it came to him. Aside from the fact that I had my own free choice and wasn't willing to join the lynch mob that all but threw him under the bus, I was unquestionably hypervigilant. However, I never felt on guard when I was around him, and my intuition was as reliable as anything I'd ever owned. And it was telling me not only was Tom not the killer but he would also essentially be the one who helped me find out who was.

CHAPTER TWELVE

As I stood there in the hospital waiting room firing off a barrage of questions at Tom, I noticed him giving me those sad, puppy dog eyes. *Oh, no you don't,* I thought to myself. *Not this time. Enticement will get you nowhere when there's a recent death in town that seems to follow you like a stray cat.*

"Tom, how did you get to the hospital?" I asked. "I had your van and my car was still in my driveway when I got home a few minutes ago. "

"I used your friend's phone to call an Uber," Tom said. "I thought to call you but your number wasn't in her phone, and still being slightly under the influence as a result of patronizing the Tunnel Funnel bar, I realized I was never going to recall your number by memory after foolishly losing my phone earlier today. So, while appreciating the fact that I was still too intoxicated to drive, I knew I couldn't sit around and do nothing after seeing the condition your friend was in," Tom said, passionately.

"Oh, I'm sure she's thankful," I said. "However, when exactly did you see her? She was still asleep in my bedroom when I left and you were passed out in my guest bedroom. Did the two of you cross paths going to the restroom or something?" I asked.

"Umm no," Tom murmured, "I was in your bedroom."

Completely shocked by the news that Tom felt more than comfortable traipsing around my bedroom, I decided to take a page out of Crystal's book and debut my fabulous acting skills. I knew I needed to keep my composure, so I stood there completely stone-faced without batting an eye.

It was the least I could do, I thought to myself. If I was going to scratch Tom's name off my suspect list, I needed to know exactly what he'd been up to. So, I decided to join in and play the game that everyone in town seemed to be so good at—vilifying Tom. I threw caution to the wind and decided that the only way I'd catch a killer was by not playing by the rules.

"So, you found Dee almost at the point of no return, huh?" I asked Tom. "Had she been stumbling around in my bedroom dazed and confused? Was that why you initially went in there?" I asked in an attempt to figure out why Tom just so happened to go into my bedroom at the most inopportune time when he's never been in there before.

"No," Tom whispered while looking down at the hospital floor. "She wasn't awake when I went into your bedroom. To be honest, I actually forgot that you left to have dinner with the Lucas's and I assumed that was you in your bed. So, after knocking on your bedroom door and not getting an answer, I just wanted to make sure everything was okay. I just wish none of this ever happened." He stood there and hung his head in his hands as if a raging hangover was hammering his brain.

Aw-Shuck's! I thought to myself. That was a pretty logical explanation. What was I doing standing here badgering Tom who'd just saved me from someone's imprudent distraught wife at a bar, when the real killer was somewhere possibly picking their next victim?

I still didn't know how Tom knew enough to bring Dee to the hospital because she had possibly been poisoned, but what I did know was Tom wasn't Ronda's killer and finding out who was, well, that took precedence over someone walking into my bedroom.

As I stood there looking at Tom, I saw him try to discretely wipe away tears. I just hate it when my friends are upset, and what's worse is when I'm the one who caused the pain.

However, before I could tell Tom that everything would be okay, he whispered to me in a hushed tone, "After going into your bedroom, Sam, I realized I needed to tell you something, or I would regret it forever if I didn't." Then as quickly as he began talking, he stopped. I could see it was hard for Tom to get the words out, and I assumed it had something to do with the crush he'd told me about earlier.

Unfortunately, because I knew Tom was in such a vulnerable state, anything he asked would require me to tread lightly when answering. I loved all my friends, but I simply couldn't keep going back and forth between my good cop and bad cop personas. It was physically draining and, if I'm being honest, I wasn't sure which one I needed to be in this moment.

"Whatever it is Tom, it's okay," I whispered affectionately. "You can tell me later when everyone is safe and sound. Right now, you need to sit down because you don't look so hot," I blurted out to an unsteady Tom. "Have you eaten anything since getting pie-eyed at that bar?" I asked.

"No," Tom replied. "Other than a protein bar, I haven't had anything to eat all day."

"Well, I guess drinking on an empty stomach will have this kind of effect on you," I said as I helped Tom into the waiting room chair. "Let me see what I can find out about Dee, then we'll stop by McClucky's on the way home," I said as I yanked my hand away, so that Tom didn't crush it as he fell into the chair.

I walked away thinking that aside from the time I learned of Jack's death, I hadn't remembered ever feeling so useless. Tom and Maureen both had been well beyond what they could possibly handle as far as drinking goes, Ronda unfortunately was tragically murdered, and her mother Dee was currently in the hospital from a possible poisoning.

Whoever was responsible wanted me isolated and suffering for sure, I thought to myself. However, I knew justice was right around the corner for my friend Dee and her beautiful daughter Ronda. So, I put that extra pep in my step and hurried over to the front desk to ask the receptionist what room Dee was in, and if she was awake.

"Hello!" I blurted out as I approached the older woman's desk. She had to be in her mid-sixties, but she looked fabulous. As I stood there staring at the woman before she answered back, I thought about what my mother told me ten years ago on her sixtieth birthday, when her friends were giving her a hard time because she was the first one to reach that milestone. She said, "Samantha, sixty is not the cut-off age for living your life; it simply means you're getting wiser, and with that wisdom you'll learn how to work with what you've got just a little bit better than most."

Even though she was a handful at times, I always received words to live by from my mother. (*Although, I'm not quite age-appropriate to call myself a Grey Cougar just yet.*) I felt as if I were coming into my own and I knew the last hurrah would come down to who could outwit whom. So, I was going to make certain that if I didn't have the wherewithal to think like a killer, at the very least I'd use what I've learned over the years to try and outthink one.

"Hello, there," the woman shouted out. "Well, aren't you pretty as a peach? What can I do for you?" she asked.

Given the circumstances—surrounded by injured people—and the fact that it was almost midnight, the woman seemed extremely vibrant and full of life. She had a hint of that southern charm that Ronda possessed, so I assumed she wasn't from here originally either.

"Oh, I'm just here to see someone who was checked in a little while ago," I replied. "Her name is Dee, well, her full name is Daphne Dee Evans." I shook my head and smiled while thinking about the conversation I'd had yesterday with Ronda in the dog park, when she'd mentioned that my dog had the same name as her mother.

As I stood there in a daze, I thought if I'd known at the time that Ronda was talking about my old childhood friend when she referred to her mother Daphne, then none of this would've ever happened. Ronda would've come back to my house and Dee and I would've talked on the phone for hours. None of my friends would be suspects, and my world wouldn't be completely upside down. Well, obviously I didn't have a time machine to change the past, but I knew the faster I accepted the fact that someone I loved could be responsible for murder, the better off I'd be.

"Okay, here she is!" The woman blurted out while checking her computer for Dee's room number. "Are you related to the patient?" she asked.

"Umm, technically, no," I whispered. "However, we were childhood friends and she's here staying with me from out of state; I don't think she has any family in St. Lux," I said.

"Goodness gracious." The woman muttered while looking at her computer monitor. "I didn't see the note attached to the patient's file," she said. "Looks like even if you were family, technically, I couldn't let you back there until the doctors know that the patient is safe from danger, and subsequently remove her from the no-visitors list. It's just hospital rules when someone is brought in exhibiting the type of symptoms Mrs. Evans is presenting," the woman said. "Obviously, we can't have too many people in and out of her room for safety reasons."

Boy, am I getting a taste of my own medicine, I thought to myself. All day I had been suspecting everyone in town of Ronda's murder, and now I couldn't even see her mother in the hospital because the doctors thought I'd be going back there to finish the job. Although I understood, I can't say I liked the irony.

As I was walking away feeling hopeless, I heard the woman yell out, "Hold your horses, honey." Instantly, my eyes widened at the thought of now being able to see my friend, so I ran back over towards the receptionist as bright-eyed and bushy-tailed as could be. When she suddenly said, "Well, I'm not supposed to do this, but why don't you come back in the morning, darlin'?"

"Will I be able to see Dee then?" I asked enthusiastically.

"Well, I can't promise you anything," the woman said. "However, if your friend is feeling better then I'll have her add your name to her approved visitors' list, and we won't be able to deny you entry."

"Oh, thank you!" I shouted out as I went to call her by her name before realizing I didn't know it. The woman, noticing the long pause in my sentence, put two and two together, then moved her long hair away from her badge to show that her nametag said 'Laura.'

"What a coincidence," I said. "My mother's name is Laura also."

"Well, if you're insinuating that I'm old enough to be your mother, then you'll have no problem visiting your friend because I'm fixin' to put you in the hospital right now," Laura said with a smile.

"Even though my mother is only twenty-seven years old," I joked.

"I like you," Laura said after she stopped laughing. "Even though I can't allow you to see your friend this second, I can tell you as of now she's doing great and it looks as if she'll be fine," Laura whispered,

"Oh, thank you so much," I whispered back, while placing both of my hands over my heart.

"You betcha. Now go get some rest, kiddo. You look exhausted," she said, as she winked at me.

I walked back over towards Tom and noticed that he'd fallen asleep in one of the waiting room chairs. "Tom," I called out as I nudged him on the shoulder. "Let's get you something to eat," By now it was a little after midnight and I was starting to drag my feet from exhaustion. However, I figured one last trip to McClucky's before calling it a night should be okay.

After helping an intoxicated Tom get to his feet, he asked me If I was able to see Dee and if she was doing okay.

"Well, I'm going to get a good night's rest tonight, then I'll be back to visit Dee in the morning," I said. "But the receptionist told me that Dee was in great shape and she looked to be recovering just fine. Like it or not, you're a hero, Tom, and I'm sure Dee would say the same," I said, lovingly. "I can't thank you enough for everything you've done for me and for this town over the years. And now saving Dee's life, I won't soon forget it." As we exited the building, I watched my good friend Tom Miller get a bit emotional while seemingly pondering the day's events.

Once we pulled out of the hospital parking lot, I knew it would take roughly ten minutes to get to McClucky's, and the whole ride there Tom sang "In your arms" by Jeffrey Connors. It was one of my favorite songs, but I didn't recall if I'd ever mentioned that to Tom. I had heard Tom's singing voice before and knew he was good but whenever he'd noticed me within earshot of him, he'd always stop. Tom was a former police officer who beat up criminals, and who'd since made the switch to a television weatherman and appeared in millions of homes every week. But even with all the glitz and glamour of being a local celebrity, Tom still had a shyness about him when the attention shifted in his direction. However, whether it was the alcohol or some other form of courage, Tom didn't seem to care about showing his more vulnerable side tonight. As I started to sing background vocals, I realized we had gotten through three renditions of my favorite song and it was now our turn to talk into the large speaker to place our order.

After Tom yelled over me into the speaker to place his order, I pulled up to the window to pay. I was hoping I wouldn't see the same young lady who'd just taken my order a little more than an hour ago, because even though I hadn't eaten any of the food that I'd previously ordered for Sean, I just knew that if it was the same girl at the window I'd get a funny look.

I got to the window and thought to myself, *If I didn't have bad luck I wouldn't have any luck at all.* Of course, it was the same girl. However, if given the option I certainly would've chosen being too harshly judged for my late-night food choices over what she was about to tell me.

"Hey!" the girl shouted out as I handed her the money I owed for Tom's meal. "Weren't you here just a little while ago?" she asked.

"Umm, yes," I responded. "However, I don't have a problem with eating my feelings, I swear."

"Oh, I'm not here to judge," the girl said with a giggle. "I just have a thing where I remember faces."

"Oh, thank goodness!" I said to the young girl. "For a second there, I thought you were getting ready to tell me some bad news. It seems like everyone I've talked to today has hit me with some sort of misfortune," I said, laughing.

"Well, I'm sorry, but I've got to add to that bad luck streak you've got going on," the girl said, looking downcast.

"What do you mean?" I asked. "Is there something you have to tell me?"

"Well, that boy that was with you earlier," the girl whispered...

"Yeah, Sean, what about him?" I asked.

"Well, he was just here," the girl said.

"Yeah, we both were," I replied. "We ordered food."

"No," the girl said firmly. "I mean he just took off not even five minutes ago. He had been sitting in the parking lot for maybe fifteen minutes," she said.

What! I thought to myself. Obviously, she wasn't as good at remembering faces as she liked to brag about because Sean was at home in bed and most likely asleep by now.

"Who's Sean?" Tom asked.

"Are you absolutely positive it was the same boy?" I asked.

"Yes, ma'am," The girl said. "I'm only bringing it up because my sister thought he was the creepy old man who like to hang out near our cars late at night, and she was getting ready to call the cops until I recognized his face from earlier," the young girl said. "I just don't want anyone getting into any trouble," she said, as she handed me Tom's order. "However, since I just saw you two together, I thought you should know, especially with a killer on the loose out there. No one's really safe being alone at this hour," she added.

"Thank you, have a nice night," I said to the girl, completely shocked by what she'd just told me. If it were true, I wasn't quite sure if I could handle it at this point. On the drive home, I gave Tom the rundown on who Sean was and why he was currently staying at my home.

"Geez!" Tom blurted out. "You've got more worrisome friends than Hallmark can make cards for."

"Tell me about it," I said, sarcastically, while staring at one of those friends.

As we pulled into my driveway, I asked Tom if he was okay getting out of the van on his own.

"Yeah, I'll be fine—see if the boy's inside," Tom responded.

I ran up the porch stairs and entered my front door after unlocking it. *Well, if Sean was gone,* I thought to myself, *he certainly didn't use the front door because he had no key to lock it back up.* As I ran to the spare bedroom where Sean should've been sleeping, I opened the door and couldn't believe it. The girl at McClucky's was right; Sean was gone!

I fell down to my knees just inside the bedroom and almost burst into tears. I knew as long as Sean was out there, he wasn't safe. But there was nothing more I could do. I hadn't the slightest idea of where a teenage boy would find solace in the middle of the night in St. Lux. So, all I could do was hope that whoever killed his mother was as clueless as I was when it came to catching the unobtainable Sean.

CHAPTER THIRTEEN

As I sat there in the spare bedroom's doorway, I finally heard Tom make his way inside, subsequently slamming the front door behind him.

"Is everything alright, Sam?" Tom yelled out from the living room. Is the boy here?" he asked.

"No," I said dejectedly. "He's gone and I have no idea where he could be."

"Aww, geez, I'm sorry, Sam." Tom consoled me as he rushed down the hallway and knelt in front of me. "Seems like you were only trying to help this kid, but maybe this is something he needs to work out on his own," he said.

Normally, advice like this would be pretty spot-on, I thought to myself, *especially when the person I was trying to help seemingly rejected my efforts at every turn.* However, this was a fifteen-year-old boy we were talking about whose mother had been murdered. So, no matter how stubborn he was, I was going to make certain that he didn't suffer the same fate.

"No!" I said to Tom emphatically. "I know I ran into Sean because I'm supposed to help this kid. Once he realizes that I'm on his side and that I'm not the bad guy, he'll be back," I said firmly.

"Can I tell you something, Sam?" Tom asked, as he helped me up off the floor.

"Of course, Tom. What is it?" I replied.

"I've just always admired how passionate you are about helping those who aren't in a position to help themselves," Tom said, warmly. "What's more, you sort of inspired me earlier today to do the same. Well, helping was my intention, but I'm pretty sure everything went off the rails in a catastrophic way," Tom said as he hung his head.

Feeling now was as good a time as any for Tom to spill the beans on his recent activities, I posed one question.

"What did I inspire you to do, Tom?" I asked candidly as we walked into the kitchen. "Well, I'm not exactly proud of my behavior this evening." Tom blurted out. "However, I can say with one hundred percent certainty that there was no malice in my heart at the time. I was just in protective mode."

Protective mode, I thought to myself. The only person on Earth I'd ever seen Tom be so protective of was his niece, Crystal. Funnily enough Crystal used to be a sweet innocent young girl (emphasis on *used to be*). However, that coupled with her speech disorder made her the victim of some horrific childhood bullying.

Regrettably, in that moment I wanted to save Tom from implicating himself. Maybe just put a small piece of duct tape over his mouth, so he wouldn't be able to tell the rest of his story. I mean, sure, I wanted to know, but not at the expense of losing all of my friends.

As I stood there contemplating, I thought to myself, *How could I be so self-involved?* Furthermore, how could I live with myself knowing I didn't do the right thing just because I'd possibly lose a friend? So, I took a deep breath as Tom and I sat at my wobbly kitchen table, then I asked him who exactly he was trying to protect.

Tom was now funneling his McClucky's fries into his mouth as if they were going out of style. He held up his free hand as if to say, "One second." After he was done chewing, he confirmed what I already knew. Tom said he was trying to protect Crystal.

"Protect her from what?" I asked.

"*From herself,* or so I thought," Tom replied. "Do you remember earlier today when I told you I had something to take care of and I mentioned that you wouldn't be able to come along with me? "

"Yes, I remember," I said calmly.

"Well, protecting Crystal was the thing I had to take care of," Tom whispered.

I knew Tom well enough to know that he didn't go around spilling his guts to just anyone. *This is a rarity for sure,* I thought to myself. However, this was now the second time today where he's opened up like this with me. Was he more vulnerable now since unburdening himself of the feelings he carried around for me, or was this his last-ditch effort in getting someone to help a compromised Crystal? Whatever it was, I sat there glued to my chair, giving Tom my undivided attention. I knew whatever he was going to tell me about his niece would either incriminate or absolve her. I just hoped for Crystal's sake that it was the latter.

"Well, I know I can trust you with my life, Sam," Tom whispered, as he stared blankly at his bag of food. "But I just didn't want you to be involved in any of this."

"Well, I'm a big girl, Tom," I blurted out. "I don't need a big strong man to save me from the big bad wolf. Fortunately, women nowadays can do more than just create problems. We can actually solve a few too," I said, as I stood and grabbed Tom a napkin, so he could wipe off the sauce from the burger that had dripped on his left cheek.

"Don't I know it!" Tom said with a smile. "I don't believe there's anything you can't do. That's why I'm telling you this, Sam, because honestly I'm not sure I can do this alone," Tom muttered as he gazed into my eyes.

As tempting as those big brown eyes are, I casually tried to disrupt the hypnotic attraction I was now under by asking Tom exactly what he'd done in his endeavor to try and protect his niece.

"Well, although I have a background in journalism, I didn't quite put two and two together when you initially showed me Ronda's photo," Tom said. "However, once we went to the Steamy Brew Coffee Shop and spoke to Crystal's boss, it all started to click. I soon realized that I'd seen that photo of Ronda before and it was on Crystal's screensaver of all places," Tom whispered, despondently.

For some reason, in that very moment a lightbulb went off in my brain, and I knew exactly where I'd seen that headband before I took it from Ronda's luggage earlier. *I was more than certain that I'd also seen a photo of Ronda on Crystal's screensaver as well*, I thought to myself. However, it wasn't just some random photo of Ronda. Funnily enough with Crystal being my favorite barista, she would often sit and chat with me when I was at the coffee shop having breakfast. I presume while chatting one day she must've sat her phone down on the table, causing the background to illuminate long enough for me to see the photo of Ronda who, coincidentally, just so happened to be wearing a pink headband with diamonds similar to the one I'd secretly taken from Crystal's bedroom just a few hours ago. *Things definitely kept pointing me in Crystal's direction*, I thought. However, I wasn't all together sure if Tom was insinuating that he knew about his niece having feelings for Ronda. So, in my roundabout way without betraying Crystal's trust, I asked Tom exactly what he thought the photo meant.

"It means that I was privy to the fact that Crystal wanted more than friendship from Ronda," Tom said matter-of-factly.

Well, since the cat was out of the bag and, technically, I hadn't divulged the secret that I'd promised to keep, I decided now was the perfect time to discover exactly who was telling the truth between Tom and Crystal.

"Would Crystal, wanting more than a friendship from Ronda, have been a problem for you?" I asked.

"Oh, absolutely not!" Tom said, adamantly. "I would've been happy for Crystal but for the fact that I knew this would've been a one-sided relationship, and I wasn't going to allow that," Tom said angrily.

Wait, what? I thought to myself. So, Crystal was wrong about the reason her uncle had for possibly wanting to kill Ronda but was right about the act itself? Was Tom actually about to tell me that he harmed Ronda to prevent Crystal from inevitably being hurt by her?

"I'm confused," I said to a now emotional Tom. "Crystal assumed you didn't know about her feelings that were starting to develop for Ronda, and even went as far as to say that she wanted to keep her secret from her stern and unyielding uncle," I said. "Truthfully, she all but insinuated that you certainly would've had a problem with who it was she was now becoming. So, are you now saying that you knew about Crystal's little crush the whole time?" I asked.

"Absolutely! I knew. Aside from the fact that I used to be a police officer, I've been in that girl's life since the day she was born and I've been a father figure to her since she was five years old. She couldn't keep a secret from me if she wanted to." Tom gave a long pause before reaching into his back pocket. "Unfortunately, she's no longer that same little girl who came into my home all those years ago," he said as he glanced at a photo from his wallet of a young Crystal perched up on his neck.

"Well, everyone grows up, Tom," I said. "It's a part of life. Heck, just look at the Grey Cougars; they're still growing!" I joked, trying to lighten the mood.

"It's not Crystal growing up that's the problem," Tom replied. "It's the fact that on any given day I can't be sure what version of her I'll be getting."

Not wanting to assume, although I was very aware that Crystal had recently started to display mood swings that'd make even the most loyal husband hide away in his mancave, I decided to ask Tom very delicately what he meant by getting different versions of Crystal.

After eating a few more fries, Tom went on to say that once Crystal started hallucinating and having trouble remembering things as they actually are, he knew he'd be in for a long week because he'd be dealing with the "not-so-pleasant-sick version of his niece."

"Crystal didn't lie to you," Tom continued. "Well, not intentionally anyway," he murmured as he corrected himself before drinking a big gulp of his slushy lemonade. "Crystal suffers from a personality disorder," Tom said. "She started showing signs a little more than a year ago. It was right around the time when Rebecca left with our kids. There was a lot of turmoil within our household at that time and I didn't know how to deal with it, so I drank. And when I realized that the problem was still there, I drank some more," Tom said, candidly.

Seeing how emotional Tom was getting while talking about Crystal, I realized that I myself was starting to become overwhelmed by empathy. Sure, I'm an emotional person, but more than that, I believe it's partially because I didn't just consider Crystal a barista at my favorite coffee shop. Somehow, over time she had become a close friend.

Holding Tom's hand, I told him that I had no inkling of Crystal's condition, then gave him my sincerest condolences for not being more perceptive. I mean, I figured something was off with Crystal when I last spoke with her in the park, but I never expected it to be something so life-changing.

As Tom sat directly across from me at my wobbly kitchen table, he looked as if there was more he needed to get off his chest. Knowing how therapeutic writing is for me, I started to get a gut feeling that talking openly like this was starting to give Tom that same sense of freedom. Although certain subjects were hard at times, I knew from personal experience that these were the type of things that you don't want to bottle up. So, unfortunately, I knew I needed to dive a bit deeper with Tom in order to get to the bottom of things.

"Crystal's condition answers a few questions," I said firmly. "However, you must've known the girl's rocky history would come into question, not to mention the fact that Crystal tried to destroy Ronda's reputation in the past. So why would you ever agree to broadcast Ronda's photo on Channel 18 News before ever having the chance to at least clear Crystal's name?" I asked.

"Well, I never agreed to anything being aired," Tom responded. "I went home early that day and my assistant handled that particular news story. Although, I *am* secretly glad it happened this way because I'm at my breaking point, and I can't afford to look like I'm hiding anything." With that, Tom sighed heavily.

All of a sudden, I started combining parts like a three-thousand-piece puzzle. "I think I've got it now!" I yelled confidently. "Tom, while you were in a panicked state you thought for a split second that your niece could be responsible for Ronda's murder. So, you went around town trying to retrace her steps until you realized you're no Barney Fife. That's when you beelined it to the nearest bar where I found you. Am I right so far?" I asked with enthusiasm.

"Yeah, about everything except the Barney Fife analogy. Where'd that even come from?" Tom asked with a confused look on his face.

"Oh, umm...never mind the reference; I heard some lunatic say it earlier today," I quickly blurted out, realizing that I didn't possess Susie's sharp tongue.

"My point is—you came to your senses and realized Crystal wasn't capable of murdering anyone," I whispered quietly. "However, I'm guessing that feeling guilty for even suspecting Crystal is how you ended up at the Tunnel Funnel Bar in an attempt to drown your sorrows," I said assuredly.

"That's impressive," Tom said. You should be on *Dateline* solving cold cases," he laughed. "Well, I'm not that good," I said modestly. "I can't seem to figure out what happened to Ronda, nor can I figure out why half the town is warning me to stay away from you," I said, causing Tom to hang his head.

"Sadly, Tom, some people seem to think you were involved in that poor girl's tragic demise," I said. "Fortunately for you, I'm not one of those people. However, I do need to know why you were spotted hanging around my house on multiple occasions by multiple people. *Please tell me*—is everything okay with you?" I knew Tom had never lied to me before and I was just hoping that he didn't start now. However, just in case he took the bait and tried to use Ronda's death anywhere in his answer, I was more than ready to hit that ball out of the park. It had only been a day since Ronda was murdered and Tom had been spotted hanging around my house way before then. *So, in no way should her murder influence his answer*, I thought to myself.

"You're right, Sam. I have been spotted at your house on more than one occasion," Tom said. "I-I just could never come up with the right words to say to you and the next thing I knew, I found myself d-driving by your house. But I'd always lose my nerve when it came time to knock on your door," Tom confessed. From his stammering, I could see he was barely able to get the words out. He went on to say that he'd just drive around in circles, hoping the words would come to him. Then he'd be able to run up to my front porch and quickly recite them to me. However, he said, the words never came, but the days came and went. At that moment, Tom appeared to be looking straight through to my soul. "I know I've done some pretty despicable things in my past," he said. "But I'm trying to learn and grow from them, however it just seems like certain people in St. Lux would rather see me crash and burn. "

That was certainly an earful, I thought to myself. I never fathomed for a second that Tom was behind my home being vandalized, nor did I think he was my creepy silhouette midnight stalker. However, it did feel good to put that theory to bed. And with Tom all but confirming a slight suspicion that was developing in the back of my mind about the townsfolk of St. Lux, I now thought it'd be wise to focus my energy on those who were starting to point the finger.

I felt in my gut that someone wanted Tom out of the equation, and whoever it was wasn't above leaving behind a great deal of collateral damage. "I don't think you were the original fall guy!" I blurted out to Tom. "I think we're looking for someone who wanted Crystal out of the way initially. But when that plan didn't work, sadly, they settled on you," I said, confidently.

Unfortunately, solving Ronda's murder won't be as easy as finding Tom's antagonist, I thought to myself. Even though half the town loved Tom for protecting the city when he was sworn in as an officer, there were those who had pure hatred in their hearts for him for the exact same reason. A former cop's enemy list could be a timely thing to try and dissect. I felt consumed by so many problems that I honestly thought the only way I'd see the other side was by starting a secret society and allocating a few of my affairs to someone who was better equipped at handling them. I was beyond exhausted and here it was almost 1:00 a.m.

Tom was still slightly inebriated and I was so sleep-deprived from stress that for a split second all I could see while looking at him was the Kool-Aid man. I didn't know if I should put him in the refrigerator or run. So, I figured sleep would be my best bet. I helped Tom into the spare bedroom and told him to hang around in the morning because our conversation ended on a cliffhanger, and I definitely needed closure. Before I could close the bedroom door, I heard him snoring.

Since Dee would be staying overnight in the hospital, I went into my bedroom where she had been for most of the day and jumped into bed. I could hear Maureen having a nightmare or something in the other spare bedroom, but I was too exhausted to move. Besides, my mind was constantly cycling between Ronda, Dee, and Sean. Truthfully speaking, there was nothing I could do for Ronda, aside from exposing her murderer. However, Dee and Sean were a completely different story. I hadn't seen Dee since we were kids and I had just recently learned about Sean's existence. But I knew with every fiber of my being, since both of them had already lost everything that was precious to them, there was no way was I going to relinquish what was left of those two angels without a fight.

CHAPTER FOURTEEN

The next morning, I was awakened by Daphne licking my face at exactly 5:45 a.m. I must've fallen asleep right after getting into bed last night because I don't recall her cozying up near my feet. Anyhow, after willing myself up, I walked into the laundry room and poured her a fresh bowl of granola.

I slowly staggered back into my bedroom because, if I'm being completely honest, nothing called to me more at 5:45 a.m. than an alluring, king-sized bed. However, no sooner did my head hit the pillow than I heard someone banging obnoxiously loud at my front door.

For goodness sakes, unless this is Jack coming back from the beyond, I'm going to be livid, I thought to myself. "The roosters aren't even awake yet," I mumbled fiercely as I made my way towards my front door. After I reached the living room, I moved the curtains aside so I could have a look at the maniac who was causing such a ruckus on my front porch. I discreetly peeked through the window and after we made eye contact, I can't say that I was the least bit surprised. It was Sheriff Hawkins and, boy, was he was furious. I knew there was no easy way out of this one, threatening a Deputy Sheriff and all to get a troubled kid released into my custody. So, I just bit down on my metaphorical mouthpiece and prayed that I'd come out unscathed.

"Top of the morning to you," Sheriff Hawkins, I said, as I opened my front door.

"Where's the kid? "Sheriff Hawkins blurted out.

"Oh, do you mean Sean?" I asked.

"No, I mean Ralphie from *A Christmas Story*," Sheriff Hawkins sarcastically said.

As I stood there unable to control my laughter, I noticed that the Sheriff wasn't in a joking mood. So, I quickly apologized, then explained that he'd caught me off-guard with that Ralphie comeback. In my heart I knew Sean had done nothing wrong, but the look on Sheriff Hawkins's face all but said he wanted to lock him up and throw away the key.

"Well, may I ask what this is this about, Sheriff?" I said, as I started to feel like a mother bear trying to protect her cub. "This wouldn't have anything to do with his vagrancy charge, would it? Because he's no longer homeless," I added candidly.

"Yes, I know, I've already talked with my Deputy," Sheriff Hawkins replied. "He told me about you putting the boy up and he also told me about you making a scene down at the station. Now I was patient with you before, Mrs. Harris, because I don't think you're involved. But if you want us to catch your friend's murderer, you have to let us do our jobs," Sheriff Hawkins said intensely. "I'm gonna need you to stay out of the way and I know it's difficult to let someone else take control, but I can assure you if Rodney Lucas gave my Deputy an order to hold someone in police custody, there must be a good reason," Sheriff Hawkins said firmly. "Whatever the boy did I don't know and quite frankly I don't care, but on the flip side, if he's innocent, he has nothing to worry about."

Sensing the Sheriff had orders even he had to follow, I didn't get the feeling he was willing to leave without Sean. So, I had to think quick on my feet. "Well, he's still asleep right now," I said. "However, if you let me talk to him first and get him some breakfast, then afterwards, I'll bring him down to the police station myself," I said persuasively.

Sheriff Hawkins, not having just fallen off the turnip truck, agreed to those conditions, but not before asking to verify Sean's whereabouts.

Oh, geez, I thought to myself. Lying to the Sheriff could end badly for me. Unfortunately, I never fully understood the concept of poker, so I continued with my bluff.

"He's in the back bedroom sleeping," I said as the Sheriff forcefully entered my front door. Then as we walked down the hallway, I started to sweat bullets, while thinking to myself the whole time: *What are you doing? Just call this thing off. You know Sean's not in there.* As we reached the bedroom door where Sean was allegedly sleeping, I watched as Sheriff Hawkins turned the handle, then pushed the door open. His plumped body blocked most of my view into the bedroom, and as soon as I was about to open my mouth to tell him the truth, I got a glance inside.

Lo and behold! There was Sean sound asleep in bed. *What in the world is going on here? Where did he come from?* I thought to myself. Refusing to show any signs that anything was wrong, I acted as cool as a cucumber until I could get the Sheriff out of my front door.

"Told you, Sheriff; he's in there sleeping like a baby," I said cheerfully.

"Well, I have orders to follow and I needed to put my mind at ease and see for myself," Sheriff Hawkins said as he followed me back towards my front door.

"Hey, Sheriff, while I've got you, do you have any leads on Ronda's case?" I asked as we stood at my front door. "You never called me last night and I never got the chance to finish my statement down at the station either," I muttered, while praying that the police were a little closer in figuring out just who this maniac was.

"Oh, I do apologize, Mrs. Harris," Sheriff Hawkins responded. "But I was tying up a few loose ends. You wouldn't believe the amount of work that comes with being the Sheriff of such a small town. It completely slipped my mind that I was supposed to phone you. However, I can assure you that my officers are working diligently on your friend's case," he said, passionately.

"I completely understand how the day can get away from you, Sheriff," I replied. "With the bomb hoax and whatever happened last night that sent every police car in St. Lux racing towards Main Street...I'm not one bit surprised that your schedule got pushed back an entire day. Funny enough, I also had a pretty eventful day myself yesterday,"

"Speaking of eventful days, it looks as if I'm needed at a domestic disturbance right now," Sheriff Hawkins said frantically after taking a moment to answer the dispatcher on his radio. "But I'll tell you what, Mrs. Harris, how about you swing by my office when you bring the kid down to the station? Then we can wrap up your statement and I'll be able to give you an update on your friend's case."

"Sounds good to me," I said. "I'll see you later, Sheriff," I shouted out as Sheriff Hawkins walked back to his extremely dirty patrol car.

"Whew!" I sighed, closing my front door. That was about as close a call as my heart could handle. A random chance encounter with St. Lux's finest set my heart racing, but it seemed to work wonders for my fatigue because I felt as rested as a vampire in spring during daylight savings time.

As I walked into the kitchen, I suddenly remembered that I still hadn't played that awful voicemail for the Sheriff. I guess, with trying to clear Jack's name—along with everything that's happened since Ronda's death—I completely forgot that I'd even had it. And I'm sure the Sheriff had a million things running through his mind, so he hadn't thought of it either. But since I was seeing him later, I figured I'd deal with one problem at a time. I decided to make a cup of tea and some toast for breakfast, while pondering the question, *What am I going to do with Sean?* I mean, surely, I couldn't hold him here against his will. That'd be no better than Rodney throwing him in a dingy holding cell, although I did grow up with four older brothers who used threats and intimidation against me whenever I thought I wanted to get out of line. But I never really had the chance to use such scare tactics myself since I was the baby in the family. Still, I figured if I could scare Sean straight, then it'd be worth a shot.

While my bread was warming in the toaster I ran into my bedroom and grabbed my phone. I wanted to call the hospital to see if there had been any change in Dee's condition. Looking at my phone, I noticed I had one missed text message from my friend Michelle Lewis, and it appeared to come through shortly after I went to bed last night.

I clicked on the message and it read, '*Sorry about the confusion, Sam, but Max can be quite maddening at times. We're just getting back home and fortunately he's fine. However, I just wanted you to know that I got the tape recorder you left on my front porch and I'll be pulling an overnighter trying to figure out who the prints belong too. Sleep tight, and I'll call you tomorrow.*'

Michelle was an angel in disguise and, boy, was I glad to hear the good news about Max. Lately, it seemed like the smallest snippet of positive news was all the reinforcement I needed to keep me going. If nothing else, it certainly ignited a fire within me to know that there were other people in the world who wanted good to prevail.

After walking back into the kitchen and buttering my toast, I heard the floor in the hallway start to creak. So, I peeked into the hall area while still standing in the kitchen to see Sean walking towards me.

"Good morning, Mrs. Harris," Sean said with the biggest smile on his face. "Well, I must say even though I was initially a little bit wary about coming into your home last night, I ended up sleeping like a baby. Did you sleep okay, Mrs. Harris?" Sean asked.

He isn't serious, I thought to myself. He left at God knows what hour last night, then comes galloping back in here like a thief in the night, and now he has the audacity to ask me how I slept. Boy, was I ever furious, and I wasn't sure how well I could hide it after tossing and turning all night, worrying myself sick thinking about the things that could've happened to Sean. Now I find out that after coming back in from having his night out on the town, he was safe and sound in my spare bedroom the whole time. As I stood there fuming, I thought now more than ever would be the perfect time to use my brother's scare-the-bejesus-out-of-you approach.

"Sean, maybe I wasn't clear in the conversation we had while driving to McClucky's last night," I said calmly. "But when I mentioned that you'd be staying with me for a while, I thought it was implied that you could no longer roam the streets at all hours of the night."

"Oh, there's a good reason for that, Mrs. Harris," Sean blurted out, interrupting me.

Unfortunately, I wasn't in the mood to be deterred. So, I hit him with one of my mother's favorite lines when I was a child, "I'm sorry, Sean," I said politely, "but, this is the point in the conversation where I talk and you listen." Sensing I had him on the ropes, I thought now would be the perfect time to go in for the finish. If the only way I could keep him safe was by using my family's unorthodox approach to the tough love method, then that's exactly what I was going to do.

After scolding Sean for the next five minutes, I told him I needed to go to the hospital and check on a friend, then I leaned over and nonchalantly whispered to him, "If you're not in this house when I get back, once I find you I'm gonna break your legs. And I'm not just going to break them a little bit; I'm going to break them a lot. Am I understood?" I said firmly, referencing Sean's favorite phrase that was printed on his t-shirt.

"I've never understood anything more in my life," Sean said, agreeably.

Feeling triumphant, I told Sean that I wouldn't be long, then headed out the front door. *Wow! What a high I'm on,* I thought to myself. That take-no-prisoners attitude was exactly what I needed going forward. I hate to say it, but I felt indestructible.

I decided to take Tom's van as it was still blocking my car. Upon arriving at the hospital, I noticed that the nice receptionist, Laura, from last night wasn't stationed at the front desk. I walked over to the woman who was currently there and who, by the way, looked as fierce as Laura did last night, and I asked her if it would be alright if I saw my friend today.

"Well, of course, sweetie. What's your friend's name?" the woman asked. After giving her all of Dee's information, the woman told me she was in room 210 and handed me a visitor's pass.

The simplicity of this interaction compared to last night with Laura definitely made me think the woman committed an error somewhere along the way. However, if it was going to get me to Dee's room to find out what happened to her, then I wasn't going to harp on it.

As I got off the elevator and approached room 210, I noticed that Dee was finally awake. However, once she turned her head and saw me, she instantly started to cry. She told me how the doctors had to pump her stomach to save her life but said other than a sore throat and feeling some mild discomfort she was miraculously okay. I leaned over Dee's bed and proceeded to give her the warmest hug. I couldn't believe I hadn't seen my old childhood friend in nearly thirty years. However, the love I'd felt for her certainly had no expiration date. As I pulled up a chair and sat in front of Dee's bed, I told her everything would be okay, even though I wasn't entirely convinced of that myself.

Sensing I had a very short window to get answers out of Dee before she completely shut down due to the unrelenting sorrow she was experiencing, I leaned forward in my chair and grabbed her hand before asking her if she remembered taking any pills at my house yesterday.

"Maybe you woke up while I was gone and needed something to help you get back to sleep?" I asked. I was hoping she wasn't the culprit who had Jack's insomnia pills scattered all over my back lawn, so I posed the question as gently as I could because I just had to know the truth.

"You know, it's funny, Samantha. I don't remember much about yesterday, Dee said, staring blankly into my eyes. "However, I guess that's due to the fact that I never dreamt in a million years that I'd have to recall such events that coincided with my daughter's death. She was supposed to bury me!" Dee cried out, "I'll never forgive the monster responsible!" she screamed as she buried her face in her hands.

Oh, boy, I thought to myself. With everything Dee's been through lately, I wasn't sure if I could completely rule out that self-medicating theory, but I was sincerely hoping that she didn't do this to herself.

"So, you don't remember anything out of the ordinary happening yesterday, or were you feeling at all ill at any point?" I asked.

"To tell you the truth, Samantha," a now more subdued Dee said, "I was too heartbroken hearing about Ronda to even worry about what was happening to me. I can't say I remember much leading up to that point. And to be honest, I'm still a bit fuzzy about what happened afterwards for that matter."

"Well, that's completely understandable," I said, compassionately. "You shouldn't have to worry about anything other than having a proper burial for your daughter. I'll handle the rest."

"Speaking of Ronda..." Dee murmured as she sat up, "I was just getting ready to go and identify her body. I was told she's in the morgue in this hospital and I simply can't go another minute knowing my daughter is lying in some cold damp basement, waiting to be identified. I have to go and say goodbye. Will you come with me, Samantha?" Dee pleaded.

Completely caught off guard but sincerely honored, I told Dee it would be my pleasure. However, as Dee stood up, we both quickly came to the conclusion that walking wasn't in her best interest. So, I ran out into the hallway and spotted a wheelchair tucked away in the corner. I wheeled it into Dee's room just as she was ending a call on her room phone, then we headed towards the elevator.

I presumed the phone call Dee made was to notify someone that she was ready to identify the body because a few steps after walking towards the elevator, the doors opened and we were greeted by the Medical Examiner.

"Hello," the man said casually to Dee and I. "Is one of you ladies Daphne Evans?" he asked.

"Yes, I am," Dee replied. "So, I guess it's safe to assume that you're Mr. White," Dee said.

'Yes!" the man shouted out as he appeared to answer with extreme pride. "My name is Scott White. I'm sorry to meet your acquaintances under such circumstances. However, as the Hospital's Medical Examiner, I'll need to be with you when you make the identification. Has anyone informed you of how this all works?" Scott asked.

"Well, I do recall hearing about the process, but I can't say that I remember much about it," Dee whispered.

"No worries," Scott said. Then he proceeded to give a thirty-minute tutorial on the entire process, and just in case we had the memory of a chimpanzee, he gave a refresher course on the elevator ride down. Once we got to the basement and the elevator doors opened, I noticed I was as jumpy as a kangaroo. My mind went racing back to just over a year ago in this very same hospital when I had to say farewell to someone that I loved. Now for reasons that I couldn't understand, I was back here and a dear friend of mine was about to have the same farewell speech with her daughter that I'd had with Jack quite some time ago. That haunts me till this day.

"Wait here!" Scott yelled as he walked through a stainless-steel swinging door. Once he came back, he ushered us into a room that had only a table and two chairs in it. So, I wheeled Dee over in front of the table and sat in the chair beside her.

As Scott entered the room, he told Dee he was going to show her a photo so she could identify the deceased.

"Oh, no Mr. White," Dee shouted. "I have to physically see her so that I can say goodbye."

In that moment, as Scott looked at the pain on Dee's face, he restored my faith in humanity. Not only did he break the rules he'd just given us in that thirty-minute spiel but he also didn't hesitate in letting a grieving mother say goodbye to her slain daughter. After agreeing to let Dee into his closed-off work space, Scott politely asked her not to disrupt the body. Unfortunately, I wasn't allowed to go in with her.

Well, maybe that's exactly what she needed, I thought to myself. Dee needed to say all of the things to Ronda that, unfortunately, she'd never have the chance to say again. I told her to be strong and that I loved her. Then Dee somehow mustered up the strength and walked the rest of the way to say her final goodbyes to her daughter.

Twenty minutes later, Dee was walking back out and instantly flopped back down into the wheelchair. I couldn't tell if she was smiling or crying at this point, so I just asked her if she was okay.

"Either I'm better than okay, or I've gone crazy," Dee responded.

"What do you mean?" I asked a more composed Dee.

"Well, I was horrified at first. But while I was talking to Ronda, she told me to stop my crying because she was in paradise," Dee said calmly.

"Oh well, that doesn't make you crazy," I replied. "You were looking at Ronda in a way that you'd never seen her before and I'm sure anyone's mind would go back to a much happier time," I said, sincerely.

"But her saying she was in paradise wasn't the weird part," Dee said intensely. "She also told me not to worry about catching the monster responsible for her death because you'd figure it out. Well, that is as long as Daphne isn't blocking the evidence," Dee said with the most confused look on her face. "It was a very weird exchange because my daughter doesn't call me by my first name," Dee proclaimed.

Oh, dear, that's not even the weirdest part of the story, I thought to myself. That was the exact premonition I'd had last night when I was trying to fall asleep. I only wish I knew what message Ronda was trying to convey when she said, "As long as Daphne wasn't blocking the evidence."

This was Ronda's second time in as many days essentially speaking from the beyond. *What did this all mean?* I asked myself. What was right in front of me that I wasn't seeing?

As I looked down at Dee sitting in that wheelchair, I whispered to her that I could feel it in my soul, and I knew I was getting pretty close to figuring out who was responsible for her daughter's murder.

"So, no!" I said emphatically, "I don't think you're crazy. In fact, I believe you're quite the contrary. Funnily enough, my dog's name is also Daphne and I'd mentioned that to Ronda the other day when I met her. However, what's really interesting is last night when I was having difficulty sleeping, Ronda came to me in a vision and we had a very similar exchange. I've been struggling with whether or not I should tell you," I said, as my eyes began to well up. "However, I just thought you'd been through so much already and you didn't need to hear about me having hallucinations about your daughter."

"You stop that crying, Samantha," Dee shouted as she wheeled herself over towards where I was standing. Then she lowered her voice and whispered passionately, "My daughter said she's in paradise and right now all I can do is take her word for it. So don't you dare feel guilty about her death, especially when the maniac who took her from me is somewhere out there showing no remorse."

As I wiped away tears, Dee reached out her arms and we embraced with a hug. She informed me that the doctors, unfortunately, wanted to keep her overnight again for more observation. But she said that she couldn't complain too much because she'd be adjacent to paradise where Ronda was currently residing.

I thought that was such a sweet way of dealing with an unfortunate loss. But the truth of the matter is nothing was ever going to bring Dee peace until she knew with absolute certainty who did this, and why.

The million-dollar questions were: Could I transform myself into the thing that made even the big bad wolf shiver? And did I have what it took to bring a murdering lunatic to justice?

As Dee and I waited for the elevator, she suddenly asked me how long it had been since Jack died.

"A little over a year now. Why do you ask?"

"Well, it's probably none of my business," Dee replied. "But when I was in my stupor as Tom brought me to the hospital I got the feeling that he was pretty smitten with you," Dee whispered.

"Oh, really! You figured that out under the influence and in all of a day, huh?" I said with a smile.

"Well, what's the matter, Samantha? You having trouble believing your best friend who you haven't seen in thirty years who's now grieving the loss of her only daughter, and who's more than likely still slightly stoned from God knows what drug? Okay, well now I totally understand your skepticism." Dee shook her head at me. "So, you should probably take the next few things I say with a grain of salt, you know, just until I'm in a better headspace."

I certainly was overjoyed to see Dee coming to terms with everything— even if it was just because she was feeling no pain because of her medication— but it seemed like everyone who was aware of Tom's little crush on me either suggested that I stay far away from him or they had us off in fairytale land building a house with a white picket fence. There was no wiggle room and it scared me half to death.

After getting off the elevator, I held the door open and told Dee that I'd be back later with some food that she could stomach. She gave me a slight giggle, then said, "That would be nice." I gave her one more hug for the road and told her to call me once she talked to her doctors, then watched as the elevator doors shut between us.

It was almost 8:00 a.m. now and I was on my way to the family court. I wanted to get a jump on filing the custody case for Sean, and I was hoping that I'd be granted temporary custody. However, in my mind, I could hear the judge laughing at me. I was a widow, I had no other children in the home, and the only thing I'd ever taken care of was Daphne and plants. I was trying to pull off the impossible for sure with asking to raise a teen who seemingly didn't trust adults.

As I drove towards the courthouse, I knew I'd be passing McClucky's, so I decided to stop and get Mr. Black and Sean some breakfast. After paying for my order and getting everyone's food, my cellphone begin to ring. I noticed on my caller I.D. that the number appeared to be from a payphone. So, I pulled over in the parking lot after leaving the drive-thru window to answer the call. That's when I heard a distressed Tom yelling at me to get back home. "What is it, Tom?" I asked frantically. "What's happened?"

Tom informed me that his former boss and the man who was soon about to be my former friend, Rodney Lucas, was at my house. Tom said that Rodney was arresting Sean for vandalism.

The nerve of that man, I thought to myself. They couldn't hold Sean for vagrancy, so he found something a little more concrete. "I'm on my way home, Tom," I said in a flustered tone. "Get back there and stop this if you can!" I shouted.

After ending the call, I pulled out of McClucky's parking lot, wondering if Sean was ever going to catch a break. *Well, there's no way I could worry about going to the courthouse now,* I thought to myself. I had to make sure there'd be a kid left to gain custody of after all of this was over. All I could think about was

Sean reaching his breaking point because I knew if that happened, it would ultimately lead him down a road of self-destruction.

As I drove home, the question that constantly crossed my mind was, *What was Rodney hiding?* I mean I'd certainly never imagined Rodney being involved in a murder before, but the level of dedication he showed in keeping Sean away from me, well, it was enough to convince me that the most dangerous people are the ones who can't afford to have their skeletons exposed. I didn't know if Sean mother's murder was somehow connected to Ronda's, but I certainly wasn't above disrupting Rodney's world to find out whether he was involved in either.

CHAPTER FIFTEEN

I pulled into my driveway just as Tom was running through my front door. Instinctively, I rushed in behind him, but as I entered I heard him say it was too late. Rodney Lucas had captured Sean. My house was a complete disaster and it looked like Sean put up quite the fight to not to be taken in by that hoodlum, who obviously used his connections down at the police station for his own personal interest.

In that moment, all I could feel was guilt because now for the second time I'd left Sean all by himself, and essentially fed him to the wolves of St. Lux. I couldn't remember ever feeling so discouraged. I turned around while looking at Tom, then hollered, "I give up, I can't win! Every time I take a step forward, I not only get knocked back a step but I also get knocked down. I don't know what I was thinking running around town like a vigilante. I can't do this anymore. I can't help anyone," I muttered in the most pitiful tone.

"Am I supposed to feel sorry for you?" Tom said matter-of-factly. "There's no way you're going to help anyone with that attitude. But I'll tell you what, Samantha..." Tom said, as he walked towards me, "You behaving like a vigilante when half the town wanted to persecute me is the only reason I didn't drink myself into a drunken stupor last night. Samantha, you not only saved my life but you also helped me to see that it's far too precious not to fight for it," Tom said, passionately.

"Oh, I appreciate your kind words, Tom. Nevertheless, I'm just your *standard woman* who's shown time and time again that I'm out of my element. I can't even keep that poor kid safe," I said, feeling dejected.

"Oh, boohoo!" Tom mocked me. "Samantha, I've watched you pick yourself up and dust yourself off too many times to count. You did it after Jack died and you continue to do it. Truthfully, as your friend I noticed how disconnected from life you were back then and how you looked as if you had nothing left to give, although you eventually pushed forward until life wasn't a chore anymore. I know you can do it again, so no more excuses!" Tom shouted as he grabbed my hand. "If you want me to stand here and agree with you that you're some *standard woman,* then that's just too bad because in my eyes not only are you not standard but you're also the type of woman who sets the standards" Tom said, as tears ran down my face.

"So, what do you say?" Tom yelled as he reached for my other hand. "Let's go get the boy out of jail and put the actual dirtbags who belong there underneath it."

As I looked into his eyes, his endearing speech inspired but one response from me. "Okie Dokie Macaroni!" I shouted, drawing a smile out of him. As I continued wiping away tears, I asked Tom if he'd seen Maureen emerge from the other spare bedroom this morning.

"Well, to tell you the truth, Sam, I had no idea she was even here."

"Oh, no worries, she's a hard sleeper, so she's probably still back there in bed," I replied. "Still, every time I turn around, I'm someone's unwilling participant in the most convoluted game of hide and seek," I griped out of frustration. "I'd better go check on her." As I walked down the hall and opened the bedroom door, the words just flew out with no hesitation.

"Yup, this looks about right," I murmured. Maureen was gone, and I was staring at an empty bed. It was as if I was in a horror movie but the audience wanted the villain to emerge victorious. I felt as if I was always a step behind whoever was responsible for all of this carnage. However, now I wasn't sure if I could even trust my good friend Maureen. I mean, I figured she'd slept her hangover off and had gone into work this morning. But she was obviously disappearing at the most inopportune times, then popping back up just long enough for me to erase her name off my suspect list. *Last night she could barely speak*, I thought to myself. Now for the second time in as many days, she's up and disappeared. Things just weren't adding up for me, and sadly, now I didn't have my best friend around to run and talk to about them. So, I decided to use that excess energy as fuel. I figured it couldn't hurt to have a little extra oomph and to have an advantage over the killer for a change.

I asked Tom to give me five minutes, then I ran out to his van and grabbed Mr. Black's breakfast which I'd promised him yesterday. I knocked on his front door and he answered with the biggest smile on his face. He hugged me like I'd never been hugged before and I thought the warm embrace was a bit odd until he opened his mouth.

"Sandra, it's so good to see you," Mr. Black shouted out while addressing me by his daughter's name. "We've got so much to talk about. But who's the pretty boy standing by your van?" Mr. Black whispered, referring to Tom.

Oh, here we go, I thought to myself. I knew what this was. Mr. Black was currently going through one of his dementia episodes. Luckily for me, I had the Midas Touch when it came time to getting Mr. Black back on track.

I found that sitting him down and telling him old war stories he used to describe in great detail to Jack and I about his time in the service really seemed to do the trick. He probably told us hundreds of stories over the years, and I'd always sit there completely dumbfounded to be in an actual war hero's presence. If being a little over the top and thinking outside of the box was good enough to help Tom, then I was certainly willing to give it a go to help the rest of my friends in need. So, I sat Mr. Black's McClucky's breakfast on his coffee table, then grabbed his hand, and sat with him on the sofa.

I started to remind him about all the wonderful things that he'd done in his past, and two stories in I seemed to have a breakthrough. Something in his eyes changed and he no longer looked confused.

"Samantha, did I go off my rocker again?" Mr. Black asked.

"Just a little bit," I chuckled.

"Well, I'm sorry for scaring you, Samantha, but not as sorry as I am that I can't remember the tiniest snippet of it, because you know how I love a good laugh," Mr. Black said, while grabbing a big slice of bacon from his McClucky's bag.

"You're going to give me a heart attack, old man," I retorted.

After laughing at Mr. Black, I stood up and walked over to his dining room table, then grabbed his medication. I knew he'd rather eat chalk than take his pills, so I stood there and watched as he choked them down with the big gulp of coffee that I'd brought him. When I'd verified that he'd swallowed his pills, I told him that I had a few errands to run but reiterated that I was only a phone call away if he needed anything.

"Who are you, again?" Mr. Black shouted.

As I stood there trying to think of another war story that would get Mr. Black back into the right headspace, he suddenly yelled, "I'm just kidding ya, Samantha! Now go, get out of here, I'll be fine," he said as he walked me towards his front door.

However, before getting outside I purposely stepped on Mr. Black's foot. *That'll teach him* I thought to myself. I just wished I had on heels.

Once outside, I ran over toward Tom's van where he was still standing. By now it was almost 8:30 a.m. and I figured we needed to get a move on if we were going to help anyone. But as I approached Tom and asked him if he was ready to go, he informed me that Crystal was on her way to meet him at my house.

"She's coming here!" I blurted out.

"Supposedly," Tom said as he handed me my phone. "While you were helping your neighbor, I heard your cellphone ringing and it happened to be Crystal calling. I answered and asked her to meet me here so we could talk. Do you mind if I catch up with you later?" Tom asked.

"No, I guess not. However, when the time comes—and I'll tell you when—I'm going to need a huge favor from you, with no questions asked," I said with a smirk.

After getting into Tom's van, I felt something just wasn't sitting right with yet another disappearing act by Maureen. I couldn't quite put my finger on what I thought the issue was, but I knew something was off, so I decided to go over to her apartment before heading to the police station to get Sean.

Arriving, I decided to give her a call, but she still didn't answer. So, I thought to use my emergency key again. While holding my breath and praying to God, I yanked on the door and miraculously it opened this time. As I walked up the stairs and opened her apartment door; right in front of me was a confused-looking Maureen lying on her sofa, I noticed that she looked completely disheveled. Her apartment appeared like a war zone and I didn't have to be a bloodhound to smell that she hadn't showered in a few days. I knew I needed to help Sean but being around that kid even for a day I knew he could persevere for a while on his own. Maureen, on the other hand, was in such bad shape that she looked one head spin away from an exorcism.

"Maureen!" I yelled as I inched closer towards her. "What's going on? Are you acting out because you've been drinking?" I asked, assuming that's what brought about her erratic behavior last night.

"You know I don't drink anymore, Samantha." Maureen said, "I'm just not feeling well."

Well, at least things were starting to look up, I thought to myself. Those two sentences were probably the most I'd gotten out of Maureen since last night. Then it hit me, as I stood there looking at a discombobulated Maureen that last night when she was staring into space looking out my patio doors, I only assumed she was inebriated. I never considered the fact that she could've been poisoned. But now, come to think of it, Maureen appeared to be showing similar symptoms as Dee. And since I now knew that Dee had been poisoned, it was very possible that Maureen had been too.

What lunatic is going around town poisoning all of these innocent people? I asked myself. I guess I had to figure out that part once I knew Maureen was okay.

As I helped her into Tom's van, I knew whatever Maureen had been poisoned with, she obviously didn't consume as much as Dee. She didn't appear to be as sick and she certainly didn't look as though she wasn't capable. It was apparent just from looking at the two women that Maureen led a much healthier lifestyle, and it certainly appeared as if she had more energy to muscle through when her body so clearly wanted to shut down. I went back inside and grabbed Maureen's purse, cellphone, and phone charger before we made our way to the hospital. Upon arriving, I ran inside and told the first doctor I spotted that I had someone in my car who had possibly been poisoned.

I think it was safe to assume that two women who'd been in the same house, now exhibiting the same symptoms would certainly be enough to get my picture up on the wall with the word "suspect" in huge print underneath it. So, as the doctors rushed over to Tom's van and placed Maureen on the gurney, I yelled out that I'd be back to see her later. I knew whatever was going on with Dee and Maureen that they'd be safer in a hospital than anywhere near me right now. So, after watching Maureen get wheeled away, I took off and headed to the police station. Inside, I noticed Charlie sitting at the front desk drinking a soda. The tension in the lobby was as thick as mash potatoes made by yours truly.

This place had definitely worn him out within the last twenty-four hours and I think it had something to do with that TV news interview he did with David Holtz, and the bomb threat he took responsibility for.

Until now I never realized what a big ball of energy Charlie actually was, and without his crazy antics to make even the most toughened person laugh, the police station seemed lifeless. However, something in my gut was telling me that Charlie had come to his senses and he no longer wanted to take the fall for something he didn't do. Unfortunately, once Charlie attached his name to the story and it was out there, wheeling it back in wasn't going to be so easy.

It appeared as though the officers began to shun Charlie because of this wishy-washy attitude he possessed. First, he said he was responsible for the bomb hoax. Now, looking at him, I could tell all he wanted to do was yell from the rooftop that he wasn't the culprit. Unfortunately, it was this back and forth that was making for one harsh work environment. Well, I didn't need to tell a distressed-looking Charlie the reason for my visit because as I approached his desk he informed me that he'd just buzzed the Sheriff. So, while I sat waiting for Sheriff Hawkins, I asked Charlie why he'd taken responsibility for the bomb hoax yesterday when it was apparent that he knew as much about bombs as I did.

"Oh, you watched that interview?" Charlie said casually. "Well, it's just a little study I was doing, and I just wanted to see how far I could push the envelope without actually confessing to a crime."

"Umm, the last time I checked, Charlie," I said sarcastically, "blowing a bunch of people to smithereens with a bomb is a crime. Besides, your reaction told me that you didn't even know there was a bomb scare until after David Holtz told you so," I added forcefully.

"Well, I guess I'm a pretty good actor, sis," Charlie muttered, sending chills down my spine as I remembered him professing the fact that I was like a sister to him.

After a few minutes, I noticed Sheriff Hawkins walking into the lobby. By this time, I was starting to rethink my entire position on Charlie. I presumed with Charlie's gift to fool anyone at the drop of a dime that he probably had one last hurrah left in him. Regrettably for me, I didn't know if I should classify him as an antihero or a suspect.

"Well, hello there, Mrs. Harris. Looks like you didn't have to bring that kid in after all," Sheriff Hawkins shouted.

"It would appear so," I said sharply.

"Well, you can come down to my office if you'd like to finish giving me your statement about Crystal Miller."

"Actually, if you don't mind, I'd like to see Sean first," I said firmly.

"Well, no I don't mind at all. Although, as Sheriff I do have to follow proper protocols and, technically you're not supposed to be back here. However, since you're helping me out, I'll let you have this one," Sheriff Hawkins whispered while smiling. While thinking of Sean, I asked the Sheriff if he knew anything about the unusual circumstances surrounding the death of his mother, Nina Griffin.

"I can't say that I'm familiar with that case," Sheriff Hawkins said. But I'll certainly look into it and see what I can find out."

"That'd be great, Sheriff," I said cheerfully.

"Oh, before you leave, can you point the way to the holding cells, Sheriff? I'm completely turned around back here," I said, a little embarrassed. After Sheriff Hawkins pointed me in the direction opposite the Yellow Brick Road, he then told me to make a left once I came upon the first hallway.

"Oh, thank you," Sheriff, I said gratefully. "I won't forget this."

As I walked down the hall, I could finally see the holding cells and I realized the drunk from last night was gone, and Sean was in there by himself.

"Sean, are you okay?" I asked in a panicked state.

"Mrs. Harris!" Sean cried out as he jumped up from the metal bench he was lying on. "Is that you?" he yelled.

I instantly closed my eyes to thank God he was okay, and the next thing I saw when I opened them was a fretful Sean already at the cell bars.

"Wow, I can't believe this," I heard Sean mutter.

"What is it?" I asked frantically. "Are you hurt?"

"No, I'm fine, Mrs. Harris." Sean replied. "I just never imagined I'd be so happy to see someone whose last words to me were, 'I'm going to break your legs,'" Sean said with a smile.

"Well, that kind of still holds true because technically you did leave the house before I got back," I said, teasing him.

"Do you think you can you get me out of here, Mrs. Harris?"

"I'm going to do everything in my power," I asserted. "I know that you're scared, Sean, but I need you to hold on just a little while longer for me. I feel like I'm starting to make progress but I'm going to need you to be strong and not just a little bit, but a lot," I said, as I reached my hand through the metal bars and grazed his shoulder.

Sean smiled then said, "I can do that for you, Mrs. Harris."

I informed Sean that I was planning on talking to Rodney Lucas as soon as I left the police station in an attempt to get him to drop the vandalism charges. I soon realized that I needed to do a bit of groveling to a man who, quite frankly, I was starting to despise. It was a tremendous effort to have to go through in order to get someone out of jail for pulling a childish prank. However, I was up for the task because, unfortunately, Rodney was the only person I knew who possibly had any intel on Nina Griffin's murder, and I wanted answers.

As Sean and I sat there talking, he told me he had no idea that Jack and I were married. He'd mentioned that he secretly followed Jack home one day and pretty much assumed he was a bachelor because he never saw anyone else at the house while he was casing it.

"You followed Jack?" I asked. "From where?" I whispered.

"He was at a gas station one day and I recognized the truck as being the same one that the person who killed my mother drove away in," Sean answered. He went on to say that the police wouldn't help him so he started his own investigation and he found out where Jack lived.

"Go on, Sean," I murmured. "What else did your investigation turn up?"

"Well, some things are still unclear to me. But, with you by my side, I know maybe we can figure it out together."

"You'll always have me by your side," I said with a smile. "And I'll gladly help you figure it out, Sean, but time's not on our side. So can you think of anything else you discovered once you were at my house?" I whispered.

"No, not really," Sean said as he looked to be in deep thought. "Well, I had a key, a very small key," Sean said. "It belonged to whoever killed my mother, and I would sometimes sneak into what I thought was only Jack's house at the time and try to open things small enough that I thought the key would fit. I wanted concrete proof before going back to the police," Sean explained.

"Well, did that key ever open anything?" I asked.

"No! It never did."

"So, what happened to the key, Sean?" I asked warily.

"I lost it in outside playing with your dog one day," Sean said. "That's why I hurried across the street when you were outside playing fetch with her on your front stoop. I thought she'd notice me and give me away," Sean muttered.

Well, Sean was absolutely blowing my mind. *I'm not sure if I'm ready for all of this*, I thought to myself. But I was nothing if not a fast learner and I now knew that the key Daphne dropped on my kitchen floor yesterday was the very key that Sean had lost. It belonged to the individual responsible for his mother's murder, and I now had it in the pocket of the pants I wore yesterday.

"I should apologize to you, Mrs. Harris," Sean said emotionally.

"You should apologize to me," I repeated. "Sean, you have nothing to apologize for."

"Well, I accused your husband of something awful," Sean whispered. "I didn't know him, but I'm sure I would've liked him. And I'm positive if he was married to you, then there's no way he's responsible for my mother's death," Sean said, candidly.

With tears starting to fill my eyes, I thanked Sean from the bottom of my heart and promised him we would bring the monster who was responsible for the death of his mother to justice. I told Sean that he'd probably never seen me while casing my house because I had the tendency to stay after school, so that no student ever fell behind. I explained to him that although the truck in question was indeed Jack's, he allowed everyone in town to drive it. From friends who went fishing and needed extra space to families that went up north and needed to pull a trailer, almost everyone in St. Lux drove that truck at one time or another. Finding the person who had it on the night of Sean's mother's murder would be like looking for a needle in a haystack. However, if I was right about what I thought happened to Ronda, it would certainly give me the confidence to look into Sean's mother's case. Sitting there, I had the most outrageous idea. If Sean was watching my house, then maybe he saw the killer without realizing it.

After all, my theory of the killer trying to shut me up by isolating me was plausible. *Especially since all of my friends were starting to look like patsies,* I thought to myself. This left the door wide open for the actual killer to try and intimidate me (or so they thought) with broken windows and threatening notes.

"Sean, how long have you been watching my house and did you, in fact, see who broke my window the other night?" I asked.

"Yes, I did," Sean replied. "However, it wasn't me, if that's what you're thinking."

"Who was it, Sean?" I asked, nervously.

Well, I couldn't believe who he'd named. In that moment, I had a chilling suspicion of who the killer actually was, but I thought it was about time I had a little fun of my own. I was about to show this lunatic that I was the thing nightmares were made of.

CHAPTER SIXTEEN

As I sat there in the police station with Sean on the wrong side of the bars, a million thoughts went racing through my mind. I knew I only had one shot at this, so I had no intentions of blowing my investigation with only circumstantial evidence. I needed proof, and lots of it.

"Sean, I have to go for a while, but I'll be back in a few hours to get you out of here," I said. "I'll be here," Sean retorted, as I tried my best to give him a hug through the bars.

When I turned around to walk out, something was still bugging me that I couldn't quite shake. Knowing I needed a clear head for the dangerous mission I was about to carry out, I asked Sean straight out for the answer to the question that was baffling me.

"Sean, where did you go last night when you snuck out of the window?" I asked. "There's a crazed maniac running around town and you willingly put yourself in harm's way! Why?" I asked firmly.

"Oh, so you knew I snuck out of your window last night Mrs. Harris. Well, I guess it's safe to assume that my window's will now be boarded shut, huh," Sean asked hesitantly.

"Well, to be honest, I wasn't exactly sure how you snuck out of the house, but I'll advised you to never commit a crime if it's this easy to get you to sing," I said calmly. "Now spill it, Sean. Where'd you go last night?"

"Well, I-I went back to McClucky's..." Sean said as his voice begin to crack.

"Hmm...McClucky's," I repeated under my breath.

So, the girl at the drive-thru window was correct when she told me she'd seen Sean again last night, I thought to myself.

"Sean why did you sneak out of the house just to go and sit in McClucky's parking lot?" I asked.

"Well, it was a tradition my mom and I had after every little league base-ball game I scored in," Sean said, as he seemed to recall a few fond memories of his mother. "We'd go there and just pig out. However, now those are some of the only memories that come to mind when I think of her lately," Sean said, as he began to get even more emotional. "I know it may sound silly to associate my dead mother with a fast-food restaurant. But when I go there, I feel at peace. And I just wanted a little bit of that peace last night. "

"Oh, I completely understand," I said to the low-spirited Sean.

"You do, but, Mrs. Harris, you seem so put together!" Sean whispered with a confused look on his face.

"Oh, how I wish that were true," I said with a smile.

"My husband and I had a special place called Stepping Stone Park. Have you ever been?" I asked.

"I can't say that I have, but the name sure sounds awesome," Sean replied.

"Oh, it's heaven on Earth," I said. "I'll have to take you sometime, Sean. It's where Jack first proposed to me and it was one of his favorite places to go.

I sometimes go there now when the urge strikes and have long conversations with him. As a matter of fact, we just had a chat yesterday," I said cheerfully.

"Oh, wow, Mrs. Harris, it sounds like you're just as lost as I am," Sean said with a smile.

"Hey, we can all use a little guidance every once in a while," I replied. "I'm sorry, Sean, that I'll never get the chance to meet your mother. But I can attest to the fact that she raised an absolutely phenomenal young man and you should never feel silly for seeking out her guidance," I told him. "Just because we can't see them doesn't negate the fact that they're just one conversation away."

As Sean started to tear up, I noticed he pulled his arm back through the metal bars that separated us and wiped the tears away.

"How did you get so wise?" Sean asked.

"Oh, gosh, I don't know the answer to that," I replied. "Many years on this planet, I guess. As a matter of fact, some little snot nose rug rat just the other day called me, and I quote, 'like a hundred years old.'" As soon as the words left my mouth, Sean and I both had a hearty laugh.

A few minutes later, before I left, I tried giving Sean another big hug through the holding cell bars. Then I told him not to blink because I'd be back before he knew it. As I rushed down the hall heading towards Sheriff Hawkins's office, my phone began to chime, but this time it was a GPS notification. Once I came to a complete stop in the middle of the hall, upon further inspection I realized that it was Daphne's dog tracker. *How'd she get such a long way from home?* I panicked with worry. Then I remembered that I put Daphne's GPS tracker on Crystal's car bumper. Well, with everything that was going on, I'd forgotten all about it. However, with my phone now currently tracking Crystal, I'd realized she'd just given me an idea I never would've thought of on my own. And I needed reinforcements if I was going to do this thing right. I started running through the halls so fast I accidentally bumped into Sheriff Hawkins, almost knocking him down.

"Excuse me!" I shouted out as I helped the Sheriff find his balance. "However, you were just the man I was looking for," I boldly stated while trying to keep my composure as best I could. I knew with only having the one chance—to right this wrong—there was no way I was gonna let anyone stop me, including the Sheriff. So, I needed to think quick on my feet in order to try and restore some sort of justice in St. Lux because, honestly, I felt as if I were the only one who could at this point.

"What are you up to now, Mrs. Harris?" Sheriff Hawkins asked with the most uninspired look on his face.

"Umm... Okay, hear me out, Sheriff," I whispered while thinking of an excuse to hurry and get by him so I could set my plan in motion. "So, I've got this theory and I wanna test it out, but there's just too many moving components to explain everything right now, and time's not on my side. I need to run, but I'll give you a ring in exactly one hour," I shouted out as I continued to run through the halls like a woman on a mission.

If this plan was going to work, I need to get a move on, I thought to myself. I now felt as though I knew who Ronda's killer was, unfortunately, I needed hardcore proof to prove it and I wasn't going to let anything get in my way.

However, before leaving the lobby, I gave Charlie a death stare that would've frightened the pants off Bruce Lee. I wanted him to know that I was aware of what he'd done, and his innocent boyish charm wasn't going to get him out of this one.

Once I got to the parking lot, all of a sudden, I started to worry. I mean, I wasn't entirely sure if my foolproof plan was one hundred percent foolproof. So, lamentably, I knew I was going to have to enlist the help of someone who I wasn't quite fond of at the moment, Mr. Rodney Lucas.

Sadly, in my opinion, it seemed like Rodney was becoming desensitized to humanity and was just one step away from being a criminal himself. However, if exploiting Rodney for all of his connections would ultimately get me the result I'd had in mind, then I can't say I felt the least bit sorry about it.

I jumped in Tom's van and headed over to the Lucas residence. I wanted to make certain that I secured Sean's freedom before I set my plan in motion because if this thing went sideways, not only would there be no coming back from it, but there would also be hell to pay.

It was almost 10:00 a.m. when I arrived and Rodney was sitting on his front porch having a cigarette. I'd loved Rodney and his wife Kathleen since we were all kids in high school and aside from Jack, the Lucas's were two of the most trustworthy people I knew. However, lately Rodney was starting to come across as an entirely different person, and it was getting harder and harder to try and differentiate between the two.

"Hey, Rodney!" I yelled out as I walked over towards the porch and sat down.

"Good morning, Sam. You come to rip me a new one again?" Rodney asked sarcastically. "Actually, I came to see if we could work together," I replied. "Even though we haven't agreed on much lately, that shouldn't stop us from putting a killer behind bars," I said passionately. "However, if you agree, there is something that I'll need from you before we start. "

"Well, I'm all in, Sam. So, what is it that you need?" Rodney replied.

After taking a deep breath, I told Rodney that I didn't like the way Sean was treated after his mother's death, and I didn't gloss over the fact that I certainly didn't like how he was being treated now.

"Vandalizing your home was without question a bad decision and I'm going to make sure he works off that debt if you decide to drop the charges," I said. "However, Sean's just a scared kid who's heartbroken because he couldn't protect his mother, and his acting out shouldn't be met with contempt, especially when he's so clearly looking for compassion," I said, emotionally. "So, I need to know if something were to happen to me that you'll have Sean's best interest at heart," I whispered.

"Of course, Sam," Rodney replied. "I just wanted to scare the kid but I don't necessarily think he's a criminal."

"Oh, thank you, Rodney," I blurted out as I gave him the biggest hug.

"Wait a minute, Sam!" Rodney yelled as he pulled back from our embrace. "Did I just hear you say in case something happens to you? What exactly are you into? Is your life in danger?" Rodney asked with a worried look on his face.

"Well, let's just say I should probably start checking my brake lines before I get in my car," I responded.

"Oh, I don't like this, Samantha. I don't want anything happening to you," Rodney said as he shook his head in disapproval.

"I've got it all under control," I said. "I promise. "

"Well, I guess you're in too deep at this point, so what's the plan?" Rodney asked. Just then as we sat on that hard concrete porch, I told Rodney that he'd asked that question at the most precise time because now I really needed him to buckle up and brace himself. After spending about half an hour explaining to Rodney everything that I'd found out thus far, he just sat there in disbelief with his mouth hanging to the floor.

"You figured all of this out on your own, Sam?" Rodney asked.

"Yeah, pretty wild, huh?" I said.

"Try impressive," Rodney retorted. "My little pretend baby sister is all grown up and doesn't need me to protect her anymore," Rodney said, as he motioned a fake tear falling down his cheek.

"Well, you can't say I didn't warn you," I joked, referencing the disagreement we'd had yesterday about him telling me half-truths.

"Anyway, you cut it, Sam, this is nice work on your part," Rodney said. "So, what do you need from me? I'll follow your lead," he whispered.

"You couldn't have better timing with your questions today, Rodney," I laughed. "Do you think you'll be able to round up a few people and get them to the old, abandoned warehouse on South Graham Road?" I asked. "Whether you get them by hook or by crook, I need them all there," I shouted.

"I not only think I can get them there but I also *know* I can," Rodney said with confidence.

"Well, that's just what I wanted to hear," I replied. "I'll make a list of everyone who needs to be there. You can handle the not-so-easily-persuaded people and I'll get all the others. Although Rodney, I should tell you," I said in a hushed tone, "I don't know with one hundred percent certainty that the person I just depicted as a monster in my story is truly our killer. So, we'll need everything to go off without a hitch and hopefully they'll take the bait," I said. "Do you still think you can get everything in place like we talked about?" I asked.

"I most certainly can. Now let's go get this psychopath!" Rodney roared.

"Let's do it!" I shouted intensely. "I'll text you the names of everyone involved. You just make sure the people on your half of the list are at the warehouse by 2:00 p.m. and I'll do the rest."

"You've got it, boss!" Rodney said with a smile.

I knew we were getting down to the wire, so I stood up from the porch, took a deep breath, then closed my eyes. Once I opened them, Rodney had his arms halfway around my body, giving me the warmest hug while repeatedly saying, "Please be careful."

I told him that I'd be as nimble as a cheetah or as ferocious as a bear in doing whatever it took to get this maniac off the streets of St. Lux. Rodney smiled, then I left on my way to go and prepare to catch a killer.

I hopped in the driver's seat of Tom's van and headed towards home. I needed to know if Crystal had told her uncle any new information to which I wasn't yet privy, and I also needed Tom at that warehouse. Shortly into my drive home, my phone started to ring, so I pulled over to the side of the road and saw that it was my good friend Michelle Lewis calling. I instantly started praying that everything was still okay with her son Max.

"Hello, Michelle," I said as I was finally able to answer her call before it went to voicemail. "Is everything okay with Max?" I asked.

"Yes, he's fine," Samantha.

"Oh, thank goodness!" I blurted out before letting out a sigh. "I hope you're calling me with good news about those fingerprints!"

"Well, actually I did get a partial print from the tape recorder," Michelle said. "I'm not willing to bet my life on the accuracy of the results just yet, but all roads seemingly lead back to one person," Michelle said confidently.

"Oh, geez," I thought to myself. "This was it." The next sentence out of her mouth would either confirm my suspicions or completely disprove them.

"Wow, I can't believe you got a match back so quickly," I said. "Well, who is it?"

"So, I don't want you to read too much into any of this because, as I mentioned before, with these speedy results the quality of accuracy can leave a lot to be desired."

I was almost positive the next thing I heard Michelle say was that the prints belonged to someone other than the person I suspected all along. *How could this be?* I asked myself. I was so confident. "Michelle, Michelle, are you there?" I shouted into my phone without any response. *Wouldn't you know it?* The reason I couldn't hear Michelle's response was because my phone was powering down. I must've forgotten to charge it last night before falling asleep and now it was dead.

As I sat there on the side of the road, I thought to myself, *If Michelle said who I think she said, then this changes everything.* It completely threw my original theory for a loop and I wasn't sure if I had enough time to come up with a different plan.

Confused but not deterred, I knew my phone would last at least five additional minutes if I powered it back on. So, I proceeded with the plan that Rodney and I discussed. I texted him the names of everyone involved and I put an asterisk by the names of the people I wanted him to wrangle up and bring back to the warehouse.

Afterwards, I got back on the road and five minutes later I was home. Tom was sitting alone in my living room, so I asked him how his chat with Crystal went.

"Not good, to say the least," Tom said. "She's not doing well and I'm not sure I have what it takes to help her get better." Tom went on to say that Crystal ran out of my house in a huff while shouting out that she was going to her sanctuary.

"Even if I knew where this sanctuary was," Tom said, "I'm not sure if I've got the strength to chase after her anymore."

"So, you're just going to give up on your favorite niece?" I shouted. "Were you never a brat when you were younger?" I asked.

"This is different," Tom said with concern. "My niece thinks I'm ruining her life, Sam." "Well, as her legal guardian you probably are," I said as gently as I could. "Lord knows my parents were constantly telling me how to dress, what music was acceptable, and don't even get me started on the first time I decided to introduce them to Jack," I yelled as I resorted back to a childhood rant.

"Are you getting to the point in the story where I start to feel better?" Tom said with sarcasm.

"The point is," I retorted, "once I was out of that bratty phase and realized that my parents were only trying to help, I don't think I'd ever been so grateful, and I'm willing to bet Crystal will feel that same way one day. But only if you don't give up on her."

"Gee, golly, Sam, the way we motivate one another we sure do make a good team, huh?" Tom shouted. "We should patent this act and take it out on the road. What do you say?" Tom asked.

"Well, that'd be the day. Two basket cases driving around the Midwest charging locals for cognitive therapy sessions," I joked as we both laughed. A few seconds later, we both walked into the kitchen once we heard the oven timer go off. I'm not sure where he'd gotten all of the ingredients, but it looked and smelled as if Tom were preparing a huge pan of spaghetti.

Tom was a man of many talents but from the looks of that spaghetti, cooking wasn't one of them. He fixed a huge plate for himself, then asked me if I wanted one as well.

I'd never been so happy to be on a health kick in my life, I thought to myself. "Oh, no I shouldn't," I said, though I knew the carbs would give me energy.

"All the more for me," Tom said as he continued to load his plate with food I don't think even Daphne would've eaten.

"Tom, I know where Crystal went," I blurted out as we sat at my wobbly kitchen table. "Yesterday I put a GPS tracker on her car because people kept disappearing on me. It's a long shot, but I think I may know who killed Ronda also."

As Tom sat across from me staring with spaghetti hanging out of his mouth, I told him about the plan that Rodney and I cooked up and how we needed everyone to be at the warehouse on South Graham Road by 2:00 p.m.

Tom agreed and said that he was willing to do anything to help keep the streets of St. Lux safer for all of his friends and family. So, I asked him if he didn't mind going on a few errands with me before we went to the warehouse. With his mouth full of spaghetti, he shook his head no, insinuating that he didn't mind at all. As I stood up to get a drink from the refrigerator, I accidentally shook the table, subsequently breaking the wobbly leg and making Tom's huge plate of spaghetti go flying all over his face and clothing.

"Oh, geez, I'm so sorry!" I shrieked. "OMG, your shirt is ruined! I'm such a klutz," I screamed. "No biggie." Tom said as suavely as he could with a huge spaghetti stain on his shirt.

Still, unable to part ways with Jack's clothing, I offered Tom the next best thing. As we walked into my bedroom, I told him that he could choose from an array of shirts that I had in my dresser drawer. I really didn't want to stick around and watch him hulk out in one of my favorite t-shirts, so I decided to hit the road and take care of a few things before heading to the warehouse. I told Tom where my car keys were and we agreed that he'd meet me there after he was all washed up. Next, I went into my office before leaving and grabbed an extra car charger that I kept in my desk, then I ran towards the front door.

Once I was in Tom's van I connected my phone to the charger, then sat there for the next few minutes trying to compose myself. I have to admit I was somewhat rattled about the plan. I mean, although I was fairly confident at this point, I still knew that there was a high probability things could go wrong.

Since I wasn't entirely sure any longer about the ploy that I'd cooked up with Rodney, I thought it would behoove me to tweak the original scheme just a little bit, if for no other reason than to keep everyone guessing where I was going, including Rodney. Although Rodney and I were somewhat cordial again, if I'm being completely honest, I still wasn't sure if he'd played a part in Sean's mother's murder. So, I thought it would be wise not to give away every secret I knew, especially to someone I couldn't trust unreservedly.

Like I'd said before, if I wanted to catch a killer, I had to think like one. And just in the nick of time, my killer instinct was starting to kick in. I knew exactly how the fingerprints on that tape recorder came into play—I think I knew it all along. I guess I just didn't want to believe it. But now that I was no longer blind there was really no need for me to call Michelle back to confirm anything.

The boldness of it all, I thought to myself. To actually sit there and lie to my face, to pretend to be a friend and make me doubt everything and everyone else around me. *The nerve!* I think I was finally able to put a face to the person who was responsible for all of this, and I'd outsmarted a pretty smart killer in the process. I had never been one to toot my own horn, but with Sean now sitting where the killer should've been, my wheels just started turning. I knew I was going to be coming full force after this dirtbag and the only thing that was going to stop this train was a derailment.

CHAPTER SEVENTEEN

As I pulled out of my driveway, I realized that I hadn't even considered the possibility that this entire thing could fail, which, I admit, was a little cocky on my part. I mean, after orchestrating such a risky plan with so many different personalities, any of which could bring this whole thing crashing down like a Jenga game, it would probably behoove me to entertain every possible scenario. That being said, I figured going back to the hospital and making sure Maureen was okay should be at the top of my list. After all, I didn't want this thing backfiring on me without checking on her well-being first.

While there, I was hoping I could stop by the morgue to check out a nagging suspicion I had. It was a long shot, but I figured after these last couple of days, God himself would've agreed—I was due for a win! I was praying that I'd be able to get in and out of the hospital without incident, or at least before getting accused of poisoning my friends and ending up in a cell next to Sean.

Once I pulled up at the hospital, I received a text message from Rodney saying, "All systems go." I knew this meant everything was going according to plan and he was about halfway done with his part of the stratagem, or the part he knew about anyway. Either way, I knew I really needed to get a move on. Coincidentally, while I was walking towards the main entrance of the hospital my phone began to ring. I took it out of my jacket pocket and saw it was Maureen calling.

"Hi, Maureen!" I shouted in excitement, assuming from her phone call that she was now okay.

"Oh, Sam, it's so good to hear your voice," Maureen replied. "Oh, I just can't thank you enough for always being there for me." As she whimpered, I said, "You hush that fuss, that's what I'm here for. Literally, that's what I'm here for. I was just coming to see you. I'm currently in the waiting area at the hospital. What room are you in?" I asked.

"Well, the doctors haven't told me much so far and they actually want to take me downstairs to run a crazy amount of tests on me," Maureen said. "Maybe you should come back in a couple of hours."

"That could work if I'm not in prison by then," I muttered.

"WHAT!" Maureen shouted out. "Are you in some kind of trouble, Sam? she asked.

"It's a long story," I said. "I'll catch up with you later. I just wanted to make sure that you were okay before I did anything."

"Well, please be careful, Sam," Maureen said intensely. "You're like a sister to me, and I'm not sure where I'd be right now if I didn't have you in my life."

"I'll be careful; you just get better," I said. After Maureen stated the doctors had entered her room, we said goodbye to one another, and I placed my phone back in my jacket pocket.

Already feeling like a criminal mastermind, I decided to swipe a badge that was on the receptionist's desk after I saw her leave for the restroom. I wasn't taking any chances. I needed to see the Medical Examiner and I distinctly remember him using his badge in the elevator to get Dee and me to the basement floor. So, when no one was looking I swiped the badge, ran over to the elevator, and hit B for basement. Once I got down to the basement and the elevator doors opened, I walked over to the area where Scott White, the Medical Examiner, had taken us yesterday.

"What are you doing down here, ma'am?" I heard someone yell, causing me to nearly jump out of my skin. "I-I was looking for the restroom," I muttered, barely able to think of an excuse.

The man, who still hadn't turned around laughed, then shouted, "Well, if your lie is that bad, I can't wait to hear the real reason why you're down here." Finally, he turned around and he sort of recognized me from yesterday. "Oh, Mrs. Evans," Scott blurted out. "Please forgive me, I didn't mean to be so harsh," he said.

"Umm, it's fine," I replied. "There's no way you could've known who I was."

"Well, you must need to say goodbye to your daughter again," Scott whispered.

Obviously, somehow Scott had gotten Dee and I confused. However, his mix-up was just the win I needed. I told Scott I wasn't there to see Ronda, but whispered that I did need to see the clothing she was wearing when she was brought in. He said that wouldn't be a problem and proceeded to show me everything Ronda had on the day she was murdered. I thanked him and hurried over towards the elevator before he realized that Mrs. Evans was the woman in the wheelchair yesterday and I was just her friend. After getting back to the lobby, I bolted off that elevator as if I was the Flash and then I placed the badge back on the receptionist's desk without being spotted.

It was already noon by the time I got back to Tom's van and I realized that time wasn't on my side. I could probably make one stop in person to try and secure someone off my list. However, the others I wouldn't personally be able to lay hold of, so I had one more trick up my sleeve. I thought of an even more diabolical way of getting my prey to willingly follow me, but I just hoped Rodney would be able to use his influence to actually pull it off.

First, however, I had to make one final stop. So, I hopped in Tom's van and headed towards Susie's Sweets. I needed to pick up that overzealous, ego-maniacal, pretentious, shallow little woman, and I also wanted a donut. Susie was certainly a different type of animal, one who typically cared about nothing or no one but herself. For those reasons alone, I wouldn't put murder past her. Fittingly so, after the information I'd recently learned, Susie was smack dab at the top of my suspect list, right beside the elusive Crystal and just above the deceitful Charlie.

However, if she weren't involved, I figured using her as bait wouldn't be the worst thing in the world, especially since at this point all I had was intuition and I needed hardcore proof. So, I wanted everyone who could've been a suspect present and accounted for, to see if I could get a killer's confession the old fashion way.

As I pulled in front of Susie's Sweets, I noticed Susie outside smoking a cigarette. *That's funny,* I thought to myself. I thought she quit smoking ages ago. "Susie, Susie!" I shouted out as I watched her flick her cigarette on the ground, then turn to go back inside her restaurant.

"I'm glad you're still here," I said as I followed her into her bakery.

"Well, you look familiar," Susie blurted out. "However, I don't see any scrunchies in your hands, so you couldn't be Samantha," Susie said sarcastically.

Oh, dear God, I thought to myself. She was like a broken record with these scrunchies. However, I needed everyone at that warehouse, so I was forced to play her game. "Yes, you're right," I said. "I'm not Samantha. Don't you remember it's me, Barney Fife?" I retorted. After Susie was done laughing, she said I did resemble Barney Fife somewhat around the eyes. Without going into too much detail, I explained that I needed her to come with me.

"Umm, no thanks," Susie shouted out, "I don't do charity."

"Well, I just assumed you wanted your scrunchie order now," I said. "It's practically ready. I just need your help loading it."

"Nice try, Mrs. Fife, but I wasn't born yesterday," Susie screamed. After taking a deep breath, I gathered myself and realized that I was going to have to sweeten the pot a little bit to get Susie to that warehouse, and I knew just the thing—or person—who could get her there.

"Susie, you devil you," I whispered. "I'll let you in on the real reason I was sent here, but if you tell I told, I'll just deny it," I said with a smirk.

"Ooh, spill it, girlfriend, you know I do love a good secret," Susie replied.

"Well, Tom sent me here," I said. "He told me yesterday that he has the biggest crush on someone in this very room, and he's so smitten with you that he didn't even say your name," I said as Susie seemed to eat up every word. "I honestly think he's secretly dying to tell you, but he needed to use me as his wingman," I muttered without batting an eye as I joined Susie in fairytale land.

"Well, that checks out. After all, I am one of the most sought-after women in town," Susie said, as I stared at her enormous wedding ring and slightly scoffed at her well-known swinger lifestyle. "If Tom's going to be there, then it's definitely my kind of party, so you can count me in," Susie blurted out.

"Great," I replied. "I can't wait to see it all unfold. If you want, you can just ride there with me; I'm on my way there now," I said, as I grabbed one of the free day-old Danish from the counter.

Susie began to laugh uncontrollably then said, "Samantha, I am Filet Mignon, and whatever upholstery you've got in your car, I don't do. Besides," Susie went on to say, "I'm going to take a lover, so obviously I have to go home and change so I'll look the part."

Well, for someone who wasn't born yesterday, once she finds out the real reason for my visit, she sure was going to be crying a lot tonight, I thought to myself.

"Do whatever you want, Susie, but here's the address," I said, as I grabbed a pen from my jacket pocket and wrote on a business card Susie had lying on the counter. "Make sure you're there by 2:00 p..m," I said as I ran outside and jumped into Tom's van. Now it was a quarter after 1:00 p.m. and I needed to be on my way to the warehouse. So, after taking the short drive there, I pulled around back and spotted Crystal's car. I was hoping she'd still be here. After all, she was the one who'd given me the idea for this location on Daphne's dog tracker after it popped up on my phone.

Once I parked, I noticed that I had a missed call from Charlie. Upon closer inspection, I noticed that he'd also sent text messages. *Was this him trying to cover his tracks?* I thought to myself. Did he now—all of a sudden—feel the need to explain everything away I'd recently learned about him? So, after reading his text, I sat there for the next few minutes putting my game face on before getting out of the van. I couldn't believe what I was about to get myself involved in. Unfortunately, playtime was over and it was now time to expose the truth. So, I got out of the van and went into the warehouse. I couldn't fathom why Crystal sought out solace in this place. The entire building was damp and eerie, the windows were busted out, and don't even get me started on the New York-size rats that patrolled the premises.

As I walked through this huge warehouse, I finally reached the back and spotted Crystal sitting on an empty bench. "Crystal, Crystal!" I called out. "Are you okay?"

"Samantha, w-what are you doing here?" Crystal whispered.

"Let's just say I'm here to catch a rat," I said with a smile. "However, I'm glad I caught you. Is everything alright?" I asked again.

"Well, I'm not sure," Crystal said as she hung her head. "My uncle convinced me to take my medication and I have to admit I do feel much better now. But I sense in my heart that I've said irreparable things to him and I'm not sure if he'll ever be able to forgive me," Crystal cried out.

"Well, that's the good thing about family," I said. "The ones that truly love you have already forgiven you. Now it's just a matter of forgiving yourself," I said as Tom walked through the door at the most convenient time.

"Crystal!" Tom shouted out.

"Uncle!" Crystal cried, as she ran into Tom's arms. "I'm sorry for everything I've put you through," Crystal shouted as she appeared to hug Tom tighter.

"I know you are, Pumpkin," Tom responded, with a slight smile as he patted Crystal's back.

"You don't need to apologize for being sick. I love you still," Tom whispered, and I have to admit I got a bit teary-eyed while eavesdropping.

However, after a while, I thought we needed to address the elephant in the room. Tom had come to the warehouse to catch a killer in one of my form-fitting t-shirts. He'd seemingly turned one of my favorite shirts into a crop top, bare midriff, and all. *Eleanor from the Grey Cougars would've been so proud*, I thought to myself. While I wasn't one to dwell on anyone's clothing choices, I was worried with Susie on her way here; she'd surely tear what was left of my shirt to pieces just to get a better view of Tom.

"Sorry about your shirt, Sam, but it was the only one that looked halfway decent on me," Tom said as he caught me staring at the stretched-out fabric.

I didn't have the heart to tell him that he looked like baby hulk, so I just nodded in agreement. While we waited for everyone to arrive, Tom asked Crystal if there was a bathroom anywhere in the warehouse, and surprisingly there was. She pointed the way and Tom took off for the restroom. The next thing I knew I heard a dog barking that sounded a lot like my Daphne, so I ran outside and there she was sitting in the driver seat of my car. *She must've jumped through my car window once she noticed Tom leaving*, I thought to myself. I hurried and opened the car door to let her out and she followed me back inside the warehouse. By now every potential suspect who was on my list had parked outside and was walking into the building. I wasn't sure how Rodney pulled it off, but he certainly had wrangled up half the town—like he'd promised.

There was Rodney, of course, Talia, her sexist father Michael, Felix and his wife Betty, Simona, the boutique owner, and in her Batmobile, Susie Lynn. A few seconds later, Sheriff Hawkins was walking through the door with Charlie

West, Deputy Hicks, and Allison Cooper, the drunk woman from the bar who seemingly had the most to gain from my downfall.

"Now that everyone is here..." I shouted. "The sooner we begin, the sooner we can get a killer off the streets of St. Lux."

"Killer," Susie repeated. "Are you still playing that scavenger hunt game? Well, I want no part of this. So, where's Tom?"

"I'm right here," Tom said, as he came strolling back in from the bathroom. What do you want with me?" Tom asked Susie.

"Mmm, are you wearing that breakaway t-shirt just for me?" Susie asked, while staring at Tom with her mouth hanging open. "Well, if this is part of the scavenger hunt, y'all can count me in," Susie said seductively with her eyes on Tom.

"Sadly, we don't have time for this spectacle," I said, referring to Susie's antics. "There's a killer amongst us and I know exactly who it is."

"Are you telling us the person who killed that poor girl you were going around town asking about is *here?*" Felix asked in disbelief.

"Her name was R-Ronda," Crystal hollered.

"Yes, her name was Ronda Evans and she was a beautiful soul," I said. "Her mother was a dear friend of mine and, as you can imagine, she's been suffering ever since she found out her daughter was tragically murdered."

"Well, who was it?" Allison blurted out. "Who murdered Ronda?"

"You see, that's the part I couldn't figure out for the longest time," I said. "I couldn't understand who could be so heartless as to take the life of a young girl. However, once all these strange things started happening after the fact, I was led straight to the monster responsible."

"What strange t-things?" Crystal asked.

"Well, for one..." I said confidently. "I have a good friend named Michelle Lewis who's a fingerprint analyst. I sent her the tape recorder that someone strategically placed underneath my deck. Unfortunately for me, that same someone threatened my life in a note that was thrown through my window with a brick attached to it. And I'll bet it's safe to assume all of this was done in an attempt to find out what I knew and, subsequently, get rid of me."

At this point, Susie, having the attention span of a gnat, started to harass Daphne in the middle of my speech. "Grrrrr!" Susie yelled before starting to stomp her feet at this poor, defenseless dog. Daphne appeared to have had enough and began to bark at Susie.

"Wow, do you understand the type of dedication it takes to irritate a dog?" Tom said to Susie.

"Careful, Tom, or I might not let you play find the apple fritter later tonight at my donut shop," Susie retorted, as a confused Tom threw up his hands.

"Please!" Sheriff Hawkins screamed as everyone involved was obviously startled by his forcefulness. "What about the tape recorder, Mrs. Harris?"

"Yeah, who did the prints belong to on the tape recorder?" Betty asked.

"Well, thanks for lassoing me back in, guys," I said, trying to ignore Susie's shenanigans. "The prints that were on the tape recorder belonged to a friend," I stated. "Unfortunately, they also belong to the same person who poisoned both Dee and Maureen. It took some time but I finally figured it out," I said, as I casually looked around the room.

"Maureen was poisoned the night of Ronda's murder when she was out for her late-night run and Dee never saw it coming. However, she suffered the same fate as Maureen the next morning when she arrived here in town. Coincidentally, both women were given water bottles, and if I had to guess I'd say they were roofied with benzodiazepines," I shouted angrily. Well, I must've struck a nerve with the responsible party because at that very moment it was like the stars had aligned, and I was finally getting the big break I'd been longing for. However, I have to admit that I wasn't expecting such a consequential gem to just fall into my lap. Someone with a guilty conscience had felt the need to chime in with a song after my roofied allegation. Usually, I loved a good song, but nothing good was associated with this one. Some brazen, callous, lunatic was humming the melody to the killer's favorite ditty, "Anything you can do I can do better."

In that moment I stood on the bench and screamed at the top of my lungs. "The monster who Sean saw throw a brick threw my window, and the person whose fingerprints are on that tape recorder belong to none other than the person who's whistling at this very second, Mr. Charlie West," I shouted as gasps filled the air and everyone figuratively clutched their pearls.

"Sam, no, I can explain," Charlie cried out as tears quickly covered his cheeks.

"Sorry, Charlie," I retorted. "But all roads lead back to you."

Susie, being the oddball that she is, started to show compassion for the one person who stood accused of the crime. "Anyone could be responsible for this!" Susie shouted. "Let's not forget we're currently listening to a woman who's wearing a denim jacket with a brown belt. I mean, she's clearly irrational! How about Felix and his wife Betty?" Susie blurted out. "I wouldn't put it past those two. They definitely look as if they get into some pretty kinky stuff, and I know from personal experience about relationships that end tragically when three people are involved. Or better yet, what about this massive hunk of a man right here?" Susie looked directly at Tom. "I mean, since Samantha's currently on this witch hunt, shouldn't we hear everyone's alibi? So, let's hear it, tank top. Where were you when those girls were poisoned?" Susie crassly said, referring to Tom's shredded shirt.

"Enough!" Sheriff Hawkins shouted. "I'm going to restore some order in here if it's the last thing I do. Although Rodney got me to come here under false pretenses, now that I'm here, what exactly are you getting at, Mrs. Harris? Charlie is a fine young man and one heck of an employee. So where do you get off accusing him of murder?" Sheriff Hawkins said firmly.

"Well, I-I have his fingerprints and the tape recorder," I said, barely able to get the words out because I'd never seen the Sheriff so furious.

"Come outside, I'd like to speak with you in private," Sheriff Hawkins said.

As I followed the Sheriff with Daphne in my arms, I noticed Charlie giving me the death stare I'd given him just a few hours ago, and it was chilling to say the least. Then out of the blue as I walked by Talia, I heard her shout out, "PONFUSION, don't let it make you lose sight of the truth." I gave Talia a quick smile as I continued to follow Sheriff Hawkins.

Once we got outside, I put Daphne down and I thought the Sheriff was gonna rip me a new one; instead, he congratulated me for my work.

"Sheriff Hawkins, you're not upset with me," I asked.

"Well, of course not, he replied. "I simply needed to create a diversion to get out of there."

"A diversion..." I repeated. "Oh, thank goodness, I thought it was about to be off with my head for accusing your protégé," I said warily.

"Well, I have to admit, Mrs. Harris," Sheriff Hawkins said, "I've been more than a little suspicious of Charlie myself as of late. I just couldn't see him for what he was until now," he said as he rested his hand on my shoulder.

Knowing I needed a conviction for Dee's sake, I didn't want to waste precious time sitting around on my hands. So, I shouted at the Sheriff, "Aren't you friends with the presiding judge?"

"We're friendly with one another, Mrs. Harris," Sheriff Hawkins said. "However, we haven't spoken since I became Sheriff."

"Well, do you think you can take me there now?" I asked frantically. "I'll tell him exactly what I've discovered, and with any luck we can be back here within minutes with an arrest warrant in our hands."

"Oh, I don't know, Mrs. Harris," Sheriff Hawkins said skeptically. "Even with the suspicion I've had of Charlie as of late, I still know he's a good kid.

I just can't wrap my head around him being a murderer," Sheriff Hawkins whispered softly.

I paused for a while before yelling, "It's the only way to get him off the streets. I mean, I know he's like a son to you, Sheriff, but the only thing we should be concerned about here is the victim. Unfortunately, the person responsible—no matter who it is—needs to be stopped," I said, passionately.

"You're absolutely right, I'll do it!" Sheriff Hawkins shouted after I'd finally convinced him to change his mind.

"Great, you can radio Deputy Hicks and have him keep an eye on Charlie until we get back," I said, realizing that convincing the Sheriff was a little easier than I'd anticipated. After chasing Daphne around the Sheriff's car, I was finally able to catch her because she hadn't fully grasped the concept of someone suddenly stopping and waiting for her to make a full rotation. We got in on the passenger side, and while driving to the courthouse, the Sheriff got a call on his radio about a home invasion in progress. I certainly knew how traumatic someone entering your home without your permission could be, so the Sheriff and I took a detour and ended up on the other side of town where the burglarized home was located.

"Stay close to me, Mrs. Harris," Sheriff Hawkins said as we entered the creepy house with boarded up windows out in the middle of nowhere.

"S-Sheriff, this house looks pretty abandoned," I said while looking around. "D-Do you think the robbers are still here?" I asked, just barely able to get the words out. Suddenly, the look of pure evil took over the Sheriff's face as he turned around and pointed his gun at me and Daphne. "Oh, silly rabbit!" Sheriff Hawkins shouted. "There were never any robbers here!"

"What do you mean, Sheriff? I heard the dispatcher call you about a robbery in progress?" I said with a confused look on my face.

"You know it bodes well for me that someone as smart as you could be so oblivious," Sheriff Hawkins boldly stated. "What you heard, you twit, was a taped recording of a dispatcher. And if I do say so myself, it's quickly becoming my favorite go-to."

"But I don't understand why would you fake a robbery," I asked warily.

"Good question," Sheriff Hawkins said in an unfeeling tone. "Let's just say I needed another little diversion to get you here."

As the Sheriff pushed me further inside with his gun pointed at my back, it started to feel as if he'd been here before. He was turning on every light in this enormous, abandoned house without missing a beat.

"Why are you doing this?" I asked. "We've already proven Charlie's guilt."

"Wrong again!" Sheriff Hawkins shouted out, looking as if he loathed the fact that I hadn't accused him of the crimes. "I'm responsible for Ronda's death and all the others too. It's just Charlie's bad luck that I had to frame him this time around," Sheriff Hawkins said as he followed his admission up with the most diabolical laugh. "Although, I'm sure I don't have to tell you this, considering I've tried pinning this murder on several of your friends, any of which should've stuck. But you just couldn't stop Nancy Drewing now, could you?"

As he pushed me and Daphne into the kitchen, I stood there mortified. *How could the Sheriff be responsible?* I asked myself. I'd just heard Charlie with my own ears humming the melody to the same song that the killer so brazenly whistled while tormenting Ronda. Had I overlooked something, or was I starting to get too big for my britches? While pondering several thoughts, Daphne jumped from my arms and ran around the island and tried to attack the Sheriff. I hurried and picked her up, then tried running away. But I only got as far as the hallway before he caught us.

"Get back in here, you little cretin," Sheriff Hawkins shouted as he pushed us back into the kitchen.

"Why are you doing this, Sheriff?" I asked. "What sick perverse pleasure do you get out of torturing me?

"Well, I could ask you that same question!" Sheriff Hawkins shouted. "Every time I'd go to frame someone, here comes Little Miss Sunshine to save the day while torturing me in the process. And with you now coming dangerously close to figuring everything out, I knew I needed to make sure you were out of the way by any means necessary," he screamed with dead eyes.

"Even by ruining the lives of innocent people?" I shouted.

"Hey, let's not play the victim here. You have no one to blame but yourself for all of this destruction," Sheriff Hawkins said. "This would've been over quite some time ago if everything had gone according to plan. I intended on framing Crystal for this murder, shortly after I witnessed her giving Ronda a fur coat. And I even took the time to obtain Ronda's photo from one of Crystal's social media accounts to do it. But when you told me about your suspicions of her, I knew any lawyer worth his salt would clear her name in an instant. So, I set my sights on Tom, but like a thorn in my behind, there you were. Thankfully, once that imbecile Charlie went around town unwittingly poisoning everyone in St. Lux, I knew I had to improvise, and it was then I knew I'd found my patsy," Sheriff Hawkins said.

"So, all of this is because of you," I said angrily. "Well, that's where you're wrong again, Mrs. Harris." Sheriff Hawkins screamed while saying I was to blame as well. "You see once we ran into the front lobby the other morning after we'd heard Mrs. Evans causing a commotion, I'd noticed, unbeknownst to him, that Charlie had given her one of my personal spiked water bottles from my work bag that I specifically told that moron to never touch, although he never knew the reason why. But once I saw she drank the entire bottle and that you were taking her to your house, I set my sights on you and everyone around you."

"You're a monster," I shouted.

"Bite your tongue before I cut it off," Sheriff Hawkins said forcefully. "Would a monster have done that girl's hair and made her as pretty as possible for when she was found? Honestly, with that fox, I felt as if I had just bagged a fourteen-point buck," Sheriff Hawkins said, smiling the whole time while seemingly enjoying the details about Ronda's murder. "I'll remember this kill until I'm old and grey. You see that little tramp Ronda was blackmailing me for years. It all started when I lived in Tennessee and Ronda caught me disposing the body of a local prostitute behind a dumpster. Instead of going to the police—and telling my superior—she chose fame and fortune. And all those fancy clothes that everyone thought made the woman she never paid one dime for any of them. That was my HARD-EARNED MONEY!" He screamed as the vein in his neck protruded out. "Well, I learned rather fast that I needed to rid the world of women like her, so a few months after leaving for St. Lux, I devised a plan for the girl who had since become an internet sensation—based off her looks and all those expensive clothes that I was still paying for—to meet me at a coffee house for lunch. It was as simple as making a fake profile, getting her to Michigan, snatching her out of a dog park, and let's just say *shooting my shot* with her once I had her here. You get it—because I shot her," he said as he laughed.

Disgusted but knowing it was important to keep him talking so I'd stay alive, I asked the Sheriff if it was also his idea to have an innocent child like Charlie harass me at my home.

"Well, I can't take all the credit," Sheriff Hawkins said, as he continued to laugh uncontrollably. "Truthfully, I did have Charlie surveil your premises for quite some time. However, he's so bad at trying to be a good cop that he had no clue it was even your house," Sheriff Hawkins said while still pointing his gun at Daphne and me. "I simply told him that the person who lived there was a prime suspect in Ronda's murder, and I knew the odds would be in my favor that he'd go rogue and try and impress me by solving the case on his own."

"So, the late-night creeper and the brick through my window was all because of you manipulating a helpless child," I shouted. "Wow, Sheriff, were you that afraid of little ol' me that you had to resort to scaring me out of town," I asked, sarcastically.

"Well, the brick through your window was just an added bonus. But I can't take credit for it because it certainly wasn't Charlie," Sheriff Hawkins said with a devilish smirk. "However, nudging Charlie in your direction so he could spy on you, well, that was genius and it allowed for the perfect cover-up. But you want to know what the best part of all of this is, Mrs. Harris?" Sheriff Hawkins asked.

"Enlighten me," I said, nonchalantly.

"Had I killed you days ago for getting in my way, there would've been no one to create such a scene in front of half the town, and seemingly help me seal Charlie's fate," Sheriff Hawkins laughed.

"Clever," I said with a sneer. "So, what do you plan on doing with me?" I asked.

"The same thing I do with all the others," Sheriff Hawkins responded. "I just hope you're not claustrophobic because I've got the perfect little compact coffin for you. And with any luck I can take care of Ronda's mother too and you guys can have a double burial," he said with a detached expression on his face.

Just in the nick of time, the entire house went pitch-black, and as I stood there holding Daphne, I shouted out, "Looks like you forgot to pay the light bill, Sheriff!"

"Who's there?" Sheriff Hawkins yelled out. "Turn those lights back on whoever you are or she's dead!"

"Your wish is my command," someone blurted out from the darkness.

But after the lights came back on in the kitchen, I noticed that the Sheriff looked like he'd seen a ghost when he spotted none other than Charlie West standing at my side.

"What is this?" Sheriff Hawkins blurted out. "What do you two think you're doing?" he asked.

"My oh my, Sheriff Hawkins," I said casually. "I must admit that I'm shocked at this reaction. You, of all people, had to have known that I was gonna need a diversion," I said as Charlie handed me a tape recorder. "You see this!" I yelled as I held up the device. "Well, this proves you're not as smart as you thought you were," I shouted angrily.

"What is that?" Sheriff Hawkins asked frantically while more than likely wishing he'd kept his dirty little secrets to himself.

"Oh, this old thing," I retorted. "Well, it's a tape recorder and it just conveniently recorded everything that's wrong with this town. However, I can't take all the credit," I said, mocking the Sheriff while using his own words against him. "You sort of inspired me after you had Charlie sneaking around my house," I shouted.

"Give it to me before I blow you both to pieces," Sheriff Hawkins yelled.

"Wow, Sheriff, you still don't get it, do you?" I replied, as Charlie and I both shook our heads. "Did you really think that I'd go anywhere willingly with you knowing you had a loaded gun? That thing is as empty as Susie's head," I said, with a smile. Instinctively, Sheriff Hawkins pulled the trigger and, to his surprise, no bullets came out.

"Oops!" Charlie yelled. "I guess I unloaded your gun this evening after you had me polish it." "Thanks again I couldn't have done it without you, Charlie," I interjected as we high-fived one another. "Are these what you're looking for?" Charlie asked as he pulled the Sheriff's bullets from his pants pocket. He then pulled a loaded gun from his waistband while dropping the bullets to the floor.

"You see, fortunately for me," Charlie shouted angrily at the Sheriff, "I started to suspect you once you let me take the fall for the bomb hoax that I knew you were behind. Unbeknownst to you, I heard your phone conversation yesterday when you thought you were alone; you know the one where you said to someone that you needed one hell of a distraction in downtown St. Lux. I wasn't quite sure what the other person said, but after David Holtz told me that the bomb scare was just a hoax, I figured that was just the kind of distraction that a guilty person needed to throw everyone off their trail. So, while devising my own plan, I decided to shake things up and take responsibility for the bomb scare. Then once Sam told me about finding a tape recorder underneath her deck, well, it all came together, and I figured you were using me in order to get rid of the one person in town who could expose you. And the more Sam and I talked, the more damning the evidence against you became. And when she mentioned the killer was whistling a particular song, I instantly knew me blaring out that same ditty in front of everyone would garner only one response out of an egomaniac like you." Charlie appeared to be holding back tears. "How could you do this to me? You were my mentor!" Charlie screamed, as he focused the gun on the Sheriff.

Seeing Charlie's emotions take over, I started to feel as though he was deviating from the plan we'd discussed, so I yelled at Charlie that the Sheriff wasn't worth it and asked him to give me the gun. After a few seconds, Charlie calmed down and handed the gun over. He then said he'd just received a text message and all the others from the warehouse heard every word of Sheriff Hawkins's confession, including Deputy Hicks, and they were all on their way to arrest him.

Realizing he had no way out of this one, Sheriff Hawkins suddenly asked me if I didn't mind explaining when I started to suspect his guilt.

"Well, I don't mind at all. As a matter of fact, I'd be happy to oblige," I said to a deflated Sheriff. "Quite frankly, ever since this morning I had a nagging suspicion that you were responsible for Ronda's murder," I shouted, as I pointed the gun at the Sheriff. "I knew Charlie had no idea where I lived. As you've mentioned before, he thought my house was where the prime suspect resided. So, once I found out it was him who planted the tape recorder it all made sense, and I knew that he was simply trying to gather evidence to appease his idol. And when I asked you to point me in the direction of the holding cells so that I could talk to Sean, I noticed the fresh scratches that were on your forearm, not to mention the fact that you never asked to hear that voicemail this morning at my house, because sadly I think we both know you already knew what was on it. However, the icing on the cake occurred at the warehouse. If you'll recall, I never once accused Charlie of murder, but you conveniently did. Actually, I purposely only mentioned the fact that Charlie planted the tape recorder underneath my deck and threw a brick through my window, but I knew it would be enough to lure you out of the shadows. With you being a creature of habit, once you took the bait I knew you'd find an excuse to bring me here," I said, emotionally. "After all, this is the location where they found Ronda, isn't it? I figured an animal like you would always run back home. So, after I talked to Rodney, we devised a plan and he came here before going to the warehouse and hid this tape recorder. I knew for a fact I'd be able to get a full confession out of you without breaking a sweat."

"Nicely done. What about this imbecile? How'd you get him to turn?" Sheriff Hawkins asked while looking at Charlie and slowly coming to terms with the fact that he'd been caught.

"Good question," I said as I mimicked the Sheriff's unfeeling response from five minutes ago when he thought he was still in control. "Once I arrived at the warehouse, I noticed that I had a few text messages from Charlie. He admitted to putting the tape recorder underneath my deck but said that he had no idea I even lived there. Unfortunately for you, the thing you didn't count on was me telling Charlie that I'd found that very same tape recorder only a few hours later after he'd hid it, and us putting two and two together and coming up with you."

"So, you two nitwits teamed up and convinced Rodney to get me to the warehouse?" Sheriff Hawkins yelled. "Well, we're not ones to brag," I responded. "However, you're not the only one who can think like a lunatic. Once I read Charlie's text messages, I instantly called him. Then we hatched out this plan as I sat in my car before going into the warehouse," I said with a devilish grin. "I told Charlie I wouldn't go as far as accusing him of murder, but I also told him that once I insinuate his guilt in front of everyone in town, he'd better weep like a baby. I knew that'd get your motor running. And like so many other cowardly murderers, once you got me alone, you'd relish in the fact that you were finally able to brag about your monstrous ways."

"You'll pay for this," Sheriff Hawkins said, as he looked at Charlie and I with pure hatred in his heart. Luckily for us, Deputy Hicks and all the others were barging through the front door at that precise moment.

"You're under arrest, Philip Hawkins," Deputy Hicks shouted. "Put your hands behind your back."

After the Sheriff was handcuffed, I walked over towards him, looked him straight in his eyes, and with a smile on my face, I blurted out, "I guess me Nancy Drewing didn't make me so oblivious after all."

"You think you've won, don't you?" Sheriff Hawkins asked indignantly.

"I know I have," I said emphatically. "As a matter of fact, I'm kind of loving the irony." I whispered softly into the Sheriff's ear as I inched closer towards him. "You see with all that talk you were doing about putting me in a small compact coffin, and here I am putting the nail in yours. Honestly, Sheriff, the next time you want to steal a girl's photo off social media, please make sure it's a current one. Now somebody get this douche out of here!" I shouted as Tom simultaneously ran into the kitchen.

However, as I turned to walk away, Sheriff Hawkins somehow got his hands free and came after me like a raging bull seeing red. Tom, recognizing the danger I was in, without hesitation, jumped on the Sheriff and gave him the old one-two. Suddenly, as I turned back around to see what all the commotion was about, I watched as a gun fell from Sheriff Hawkins's hands onto the floor. Somehow, without drawing attention, the Sheriff had gotten his hands free by using his own keys. Then he casually grabbed the Deputy's firearm—all within a matter of seconds. Tom was the only one who noticed and he'd put himself in harm's way just to protect me.

In that very moment I'd glanced over and realized that Tom was trekking down treacherous roads right by my side. Just as Mr. Black wisely said a suitor should. Shortly after the kerfuffle, Deputy Hicks gained control over Sheriff Hawkins and escorted him outside. I immediately thanked Tom, then gave him the biggest hug. Just then everyone from the warehouse came barging into the kitchen and simultaneously gasped. Someone said loudly, "So the rumors are true!" and everyone began clapping.

Tom and I both smiled, then I bashfully said, "Wouldn't you all like to know!" Once we were all outside, I watched Deputy Hicks put that animal, Sheriff Hawkins, in the back seat of his patrol car. Then Talia came over and asked if I'd known all along that it was the Sheriff.

"Well, I had my suspicions," I said. "However, they were more than confirmed when I purposely put Daphne on the ground and chased her around the Sheriff's patrol car. I saw with my own eyes Ronda's broken heel on the back floor, tucked underneath the passenger seat. I'm not sure if he knew it was back there or if he just wanted a small keepsake. But the clues Ronda had been giving me up until that point became crystal clear in that moment."

"Ooh, were you hearing voices from the beyond?" Talia asked, her eyes wide with intrigue. "Do I have another news story to prepare for?"

"I'm not exactly sure what you would call it," I said. "However, Ronda came to me after her death in a vision and said, 'If I wanted to solve her murder the evidence would be right in front of me.' Then she started to laugh and said, 'As long as Daphne wasn't blocking it.'"

"It wasn't until I saw that shoe in the back of the Sheriff's patrol car," I said emotionally, "that my mind was forced to go back to the day I met Ronda. I distinctively remembered Daphne sat on her shoes and blocked her from leaving. Subsequently, everything started to click on all cylinders when I needed it the most. Then once I saw Ronda's broken heel with the clothing she had on when she was taken to the morgue, I instinctively knew that the thing she had been referring to—as far as Daphne blocking—were simply her shoes. Heck, even your little portmanteau word 'ponfusion' helped," I said with a smirk.

"Oh, did you like that?" Talia asked with a smile.

"Oh, I loved it," I replied. "Philip and confusion, those two words go hand in hand, so I assumed you were telling me not to get distracted by Philip Hawkins's trickery," I said.

"Like I said before," Talia added, while grinning from ear to ear, "You're a regular encyclopedia."

"Just out of curiosity," I asked Talia. "What on earth made you suspect the Sheriff of being involved to give me such a warning?"

"Well, to be honest," Talia said. "I'm nothing if not astute and it just so happens that I took several scans around the room when we were at the warehouse, just out of habit with having a journalism background and all. However, one of the last scans I remember doing was when you'd mentioned the person responsible for Ronda's murder was amongst us in the crowd, I discretely noticed that the Sheriff was the only one whose body language changed drastically."

"Good catch!" I said as we both smiled.

Right then, Tom and Charlie walked over towards us, and Talia made a quick break so she could get a jump on this unbelievable story that would no doubt be on tonight's news.

"So... decent work in there," Charlie said, looking emotional.

"Right back at ya," I said cheerfully with a wink.

"Just to clear the air, Sam, I never threw a brick through your window."

Well, if that egomaniac Sheriff Hawkins didn't fess up to it, and now with Charlie not taking responsibility for the threatening note, this could only mean that someone else wanted to scare me out of town, I thought to myself.

"We definitely have to talk later," Charlie said, snapping me out of deep thought. "However, I'll let you two lovebirds be for now. I should probably get home anyway and try to convince my mother that I haven't actually murdered anyone," Charlie joked.

After a quick laugh, I told Charlie to bring his mother and little brother over to my house for dinner tonight and I'd be more than happy to explain the whole thing.

"Oh, boy, that'd be great because I sure could use my big sister as backup," Charlie whispered.

"Well, it's a date," I replied while smiling from ear to ear at the thought of Charlie still feeling close enough to me to refer to me as his sister. "I guess, typically this would be the part where I'd give someone my address who's never cordially been invited to my home. However, I think you've been there a time or two," I said, drawing a laugh out of Charlie.

"Yes, I'm definitely sorry about that, Sam," Charlie said.

"Water under the bridge," I replied. Then I gave Charlie a big hug and Tom and I watched as he drove away.

"And then there were two," Tom said.

"Well, technically, three. Here comes Daphne," I said as I watched her run towards us after Crystal put her on the ground. A few seconds later, Crystal walked over and thanked me for not giving up on Ronda. Then she thanked me for not giving up on her. It was one of the most pleasant interactions I'd had with her in quite some time. She sincerely seemed like the old Crystal and I was ecstatic to even have played a small part in that. I asked her to stop by sometime so we could chat. After she gave her uncle a hug goodbye, she said she'd love to.

Right then, everyone seemingly gathered in the same general area and after we all talked about what had just happened, a few minutes later we all said our goodbyes and I found myself standing in front of Tom's van that he'd driven over from the warehouse. I was going to catch a ride back into town with him since the person who'd brought me here was currently on his way to jail. I turned around and Tom was right on my heels. Then I heard him yell out my name and say he had something particularly important to ask me that couldn't wait.

Well, this is it, I thought to myself. He was going to ask me out again. I couldn't believe I was feeling such emotions. My heart was pounding, my hands were sweating, and I just wanted to yell out the words, "Yes, I'll go out with you" before he realized what a mess I truly was and changed his mind.

As Tom composed himself to ask his question, I had the word "Yes" ready to fly off my lips. So, when he was ready, I didn't plan on hesitating this time.

"Hey, Sam," Tom said.

"Yes!" I blurted out in excitement.

"Well, I'm a little bit nervous about saying this," Tom whispered timidly.

"Just take a deep breath and say what you feel," I said gently.

"You know what? You're right, Sam, you're the best. I don't know why I'd ever be nervous around you," Tom said with a smile. Then he went on to say that Susie had told him that I'd promised his mind, body, and soul to her. "Fortunately," Tom said, "Susie's willing to let me keep my mind and soul. But my body, she said, belongs to her. Do you have any idea what she's talking about?" A very confused-looking Tom stood in front of me.

"Well, obviously, Tom, I can't lie to you," I said frantically. "I will, however, tell you that the woman is a lunatic, and I wouldn't be that surprised if someone told me she eats hamsters," I added, momentarily deflecting all of Susie's indirect jabs that seem to wreak havoc on my life.

"Oh, good," Tom said. "Because you're the only woman I want to belong to. But only when you're ready, of course," Tom said with a grin.

"Tom, do you want to have dinner?" I blurted out, no longer willing to play coy.

"Sure, you mean tonight with Charlie and his family so I can act as your buffer?" Tom replied. "Sounds like a fun time. Count me in."

"Well, not quite," I said. "I mean just the two of us. I was thinking tomorrow night, maybe at a restaurant?"

"Oh, geez I don't know what to say," Tom said, as he casually looked away from me.

Dear God, was I too forward? I thought to myself. *I've got to find some way out of this before my face turns as red as a stop sign.*

Then—like he'd done so many times before—Tom swooped in to save the day by saying, "Oh, I'm really bad at trying to be suave, huh. Of course, I'll have dinner with you!" He shouted this out as he raised both arms into the air. After he was done geeking out, he planted one on me that would've instantly made Susie's knees buckle.

"Well, I'm not sure if that was appropriate, but I've been wanting to do that ever since the other day at your house," Tom said.

"I'm not sure but I think it was highly inappropriate that you stopped," I blurted out as Tom kissed me again.

After gathering my composure, I asked him if he could make good on that favor he'd owed me.

"Of course, anything, Sam. What is it that you need?"

"I was just wondering if you could go to the police station with me. I need to pick up Sean," I said emotionally.

"Sure, I can do that," Tom replied as he held my hand.

"By the way, not that I'm not grateful Tom but I was wondering how you knew enough to rush Dee to the hospital last night?" I asked.

"Well, being a police officer for all those years I've seen more than my fair share of glassy eyes," Tom said. "I knew instantly when I went into your bedroom and saw her disorientated state that it was far more than despair from losing her daughter."

"Wow, talk about being in the right place at the right time," I said. "But you know with everything I've uncovered today, there's still one thing that's baffling me."

"Oh, yeah, what's that?" Tom asked, leaning on his van's door.

"I still don't know how Jack's bottle of insomnia pills got spread across my backyard," I said. "It obviously was intentional, and I knew Dee hadn't taken any because I knew the exact number of pills Jack had left in the bottle and they all were accounted for once I retrieved them off the lawn. Honestly, I just get the sense that someone is playing a dangerous cat-and-mouse game and I don't know who it is, but in my heart of hearts I feel like the Sheriff isn't responsible for this one."

"Well, maybe some mysteries just aren't meant to be solved," Tom whispered as he opened my door.

"Or maybe some mysteries just need a deeper look," I retorted.

Surely, I couldn't tell Sean that whatever happened to his mother was a mystery that wasn't worth solving, I thought to myself. Unfortunately, as I hopped in the passenger side of Tom's van I was overcome with bittersweet emotions. I was excited about getting that monster Sheriff Hawkins off the streets of St. Lux, but the fact that Ronda wasn't here anymore was heart-wrenching, to say the least. However, I think solving Ronda's murder ignited a fire within my belly that I didn't even know had been a spark. I was going to find out what happened to Sean's mother and give him closure if it was the last thing I did. And with my life currently playing out like one of my crime novels, I was certain that my next chapter would be quite riveting.

ACKNOWLEDGMENTS

I have to start by thanking my awesome husband, Scott. From always lending an ear whenever I had a funny Joke I wanted to try out to giving pivotal feedback even if I was reluctant to accept it at the time. He was as important to this book getting done as I was. Thank you so much, Dear.

With sincere gratitude, I would like to thank everyone at BookBaby who helped me on this project. I put my trust in you guys and you delivered tenfold, I'll forever be grateful. Special thanks to the production crew and in particular Sunshine Tucker, who created the most amazing cover design.

My editor, Deborah Denicola, has been indispensable in bringing this book to life. Her wisdom, guidance, and moral support was second to none.

I also wanted to thank my mother Deborah Hearn, and my sister Tina. Both of whom encouraged me endlessly and now my dreams of being an author are fulfilled.